WH WILLOW'S VISION

THE INDIAN PRINCESS JUST BEFORE
HER DEATH GAVE HER NEW BORN
SON A NAME WHICH WOULD SHAPE
HIS DESTINY INTO THE WILD
UNTAMED LAND OF INDIAN TERRITORY

Louise Self McGuire

LOUISE SELF MCGUIRE

outskirtspress

DENVER, COLORADO

White Willow's Vision
The Indian Princess Just Before Her Death Gave Her New Born Son A Name Which Would Shape His Destiny Into The Wild Untamed Land Of Indian Territory

Cover Photo by Carlos McGuire. All rights reserved - used with permission.
Interior art by Louise McGuire

Outskirts Press, Inc.
http://www.outskirtspress.com

ISBN: 978-1-4787-1977-9

Outskirts Press and the "OP" logo are trademarks belonging to Outskirts Press, Inc.

PRINTED IN THE UNITED STATES OF AMERICA

*I dedicate this book to my
dear husband Carlos and
our daughter Sandra for
their constant encouraging
support in my writing this book.*

FOREWORD

This novel is the adventure of two families from 1846 to some years after the Civil War had ended.

The novel is a work of fiction, but I have made it as historically correct as I possibly could.

The book has a wide range of happenings from jam-packed excitement to beautiful blossoming romances.

The two families make their way from the rich land of Oregon to an untamed, sometimes hostile land with little to no law enforcement, which in turn invites the intrusion of renegade outlaws.

It's a land overflowing with Native American Indians striving to adopt the skills of farming when their nomadic ancient roots, passed down to their present lives, are all that they have known.

This is the land where the Trail of Tears ended, a land referred to as Indian Territory, which later became the State of Oklahoma.

This is a story of Scott McCord, an Army officer who uses his influence to try to help the Indians who are striving to live at peace with the white man. His pursuit is to do all that he is able to protect them from those who want to exterminate the red man.

Scott falls in love with and marries a beautiful Shoshone Indian princess called White Willow.

—————⟫(◉)⟪—————

Black Kettle speaks: "Strong Eagle, we have been forced to sign the Medicine Lodge Treaty, the Cheyenne and Arapaho had to leave our homeland in what the white man calls Kansas and Colorado. We have been forced to move south to Indian Territory to a reservation west where the Washita River flows."

—————⟫(◉)⟪—————

When Black Kettle returned to his lodge, his wife, Medicine Woman, was waiting for him. She was very troubled and spoke of a vision that she had that night in her sleep. She said, "As I stood and looked out into the night, I saw dark shifting shadows in the snow and there beneath the willow tree a wounded mother wolf, mourning for her little ones...."

—————⟫(◉)⟪—————

"Yes, Chuck a rustling in the woods...." Before anything else could be said, soldiers came vaulting on horseback toward the village from all directions!

A flaxen-haired man on a gray mount appeared bounding over a fallen tree, his eyes wild with brutal excitement with a blazing Colt in his right hand!

—————⟫(◉)⟪—————

Lucinda slid off the side of Jack and let the reins fall to the ground. Jack joined Star at the edge of the water.

Lucinda found a shady spot next to a bulky old tree trunk. She lowered herself down onto the cool green grass and lay back against the tree. The flicker of the sun through the thick overhang of the high, leaf-covered limbs sent sparkles of golden light onto Lucinda's cold black hair, and down onto her clothing and all around her.

Chuck turned to speak to her, but instead he just stood a moment to take in the tranquil picture, and then he said, "You look so beautiful sitting there. Lucinda, you are my sweetheart, aren't you?"

Chuck turned and sat down beside Lucinda, took her in his arms, and kissed her....

Chapter 1

Oregon Territory, October, 1862

From the bedroom window, a gentle morning breeze ruffled the sheer floral curtains and tiny twinkles of light fell across the old weathered face of Jeremiah Collins.

As he lay propped up with two soft feather pillows, his daughter Rose came into the room and sat on the edge of the bed and said, "Oh, Papa -- stay with me just a while longer... what will I do without you?"

Jeremiah grasped his daughter's trembling hand and brought it up to his thin, pale lips, and gave it a gentle kiss.

"You have the farm, Daughter, and it's free and clear. You'll be better off without me; you've been burdened with the care of your papa too long. It's about time now for you to make a life of your own instead of taking care of an old invalid like me. This old heart's given out, but you still have your whole life ahead of you."

Rose laid her head on her father's chest and said, "Not so, Papa; the care I've given you was never a burden...you know I love you. Since Momma and little Billy died, you're all the family I've had. All the rest of our relations are still back in Missouri."

"I know that, Rosie Ann, and you know how much you mean to me—my little sunshine girl— but you need to let me rest now."

Jeremiah's tired old eyes closed, and with a long sigh, his hands fell limp.

Rose's mind went sailing back to her childhood when her papa first called her his little sunshine girl.

I remember that warm summer day; we were walking home from church down that little country path through the woods … Papa, Momma, and little Billy and me.

The fields on each side of the path were filled with all varieties of wildflowers. They were so beautiful -- I ran ahead and into the meadow, picking flowers and singing. By the time they caught up with me, I came out of the field with my fist full of mountain sorrel, blue-eyed Marys, and bunches of Queen Anne's lace, and some wild iris and others wildflowers that grew in those Oregon fields.

"There's my little sunshine girl with her cheeks all aglow," Papa said with a big smile.

"Oh, Papa -- am I really your little sunshine girl?"

"You are, Daughter; I thought that when I saw you in the field of wildflowers with the sun shining all around you," Papa said with a chuckle.

"These flowers are for you, Momma!" I remember saying.

"Well, thank you, Rose. Jeremiah, look -- she even found the purple iris that I love so much. We'll put them on the table for a centerpiece when we eat our lunch."

Old Doc Davis brought Rose back from her memories as he walked through the bedroom door and asked, "Rose, how is your papa today?"

"Not so good, Doc; I think he's losing ground. Please, can't you do something?"

The old doc lowered his silver-gray head, gave a reluctant sigh, and said, "I'm afraid there isn't any more that I can do. We just have to keep him comfortable with as little exertion as possible. Rose Ann, come over here and sit down. I need to talk to you."

Rose began unconsciously moving her long slender fingers on the side of her gingham apron and gathering it up into a little wad, as she had done so many times before when she was anxious. She walked over and lowered herself down onto the sofa where the doctor was seated.

He leaned over and ever so gently patted Rose's hand and said, "You have to accept the realization that your papa's heart is giving out and he could pass from this life at any time.

"Rose, your papa told me that he's ready to go to that deep sleep in the grave until the time to come when he will meet his Savior. He just wants to know that you will be all right and will be prepared to let him go. He asked me to talk to you, Rose; he's just too weak to cope with the emotion of talking to you himself. After he's gone, he wants you to sell the farm. After that, he said, you will have plenty of money to buy your passage back to Missouri and make a fresh start in a land where you will have family.

"As you know, he has two sisters and a brother in that part of the southwest, and he is sure that you can get all the support you need from them. He contacted your Aunt Mary and she said there are many rural schools springing up and they're in need of teachers. With your Oregon education, she is sure you would qualify to teach. There's such a need for teachers that even some with only an eighth- grade education are teaching."

Doc Davis had been the Collins' doctor as well as the

family's friend and consultant for many years -- not only the Collins' doctor but all the families in this farming community and the small town of Dayton. He had worked tirelessly during the influenza epidemic that took the life of Rose's mother and little brother Billy as well as many others before the virus had run its course.

The old doc had delivered Billy and many of the other children who lost their lives that winter. He was never quite the same after that; his hair seemed to go gray overnight, and his timeworn shoulders slumped forward as they never had before.

Rose sobbed, "This is too much for me to take in all at once. How can I think about losing my papa and the only home I've ever known?"

"I know, dear, but you just have to take it one day at a time and let God help you, He's there for you; all you have to do is ask, and He'll give you the strength to get through whatever comes."

"You're right, Doc, and I know that is what Papa would say too. God has always been there for him, and I know He will be with me."

There was a knock on the front door. Jessie Adams opened the screen, walked in, and called: "Miss Rose, is it all right if I come in?"

"Yes, Jessie. I'll be right there."

Rose dried her eyes and smoothed her frazzled hair before she stepped into the entryway where one of her hired hands was waiting.

"What can I do for you, Jessie?" she said, still trying to gain her composure.

"I just wanted to let you know that Dan and I have finished clearing the northern ten acres for planting the winter wheat and we wanted to know if it was all right if we take off a little early -- or is there something else you want us to do?"

"That's fine; you've done a good day's work. Tell Dan that too for me, Jessie. You all go on now, and I'll see you both tomorrow."

Jessie said, "Okay, ma'am. I'll give Dan your message." He turned to leave, but then he hesitated at the door, turned back, and said, "Miss Rose, you seem upset. How's Mr. Collins? He's not worse, is he?"

"I'm afraid he is, Jessie; I don't think we'll have him much longer."

"I'm real sorry for that, ma'am … if there's anything I can do…?"

"Not now, Jessie -- but if I need you later, I'll let you know."

Rose Ann Collins was a beautiful woman with eyes as blue as robins' eggs and fringed with long dark lashes. She had healthy pink blushing cheeks, full lips, and a mantle of long, naturally curly auburn hair, which she usually wore in a loose bun a little way back from the crown of her head. At times the unruly ringlets would find their way into her eyes and onto her rosy cheeks and down onto her neck— which was becoming to her appearance, but a nuisance to her when she was working.

She was now twenty-three, and by some considered an old maid. She'd had many suitors down through the years, but she never had time for courting after her mother died. Since then, her whole life had been dedicated to her papa and the farm.

Rose turned and walked back into the parlor to finish her conversation with Doc Davis. As she moved into the room she saw that Doc had relocated from the couch and was standing by her papa's open bedroom door.

The old doc had a dejected expression when he looked into

Rose's eyes and said, "I came to check on Jeremiah and I found him…I found him… he's gone, dear… I'm so sorry.

"I'm going to send Mrs. Davis to stay with you and when I drive my buggy by Susan's home I'll stop by and tell her the sad news, and I'm sure she'll come right over to stay with you too. You don't need to be alone now, dear."

Chapter 2

Rose woke from her troubled sleep and just for an instant she thought, *Oh, I had better go see what Papa wants for breakfast.* But then the reality that her papa wasn't with her any longer and the sickening feeling in the pit of her stomach returned and filled her with overwhelming grief. In the morning silence she remembered, *This is the day of Papa's funeral.*

Rose thought, *I have to be strong*, and then she prayed, "Please God, help me to take care of my duties today; give me the strength to do what is expected of me."

As she rose from her bed, the morning light fused its way through the stained-glass window in her bedroom and sprinkled multicolored hues across the floor.

She pushed her luxuriant ringlets back from her face and from under the collar of her long brocade robe, and walked down the winding staircase and into the kitchen. She opened the heavy cast-iron door of the cookstove and began to kindle a fire from the smoldering coals when she heard a knock on the front door. She hurried to the front of the house and opened the door, and it was her dear friend Susan Delany.

Susan had been her best friend since grade school, and here she was again this morning to give comfort to her dear friend.

"Oh, Susie -- I'm so glad you're here; come on into the

kitchen. I was just getting ready to stoke up the fire and make some coffee."

Rose and Susan set at the oak table drinking coffee and eating some muffins that had been brought by some of the neighbor ladies, among an abundance of other food that they so generously supplied.

It was a chilly autumn day. The sky was engulfed with dark looming clouds, and a drizzling rain had begun to fall.

Rose said, "The minister was by yesterday and he told me they had set the time for the graveside funeral to begin about ten this morning."

"Then we had better go upstairs and get you ready, Rose."

Rose pulled her black cotton stockings up over her slim white legs, secured them into her garter belt, and slipped into her pantaloons and lace-covered camisole.

"Susie, would you please help me with this corset? But don't pull the strings too tight; this is a day when I'm going to need to be a little more comfortable."

"Rose, you have such a small waist…no one would even notice if you didn't wear a corset. I do understand how you feel, though; I didn't wear mine today. with this black dress and long jacket, I didn't think I needed it."

Rose turned and looked over at her friend, "No, Susie -- with that outfit, you look fine."

Rose stepped into her long petticoats and opened her wardrobe and brought out a black linen dress with a jacket that matched. Susie helped her slip into the dark mourning ensemble. The skirt was fully gathered to the back with the fullness at the bustle; the length was down to her black high-top lace-up shoes.

The sleeves of the dress were long with black lace on the

bottom, which would protrude out of the jacket onto her hands. The jacket fit tight around her bust and waist, with two distended linen points down her midriff.

She walked to her dressing table and picked up the black and white cameo that her momma had given her on her sixteenth birthday, and pinned it to the neck of the blouse of her dress.

As she stood looking at her reflection in the mirror, her thoughts went back to that special day when she received the gift; her momma had been so pleased that Rose liked the cameo.

Rose Ann prayed, "Oh, if only momma was still here! I need her so much -- but I am so very thankful, Father, that you have given me Susan for such a dear friend."

The Collins family left the state of Missouri in 1846 just after the trail had been cleared for wagon trains to cross into Oregon territory.

They had eked out a living in the state, but it was beset with harsh winters, and was an untamed land with many dangers from Indians as well as renegades.

They had heard of the rich land and mild weather in Oregon Territory and decided to chance the dangers of the long journey.

It was a lengthy arduous journey from the Missouri land to Oregon City. They left and joined a wagon train at the beginning of spring and arrived at Independence Rock the early part of July.

The wagon master told the people this meant they were on schedule and should be through the mountains before snowfall. It was a hard, grueling trip but they did arrive at their destination before the end of October.

The family discovered that the sacrifice they had made, leaving their home and traveling such a great distance under such primitive conditions, was well worth the perils they encountered, when they learned that all that they had heard about this Oregon land and the Willamette Valley was true, from the rich dark topsoil, two feet deep in some places, to a climate that would grow just about any crop that they chose to place into its fertile fields.

Jeremiah described this Oregon land as a land as close to what he had imagined the earth would have been like in its early beginning -- as close as he could imagine the ancient garden of Eden would have been like, with a shower of rain to water the fields almost every day but not enough to drown the crops, and winter so light that some crops could be grown year- round.

Little Rose Ann was two years old when they started their journey, but had turned three by the time of their arrival. Soon after their coming, little Billy Ray was born and the family settled down on a 350-acre farm a few miles from Oregon City.

The friends and neighbors gathered at the little family cemetery where Joan Collins and little Billy lay at rest.

They were all gathered around the concealed open pit where the pine box would soon be lowered into the still and quiet resting place for Jeremiah Collins.

The steady rain mixed with crimson autumn leaves fell around them and onto the dark umbrellas as the minister gave his heart-warming eulogy, after which, Martha Jane sang the old song "When we gather at the river."

Rose's heart was heavy as she and her friend Susan walked back to the farmhouse; they shook the raindrops from their umbrellas and stepped into the front parlor, where Rose turned the openweave net veil up over her black wide-brimmed felt hat and hung it on the rack close to the front entryway.

They heard the chatter from the kitchen as some of the ladies from their church had arrived ahead of them and were busy preparing food for all the neighbors, who would be stopping by to give their support and condolences.

Old Doc Davis arrived with his friend Henry Smith; the town lawyer, Jim Jackson; and the mercantile owner, Alford Claybrook.

Mr. Claybrook had lost his wife Molly when she gave birth to his little son Dan. Little Danny was now two years old and a handful to keep up with, as any two-year-old could be.

Alford owned the mercantile store in the small settlement close to The Dalles. He and his daughter Jenny and his little son had their living quarters in the back of the store.

Jenny was ten years old when her momma died, and even though she was such a young girl, her papa depended on her to take care of her little brother and much of the cooking and cleaning. He helped whenever he could, but he had the responsibility of the store.

When it was time for Jenny to attend school, a neighbor lady, Miss Ida May, was hired to help in the mercantile and to see to Danny's needs.

Alford delivered groceries to the Collins farm when Jeremiah was still alive and before he became bedridden. On one of those days, Jeremiah answered the door.

"Come in Alford, here, I'll give you a hand with all the provisions." Alford followed Jeremiah into the kitchen and set the groceries down on the table.

"How's your little family, Alford? I haven't seen that little Danny in a while -- I bet he's getting to be a big boy now."

"Yaw, and he's getting to be quite a handful, too; into everything."

Jeremiah called up the stairs and said, "Rose would you please come down here? Mr. Claybrook is here with the groceries."

Rose came down the stairs and into the kitchen and said, with her bright and happy smile and a little mischief and impertinence in her voice, "Yes, Papa; I heard the wagon pull up and I was just getting ready to come down."

She walked over to her papa, rose up on her tiptoes, and kissed him ever so gently on the cheek. She then spun around toward Alford and spoke to him in a delightful little voice, "Mr. Claybrook -- how are you today?"

Alford, with a lump in his throat, replied, "I'm fine, Miss Rose."

But Alford was thinking, *What a sweet little beauty you are, Rose Collins. You fill the room with your presence -- such loveliness sets my heart to pounding—you look as demure and modest a little housekeeper as this old house could have.*

He hadn't thought of a woman like this in a long time and he wasn't sure he liked it; his heart was still not over the loss of Molly.

"Mr. Claybrook, it's the time of the day when Papa and I have our afternoon tea; would you like to join us?"

"I would love to, Miss Rose, but I have to get back to the store and I have one more stop to make before I return. Maybe I can take a rain cheek on that invitation."

"Certainly you may; whenever you're making deliveries and you have time, please stop by -- or just come anytime and bring Jenny and little Danny, I haven't seen them in a while."

Rose was thinking, *Mr. Claybrook is such a fine man and he takes such good care of his children, and I know it hasn't been easy for him since his wife died. I do find him very attractive with those rich brown eyes that seemed to sparkle when he looked at me.*

There's ruggedness about him, a manliness that causes me to feel that I would be safe in his presence. I don't think any man in town would want to have a confrontation with him...but I have also seen him with Jenny and her little brother, and he's very loving and tender with them.

Jeremiah walked Alford to the front door, but just for an instant he looked back at Rose busy in the kitchen preparing her papa's tea, and he felt such a swell of emotion as he saw a young women with such deportment and the complexion of a princess, a perfect sweet little angelic daughter with such character as to take such good care of her ailing papa.

Chapter 3

A few days after the burial of Jeremiah, Rose had her hired hand Jessie to hitch up her horse Snowflake to the buggy. Jeremiah had bought the white mare for her a few years before; she loved Snowflake and the horse loved her.

Rose was an excellent rider and when she galloped Snow through the fields with the wind blowing her hair back over her shoulders and Snow's white mane flowing through the air, she had such a feeling of freedom, and all the stress of seeing her papa ill would fade from her mind. It was just her and her Snowflake riding across the meadows.

But now it was time for Snowflake to be hitched up to the buggy and take Rose to her destination. Rose Ann had a promise to fulfill and she didn't want to put it off—even though her heart was still in such a sad state, she wanted to get this undertaking completed: the promise she had made to her papa before his death.

He had told her what he wanted inscribed on his headstone, and the inscription was very important to him.

Rose had made arrangements for Susan to accompany her on the trip to the stonemason who would inscribe and deliver the headstone and put it into its place in the little family cemetery, just about a mile north of the farmhouse.

It was a beautiful autumn day, with a slight chill in the air. Rose pulled her shawl tight around her shoulders as the wind blustered down from the northern summit.

Snowflake pulled the buggy to the front of Susan and her husband Eddy's home. Rose pulled back on the reins and said, "Whoa, Snow; we're here, girl."

Eddy stepped out on the front porch and called, "Susie's not quite ready, Rose -- you want to come in and wait for her?"

"Oh no, I'll just wait here, Ed. But tell her to get a move on; I have to get back to the farm before evening, you know."

"Now Rose, you know how my little wife is -- she just never gets in too much of a hurry. But I will see what I can do to help her along."

About that time, Susie appeared at the front door, waving her hand in the air and calling, "I'm ready, Rosie; I'm coming!"

As Snowflake pulled the carriage down the one-lane country road, the lingering brisk northern breeze blew showers of bright-colored leaves across their path and all around them.

The forest was on fire with the colors of the season. The tall sycamores were the color of sunshine -- bright golden yellow with a lingering lime green on the side that had been hidden from the last frosty night—all the trees brilliant with the colors of the season: russet-orange, candy-apple and dark ruby reds and lemon-yellows.

The Cascade Mountains in the far distance were a deep, cold, blue-green strewn with flaming colored saplings, and the golden, flickering aspens in the foothills.

"I really wish you wouldn't move back to Missouri. I don't know what I will do without you, Rosie; we've been friends ever since I can remember." Susan said with a sad note in her voice.

"I know, Susie, but it's what Papa wanted. It's too hard out here for a woman alone, without family to count on."

"You need to let me and Eddy be your family -- you know that you can count on us to be there for you."

"But Susie, it's just not the same. You and Ed will be raising your family, and you have aunts and uncles who live here too, and you still have your momma close. But I have no family here, and I have to do what is best in the long run…and I'm afraid that is selling the farm and going back to where I can be close to my family."

"I guess you're right -- but I will miss you."

"Oh, Susie…we'll stay in touch, and now that the Transcontinental Railroad has connected us to the Midwest, you and Ed can visit us in Missouri. It will be a wonderful experience for you both -- and times are changing; it won't take six months to get there. Traveling by the old covered wagon is soon to be a thing of the past. They say by rail it will only take about five days, and then a short stagecoach ride on to where we'll live -- so you see, Susie, we will see each other again."

Snowflake's hooves began to click on the cobblestone drive that they turned onto, which would lead them to the stonemason's business.

As they drove close to the whitewashed rock building, the front yard was strewn with gravestones, and Rose's heart sank as she thought of having to choose a stone for her papa's grave.

"Susie, I don't know whether I can do this. It really is too soon. I should have listened to you and Eddy -- I should have given myself more time to adjust to my papa being gone."

"It's all right, Rosie; we're here now, and I'm with you. Come on -- we can do this together."

Rose removed the white hanky with violets embroidered

in the corner, which was tucked in the sleeve of her dress, and dried her tears; trying to gain her composure, she climbed down from the buggy, ran her hand down the side of Snow's pallid neck, and draped the reins over the hitching post in front of the building.

As they entered the establishment, a bell rang from the top of the door and an old man walked in from a back room and said, "Good mornin', ladies -- and what can I do for you this grand day?"

Rose walked over, extended her hand, and said, "I'm Rose Collins, and this is my friend, Susan Delany."

The old man stepped over, took Rose's hand in his, gave it a gentle shake and said, "I'm glad to meet you. My name is Sam Jones. What can I do for you two ladies?'

"Mr. Jones, my papa, Jeremiah Collins, is recently deceased and I've come to order his headstone."

"Did you see a stone to your liking in the yard? If not, I have some in the back."

Rose picked out the stone that she thought would have suited her papa. She gave the proprietor the dates of her papa's birth and death and then she said, "I want this special inscription on the lower part of the stone -- it was a request made by Papa before he died, and it was very important to him.

"The inscription that I want is a line from a song in our church hymnal. This is what I want written:

" 'The mossy old graves where the
Pilgrims sleep will be opened
As wide as before—and the
Millions that sleep in the mighty
Deep will live on this earth
Once more.' "

"Rosie, I'm very curious to know what the lines from the song mean," Susan asked on the way back to their homes.

"Susan, my papa taught me about a God of love and mercy and fairness. The more I learn about His plan for mankind, the less fear I have, and the more I trust our heavenly Father.

"God wants us to worship Him out of love, and not fear. He wants our obedience because we have learned what a wonderful loving Father He is by viewing His creation and His written word.

"Back in the middle ages, Satan fabricated in the minds of men the concept of a God that would torture the unrepentant in a burning hell where they would live in unimaginable torment forever.

"These men with the evil mind of Satan tortured and killed all those who wouldn't espouse to their teachings, in what history calls the Inquisition.

"True Christians who wouldn't conform to the beliefs of this large rich church were tortured in horrible, unspeakable ways in the name of Christian religion -- but in reality, it was in the name of Satan.

"Their thinking must have been, 'If the God we worship is a God that would torture His creatures in hell forever, then He must be pleased if we torture those who don't believe the way we tell them to.'

"Instead of this hideous torture, God tells us in His word that we are to love our neighbor as ourselves. We are to do good to those who despitefully use us and persecute us, and to love our neighbor even if they are our enemies. This is God's mind—this is His heart!

"In reality, Susan, all people -- good, as well as evil -- go to one place when they die. The Bible says they go to their grave awaiting a resurrection.

"There are many scriptures that are twisted to make people think they don't really die, but that they either go to heaven or a tormenting hell.

"Emotionally, people like the idea that when a loved one dies, they don't really die but they go to heaven in the arms of those who have gone before them, instead of only being asleep in their graves. They don't usually like to think about or talk about the other place they may go.

"The problem is if that we believe no one really dies but the good instantaneously go to heaven, then it seems that we would have to believe the bad go to a torturous hell where they burn forever.

"Susie, I have always been so very thankful that I had parents that were religious but didn't teach an ever-burning hell; they understood the truth of this, not like most children that have to fight back that horrible fear.

"It is wrongly taught that human beings have an immortal soul that can't die. That is the first recorded lie that Satan told.

"He said to Eve in the garden, *'You will not surely die.'* When it is recorded that God told Adam,

"'Of every tree of the garden you may freely eat: But of the tree of the knowledge of good and evil you shall not eat, for in the day that you eat of it you shall surely die.'

"Satan was calling God a liar when it was Satan that was and is the father of lies! Satan's lie is that we humans can't die because we have an immortal soul. God says we can die Satan says we can't. Who are we going to believe?"

"Rose -- God, of course; I will believe God!"

"Susan, we can search the scriptures from Genesis to Revelation and we won't find the words immortal and soul used together. In fact, the Bible tells us, *'The soul that sins will die.'* The only one called immortal in the Bible is God himself. He is immortal.

"There is one particular passage in the book of John, Christ speaking, where His words are twisted to try and prove that Christ said, 'No one really dies.' But I have to tell you, Susan, it is a well-known fact that when the King James Version of the Bible was translated, some mistakes were made. If we look at the original Greek translation of this passage, the true meaning of Christ's words come clear."

"Really, Rose? Tell me what the real meaning of Christ's words was."

"Susan, the incident is recorded in the eleventh chapter of the gospel of John.

"Christ's good friend Lazarus had died and Christ was going to bring him back to life in a resurrection. This was to be another miracle to convince the people that Christ was the Son of God.

"Christ told his disciples, *'Then Jesus said to them plainly, "Lazarus is dead." Then Martha said to Jesus, 'Lord, if You had been here, my brother would not have died. But even now I know that whatever You ask of God, God will give You.'*

"Jesus said to her, 'Your brother will rise again.'

"Martha said to Him, 'I know that he will rise again in the resurrection at the last day.'

"Martha understood about the righteous rising from their graves to meet Christ at His return, *'At the last day.'*

"*Jesus said to her, 'I am the resurrection and the life. He who believes in Me, though he may die, he shall live…'*

"The King James Version of the Bible has for the next verse: *'And whoever lives and believes in Me shall never die.'*

"Now this seems a contradiction of what Christ said just before this, because He said, *'Though he may die, he shall live.'*

"Christ had just said that those who believe in Him, 'though they may die,' (be dead the way Lazarus was dead) would live, or be resurrected to life.

"But then He is misquoted as saying, 'Whoever lives and believes in Me shall never die'? But he just said they would die.

"The way to understand Christ's message is to know what the original Greek manuscript truly says translated into English.

"This is the true translation: *And to her Jesus said, 'I am the resurrection and the life; the one believing in me though he die, he shall live; and everyone living and believing in me will not die forever.'*

"Susan, have you ever wondered about all the people that have lived on this earth down through the centuries -- billions who have never had a chance to know the true God?

"Look at China and other pagan nations that in past centuries have known nothing about the true God -- only their pagan gods -- and one can't inherent the Kingdom of God by worshiping pagan gods. The true God calls this kind of worship an abomination.

"If one studies the Bible, one will discover that for centuries God was mainly working only with Israel; the rest of the people on earth, God wasn't revealing Himself to in the same way He was to Israel. It wasn't until the New Testament Church was established that the Gentiles were allowed to have their opportunity to be part of the family of God.

"Susan, I've read in the Bible that the only way into God's Kingdom is through Jesus Christ. Did all these people have a chance to know Jesus as their savior?"

"No, Rose; they couldn't have known Him."

"Then what has happened to all those billions who have lived and never had their chance to know Christ? Are they in their graves, or are they burning in an ever-burning hell with no hope?"

"Oh, Rose -- that would be so unfair if it were true."

"Susan, according to God's Word, no one's burning in hell. The Bible says there will be a future lake of fire where the incorrigibles will be destroyed, die in that fire, be burned up and perish. The Bible says they will be ashes under the soles of the righteous.

"This is really God's mercy -- if He allowed the rebellious to live forever, there could never be peace for them, or for anyone around them.

"Susan do you remember this scripture? I think everyone remembers John 3:16 -- *For God so loved the world that He gave His only begotten Son, that whoever believes in Him should not perish but have everlasting life.*

"The word perish in this scripture means not only to die, but to no longer exist. Those who have their chance to know Christ and reject Him will perish, but those who believe and obey will have everlasting life. If the incorrigible live forever in a burning hell, then they would also have everlasting life. But the Bible says they will perish, that they will experience what the Bible calls 'the second death.'

"Susan, the understanding of God's plan for those He has created takes much study and time, but I will tell you this much: according to the Bible, God is not trying to save the whole world at this time, in this age, but He is preparing a people to be teachers in the world to come.

"If during this age there is a battle going on between God and Satan for men's souls, then Satan would be winning. Under those circumstances, it would seem that Satan was mightier than God. We know this isn't true.

"If Almighty God is intending to convert the world to Him during this age, He would be succeeding in doing so. But this is not happening, so what is going on?

"You see, God has a seven-thousand-year plan. He has given mankind six thousand years to try and rule himself and to learn his complete incapacity to do so -- but God has reserved the last thousand years of His plan for His own rule.

"Jesus Christ will return to this earth and gather his saints to Himself in what is called 'the first resurrection'; these are the pilgrims that are now asleep in their graves in the line of the song.

"He will then take charge of this earth and the world will be renewed during the thousand years of His rule, and it will return to the way it was in the beginning, possibly even like it was in the Garden of Eden. The Bible says during this time *the desert shall rejoice and blossom as the rose. The water shall burst forth in the wilderness, and streams in the desert.*

"The Bible says during this time; *the wolf shall also dwell with the lamb, the leopard shall lie down with the young goat, the calf and the young*
    lion and the fatling together; and a little child shall lead them. The cow and the bear shall graze; their young ones will lie down together; and the lion shall eat straw like the ox.

"*They will not hurt or destroy in all my holy mountain, but the earth will be full of the knowledge of the Lord as the waters cover the sea.*

"The Bible also says during this time the people will say: '*Come and let us go up to the mountain of the Lord, and He will teach us of His ways, and we shall walk in His path.*'

"They shall beat their swords into plowshares, and their spears into pruning hooks; Nation will not lift up sword against nation, neither shall they learn war anymore."

"Susie, can you even imagine a world with no war, when there have been wars all of our lives?"

"No, Rose -- I can't imagine a world without war. Can you?"

"I can now that I've learned about God's plan, and I pray every day for that blessed day to come when there will be a world of peace and happiness -- and even among the animals there will be peace.

"But to further answer your question about the line from the song in the old hymnal, 'The millions that sleep in the mighty deep will live on this earth once more.'

"Here's what the Bible says is to happen after the thousand year reign of Christ and his saints, when the world has been renewed like the Garden of Eden.

"It says: *But the rest of the dead did not live until the thousand years were finished.'*

"When the thousand years are completed, it will be time for what the Bible calls the *White Throne Judgment Period.*

"Susan, can you even imagine what it will be like when all the millions of people that have ever lived and not had their opportunity to know Christ will come out of their graves and be shown this new world? What a glorious day that will be!"

"Yes, Rose -- and when they see the new beautiful world full of peace and happiness, surely there will be very few in that resurrection that won't accept Christ and His laws."

Chapter 4

"There's a storm moving in, Susie, so we'd better hurry and get back home before it overtakes us." Rose flipped the reins and said, "All right, Snow, let's pick it up! Let's go, girl!"

They could see the ominous dark blue-black clouds rolling in from over the mountains and the threatening streaks of lightning flashing down into the foothills. The lightning and the booming thunder were very frightening to Snow. The hard gusts of wind blew the buggy sideways. Snowflake's long white mane ruffled in the wind; her eyes were wild, and her nostrils flared.

"Look, Rose -- what is that up ahead lying in the grass?"

Rose pulled back on the reins to slow Snowflake, and as they drew closer they could see it was a dog, lying very still; the way it was stretched out on its side, they supposed that it was dead.

"Oh, poor thing—looks like she's been shot…wait a minute!" Susan exclaimed. "That's not a dog, it's a wolf! It must have been some wolf hunters that killed her."

"Look at her tummy; she's been nursing some pups. I wonder what happened to her puppies? I think we should see if we can find them."

"Are you crazy, Rosie? What if some of the pack is still hanging around? And the storm is almost upon us—I think we should just leave and head for home."

"Well, you can stay here in the buggy, but I'm going to look around."

"All right, I'll come -- but let's not take too long or go too far into the woods – okay, Rose?"

"All right, all right -- come on, fraidy cat; we won't go very far. Just a short look around and then we'll head for home."

The wind was whipping their skirts as they climbed down from the buggy, and as they stepped into the thick woods, the leaves were blowing up and all around them. They began to feel large drops of rain stinging their faces, and claps of thunder roared overhead.

They didn't have to wander very far into the woods before they came upon three wolf pups that had been shot.

"Oh, poor little things -- I wish we hadn't seen such a sight."

"Me too, Rose…and we better go; there's nothin' we can do here."

"Wait a minute -- did you hear that!? It came from over there, Susie. I can hear something whining! It's coming from those bushes."

Rose pushed the bush back and to her surprise, a lone pup, partially concealed in a clump of wet autumn leaves, was staring up at her. As she bent over to pick up the frightened little critter she said to Susie, "Well, look what I found behind this bush. He must have been hiding back here and the hunters didn't see him. Poor little fellow; I bet he's really scared and hungry."

"Rose, look -- his markings are different from the other pups. They're gray wolves like their momma, but this one's almost completely white with some mixed gray on the ears and down his back."

"There are no white wolves in this part of the country, Susie -- he must be half dog. Old man Williams has a white husky and I've heard he sometimes runs with the wolf packs and comes in all chewed up -- maybe he's this pup's papa.

"Come on, let's get us and this little fellow home and out of this storm."

"Oh, Rose -- let me hold him while you drive us home. He is so cute…just a little ball of white fur with those tiny wild wolf eyes."

Rose and Susan took their rain cloaks out from under the buggy seat where they had stored them earlier as a precaution against such a rainstorm.

Rose dropped her friend off and took the little wolf-dog puppy and wrapped him in her shawl close to her on the buggy seat, and draped the tail of her cape over him.

Even though the buggy had a cover over the top, the rain was still blowing in from the sides. The puppy snuggled close to Rose and stopped his incessant whining, and she headed Snowflake toward home.

The worst of the storm was moving away and the wind had subsided by the time they reached the farm house.

Rose pulled the buggy up in front of the barn and called, "Jessie, have you milked Myrtle yet?"

"Yes, Miss Rose, and the milk's in the kitchen on the counter."

"Jessie, come see what I've brought home, and you'll know why I need fresh goat milk."

"Hey, Miss Rose -- where did you find that little feller? He looks like a wolf. Miss Rose, you can't keep a wolf pup; the

sheep herders and some of the cattlemen around here are trying to wipe out the wolf population. They would never stand
for you raising a wolf."

"Now Jessie, have you ever seen a white wolf in these parts?
He's only half wolf, and I suspect Old Man Williams' husky is
his papa. If that's true, Jessie, then this little guy is half husky
and we know that breed of dog is very gentle -- so Jessie, don't
you worry; this little fellow is going to be a friend to the family... just you wait and see."

"All right, Miss Rose, but I wouldn't spread it around that
he is even half wolf. You'll need more than goat milk to feed
that pup -- you'll also need some kind of gruel to mix with it.
The best thing is rice. If'n ya have some rice, cook it and mash
it up into gruel, and then mix in some goat milk to thin it."

"How'd you know all that, Jessie?"

"Oh, I raised some pups when my old hound dog Sally died
after having her litter. Charlie Lucas, the vet told me what to
do and I saved all them puppies."

"Well, this little guy needs something to satisfy him right
now, so he's going to get some of that goat milk until I have
time to cook the rice."

"I'll help ya with him if ya want me to, Miss Rose. We'll
have to see if he can lap yet -- if he can't do that, we'll have to
feed him with something he can suck."

"All right, Jessie. I can use your help, but first would you
unharness Snow and rub her down, and give her some feed?
We got caught in the storm and she's pretty tired from fighting
the rain and wind."

Rose and Jessie managed to get enough of the goat milk
down the small pup to satisfy his hunger, and he fell asleep
curled up in Rose's shawl. When she tried to retrieve her wrap

he would wake up and start whining again. She said, "All right, little fellow, but I want that shawl back tomorrow."

Rose thought as she got ready to retire for the night, *What an emotional day this has been, ordering my papa's headstone and then finding the dead wolves and fighting the storm -- but that sweet little varmint we found was the highlight of the day. What if we hadn't gone into the woods? He would have starved to death or been killed by some other wild animal.*

That's what I'll name him; I'll call him Storm, because we found him in the middle of a rainstorm. Yes, I like that for his name. My little wolf-dog puppy, Storm.

The next morning was a gloriously beautiful day; the sky had cleared and the air smelled as fresh as honeydew after the rainstorm had cleared the air the previous day.

Little Storm was whining and yapping from inside the crate Rose had placed him in the night before. She lifted him up and carried him into the kitchen where she had prepared the rice gruel and goat milk. He ate until his little tummy was protruding and he could eat no more!

Rose said, "Storm, it's not going to take you long to grow up, with your appetite."

She cupped her thumbs under Storm's front legs with her fingers over his back and held him up and looked him square in the eyes and said, "What a pretty fellow you are, with that little wolf face and slanted amber eyes -- we're going to be great friends, you and I, 'cause I really need a little fellow like you right now. And you, Storm, you need someone to take the place of your momma -- and I guess I will have to do that for you."

She placed the puppy back in the crate after removing her shawl and placing a nice soft blanket in its place, and Storm fell fast asleep.

Rose walked to the barn. Jessie and Dan were busy with the chores.

Jessie and his wife and three children lived in the four-room log cabin on the Collins' property. They were given free rent and a modest salary for taking care of the farm, especially since Jeremiah had become ill.

He had worked for the Collins family for about twelve years now; Jeremiah had always been pleased with him as a hired hand, and also he had become an indispensable friend of the family.

His wife Lucy and their children helped in the fields and with the sheep and other animals, and whatever chores needed to be done.

Kip was their eldest son, who had just turned thirteen last month. He liked the horses, and especially the palomino named Nick.

He and Rose had been riding together several times, Kip on Nick and Rose on her horse Snowflake.

Rose had enjoyed their riding together, but she did have to call the boy out the last time they rode because he wanted to run Nick into the ground instead of taking time for him to rest. Old Nick wasn't up to what that boy wanted to lay on him!

Rose told Jessie, "I don't want Kip riding Nick by himself until he learns not to run him that way -- if he wants to ride alone, give him one of the younger horses."

Jessie said, "Yes, ma'am. I'll see to it."

Kip was a good boy; he just needed his papa's firm directing.

He and his border collie Tom took care of the Collins' small herd of sheep, and at times when needed, his sister Bell helped him. Bell was now ten years old and a great help to her momma, taking care of her little sister Janie and some of the kitchen chores. She was also a good little milker; sometimes when her papa was busy he would have Bell milk Myrtle.

Bell came out of the chicken coop where she had been gathering the eggs and said, "Hi, Miss Rose; we got a lot of eggs today."

"Come on, Bell -- bring them into the kitchen, and I have something I want to show you."

"What is it, Miss Rose?"

"Come on in and you'll see."

They walked into the kitchen and set the egg basket on the table.

"Look what's sleeping over here, Bell."

"Oh! Miss Rose, a puppy! He is so cute! Can I pick him up?"

"Well, all right, you can hold him and take the little fellow outside to do his business. Bell, his name's Storm because Miss Susan and I found him in a rainstorm."

"Oh, Miss Rose, I like that name. Come here, little Storm, and we'll go outside."

Jessie saw his little daughter with the puppy and he said to her, "Don't you get too attached to that wolf pup, 'cause he may not be around here very long."

Rose gave Jessie a strong look and then said to him, "I thought we were going to keep that fact confidential -- and you need to accept the fact that this pup is here to stay!"

Jessie wheeled around on his heel and headed back to the barn where Dan was working.

"Jess, did you say that was a wolf pup! What's she doin' with a wolf pup?" Dan exclaimed.

"Oh now, Dan, I spoke out of turn; that pup's only half wolf, and his papa is probably Old Man Williams' husky. Miss Rose knows what she's a doin.' Don't tell anyone what I said. I just got up kinda cranky this mornin' and spoke when I should have shut ma mouth."

"All right, Jess, I'll keep the secret. We don't none of us want it to get out that Miss Rose has a puppy that's even half wolf."

Jessie was a little sensitive about the wolf pup because a few months before when Kip and Tom were in the field checking on the sheep, they saw in the distance some wolves gathered around something. Before Kip could stop his collie, Tom took off like a shot toward the wolf pack. When the wolves saw the dog and the boy running toward them, they headed for the brush -- all except one lone wolf that wouldn't budge from the food he was enjoying. When Tom arrived he jumped on the wolf and a bloody fight ensued. By the time Kip arrived the wolf had run into the brush and Tom lay on the ground wounded. There was a dead lamb on the ground beside him, half-devoured.

Tom had a big gash on his side and Kip took his necker-chief off and wrapped it around the dog's body and then he whispered, "Come on, Tom, let's get out of here -- you hear me, Tom? Come on, get up…you're too big for me to carry, but come on and I'll help you. Come on, boy -- those wolves will be back after the rest of that lamb!"

Tom looked up at Kip and whined. He reluctantly got up to his feet and began to limp over to his master. Kip bent over and put his hands under Tom's body and helped him along until Tom was able to walk some on his own.

When they got close to Kip's home he saw his momma in the garden and he called, "Momma, we need help." Lucy threw the garden hoe down and ran toward her son. When she got there, she and Kip were able to carry Tom to the barn.

Lucy went after disinfectant and cleaned out the gash on the dog's side. She said to her son, "Now Kip, I'm going to have to sew up that wound, so you're going to have to talk to him and keep him still. It may even be necessary to tie his mouth shut if he tries to bite."

"All right now boy, you know Momma's tryin' to help you, so lie still, and it'll be over in a minute."

Tom looked up at Kip as though he understood what his master was telling him.

When Jessie came home, he was told what had happened and he said to Kip, "From now on when you're in the field with the sheep, I want you to carry the rifle. If you would have had a gun you could have driven those wolves off before Tom even got to any of them."

Tom's side healed in a couple of weeks, and he was up running around as if nothing had happened.

Chapter 5

After Bell brought the pup back in the house and into the crate, Rose took some of the eggs from the basket and told Bell to take the rest to her momma.

When she had left, Rose asked Jessie to saddle Snowflake.

Jessie said, "Miss Rose, I spoke out of turn a while ago. I hope you'll forgive me."

"Yes, Jessie; I understand your feelings, but you don't have to worry about Storm. I'm going to town to see our lawyer Henry Smith about Papa's will. I'll be back by lunch time."

Rose walked into Mr. Smith's office on the corner of Maple and Spruce Streets.

"There you are, Miss Rose; I've been waiting for you. I hope you had a pleasant trip into town?" Henry Smith commented.

"Yes, I did, sir, and I hope we can set a date to read my papa's will."

"How about next Thursday? And I want you to tell Jessie to come for the reading. Jeremiah has made some provisions for him in the will."

"Yes, Papa and I talked about Jessie and his family before he died. Without Jessie and Lucy and the children, I would have never been able to devote so much time to taking care of Papa. We both agreed on what is written in his will, but Jessie knows nothing about it."

"Well, Miss Rose, now's the time to tell him that he is in your papa's will -- but that's all I would tell him, if I were you. It will all be revealed next Thursday, say two o'clock in the afternoon?"

"That's fine, Mr. Smith. We'll see you then."

Rose mounted Snowflake and rode her to the hitching post in the front of Alford Claybrook's mercantile store. She opened the door and walked into the establishment. Ida May was behind the counter.

"What can I do for you, Miss Rose? Is there anything I can help you with?"

"Miss Ida, here's my list -- and I hope you have gotten some of those canned peaches in by now."

"Yes, I have. How many cans do you want?"

Just then, Alford came in the front door and Rose turned and looked at him. Their eyes met just for an instant before Rose lowered hers and said, "It's good to see you, Mr. Claybrook."

Alford pulled his hat from his head, his brown hair tumbling across his brow, and he said, "Miss Rose, how are you coping with your loss?

"It's good to see you out and about…and I do wish you would call me Alford instead of Mr. Claybrook. I think we know each other well enough for that, don't you?"

Rose looked up at Alford and saw his soft empathetic eyes smiling down at her, and it gave her such a warm delightful feeling that she said, "Yes, Alford, I think we do."

"Rose, I hope I'm not being too forward, but I would like to…I would like to come calling. Maybe we could go for a ride together, maybe have a picnic? Am I being too forward? Just tell me if I am."

"No, Alford -- I think I would like that."

"How about tomorrow? I'll bring the lunch and ride my horse Jo out to your place about eleven?"

"That's fine, Alford, but you don't have to bring the food. I'll prepare the lunch."

Rose bowed her head shyly but brought her eyes up to meet his, her face flushing, and said, "I'll see you then, Alford."

Ida May interrupted the moment and said, "Miss Rose, I have all that you ordered ready for you."

Rose gathered up her supplies and put them in the bags behind the saddle, and headed back to the farm. Her heart was still beating fast and her mind was in a whirl at the thought of Alford coming tomorrow.

The next morning was a beautiful fall day. The sun had made its way up over the horizon and was standing at lofty attention in the eastern sky.

Rose poured herself a cup of coffee, and picked up her little Storm and walked out onto the porch in front of the house. The air smelled sweet with the scent of the yellow roses vining up the trellis at the south side of the veranda.

Although the forest was strewn with golden beauty and the chrysanthemums were at their glorious height, the wild little critters of the forest knew it was time to gather for the winter months which, they understood, were just around the corner.

Rose set Storm down on the soft grasses and he scampered and wobbled around with his nose to the ground, sniffing here and there. Then he looked back at Rose with those little wolf eyes, as if to ask about that big wide world out there.

Rose walked out, lifted him up and set him in her lap, and swung back and forth in the porch swing watching the squirrels gather nuts from under the hicker-nut tree.

She said to Storm, "All right, little guy, it's time for me to get a picnic lunch ready -- so it's back into the house for both of us."

Rose gathered up cold fried chicken, left over from the day before, biscuits and fried apple pies and packed them into the her saddle bags.

She thought to herself, *It's been so long since I've had a fellow to call, and I am excited but also nervous because I find Alford very striking. Oh, but I mustn't let him know how I feel -- not this soon; after all, this is only the first time for him to call. How do I even know if he really wants to court me?*

She walked up the stairs and into her bedroom and dressed in her plaid cotton riding skirt that was split up the middle.

The fashions were beginning to change and women didn't have to ride sidesaddle any longer, although there were those who still disapproved of womenfolk riding astride a horse, but in that regard the split skirts had solved the problem of immodesty.

The long skirts were sewn and split up the middle but because of their fullness, it wasn't apparent until one mounted a horse.

Rose took a long-sleeved white blouse from her wardrobe, and her brown leather vest that matched the large-brimmed felt hat that her papa had bought for her a few years back.

She remembered what her papa had said when he gave her the hat. "My sweet little Rosie, I bought you this bonnet to keep the sun from your fair skin."

She pulled on her brown leather boots, took her hat in hand, left it with the lunch she had prepared, and went to the barn to ask Jessie to saddle Snowflake.

"Where you headed this morning, Miss Rose? I heard from

some of the men in town that a cougar had come down from the mountains and was after some of their livestock, so if'in your goin' ridin', ya better take your rifle and be on the lookout."

"Jessie, I'm not riding by myself today. Mr. Claybrook is coming this morning and we're going riding together."

"Oh, is that right, Miss Rose? Well, all the same, you need to be careful."

"Now Jessie, don't you worry; we will be fine. While we're gone, I would appreciate it if you would have Bell or Kip check on Storm."

"Oh, I won't have any trouble getting either one of them to do that, Miss Rose."

"Jessie, I also wanted to tell you that I saw Henry Smith yesterday and set a date for the hearing of Papa's will. The lawyer said he wanted you present."

"Me, Miss Rose? Why does he want me to be there?"

"Jessie, you'll just have to wait and see, but I can tell you this much -- Papa did leave you something in his will. We can go in together next Thursday at two o'clock."

"Okay, Miss Rose."

As Jessie turned his back toward Rose and began to walk into the barn to saddle the horse, he was scratching his head and saying, "Now I wonder what Mr. Jeremiah could have left me?"

Rose went back into the house and fed Storm his gruel mixed with a little chicken.

Her little mixed-breed puppy was growing like a weed, and his appetite was growing too.

Chapter 6

Rose looked at the clock on the mantel and it was nearing eleven. She picked Storm up in her arms, walked out onto the veranda, and sat down in the swing with Storm in her lap, watching down the road for any sign of Alford.

It wasn't long until she saw him coming on his dappled gray stallion.

She thought to herself, *Alford's horse is a beauty, but not as good-looking as the rider.*

Alford saw Rose on the front porch and waved to her. She rose up from her seat with Storm on her arm, and waved back. As he rode up into the yard, her breath left her for an instant, for he was so handsome in his high riding boots and leather jacket. Those deep brown eyes met hers again and he said with a smile, "What do you have there, Miss Rose?"

Rose, regaining her composure, said, "Come see what Susan and I found in the woods a few days ago. He's part wolf and part dog; don't you think he's beautiful?"

"Well now, let me see the little fellow."

Alford took him from Rose and raised him up in front of his face and said, "You are a handsome little guy, aren't you? Rose, how do you know he's part dog?"

"I'll tell you the whole story later, Alford, but now I guess we had better get ready for our ride -- don't you think?"

"Yes, I do think; I'm anxious to get started, too."

When the saddle bags containing their lunch were draped over Snowflake's hindquarters and a rolled-up quilt with a tablecloth inside was tied just behind the saddle, Rose and Alford were ready for their ride.

As they rode down the dusty country road, they cut across to the meadow.

"Where are you taking us, Rose?"

"You'll see -- we'll be there soon. It's one of my favorite places in all our land."

They galloped the horses through the wide field and walked them over a rocky pathway close the edge of a deep ravine. A little way farther, and they came to a sparkling blue- green waterfall cascading down and onto the smooth mossy rocks below, and into a flowing, bubbling stream. The water was shallow, and they guided the horses over the slippery rocks to the other side and into a beautiful valley surrounded by tall pine trees with a mixture of golden aspens.

Rose said, "This is the place I wanted you to see. Isn't it beautiful here?"

Alford said as he looked around, and then back into Rose's blue eyes, "Yes indeed, Rose; there is much beauty here."

Rose dismounted Snowflake and walked a few steps; with her arms extended out and upward, the palms of her hands toward the sky, she whirled around, her hat hanging from its cord and onto her back, her auburn hair flowing in the breeze and she said, "Oh, Alford … it is so…so lovely here, and I have so many memories of this special place, where our family spent many wonderful hours."

Alford dismounted Jo. The horse walked over to Snowflake,

and following her lead, began to graze on the welcome grasses.

"Look Rose, over there, just at the edge of the forest -- a doe with her fawn."

"Yes, I see them! But now they've disappeared into the thick woods."

They spread the quilt in a shaded area close to the brook, lay the cloth upon it, and spread out the food.

They ate while they talked; Alford told Rose that he had been very lonely since his wife died and how hard it had been for Jenny and Danny without a mother to care for them.

He said, "Since Papa passed, my sister Alice has come to live with us. She's fifteen now, and she and Jenny are asking questions that I don't know how to answer. There are just things I can't teach them. Miss Ida's some help, but she can't fill in for a mother."

"Why, Alford -- I'll be glad to help with your children, and Alice too -- that is, while I'm still here. You can bring them out to the farm anytime."

"What are you saying, Rose -- while you're still here? Where are you going?"

"Haven't you heard? As soon as I can sell the farm, I'm moving back to Missouri where the rest of my family lives. Papa didn't want me to stay in Oregon Territory without any family."

Alford looked very dejected and he said, "No, Rose; I hadn't heard."

And then Alford said, "You know, Rose, I have a sister who lives in Indian Territory and she's been after us to come visit. She would even like for us to move out there."

"Really, Alford? Are you considering it?"

"I just may give it serious thought -- at least it's closer to Missouri than Oregon Territory. I know, Rose, that was rather bold of me to say, but you have to know…I care for you."

Rose didn't say anything, but she was thinking, *Yes, Alford; and I also care for you.*

Instead she just said, "Alford, I would like to invite you and the children to come have Thanksgiving dinner with us. Doc Davis and his wife are coming, and Jessie and his family."

"That sounds wonderful. We'd be glad to come."

Rose said with a big smile, "Well, then it's settled. We'll have Thanksgiving together!"

"Now, Rose -- you were going to tell me about that little pup you found and why you're saying he is only half wolf."

Rose told Alford the whole story of how she and Susan had found Storm after his mother and siblings were killed, and the different markings that he had from the rest of the wolves.

"Yes, I bet Old Man Williams' white husky is Storm's papa. If that's so, it may be a good mixture. Huskies are known for their gentle nature, and that may help to offset some of the wild ways of the wolf."

"That's what I'm hoping for, Alford. I wanted to ask you not to spread it around that I have a wolf pup -- even if he is only half, some people wouldn't like me keeping Storm as a pet."

The sun was dropping farther into the western sky and the air was turning into an icy chill. Rose and Alford decided it was time to head back to the farm.

Unbeknownst to them, the cougar that Jessie had warned Rose about was in the near vicinity of their pathway home.

Even though Rose and Alford had no idea of the danger that lay ahead, they had noticed that Jo and Snowflake had become restless and somewhat jumpy.

They gathered up all their belongings, and Alford placed his hand on Rose's left arm and gently helped her into the saddle.

As he looked up at her beaming smile he thought to himself, *She is such a beautiful person -- not only is she elegant in appearance, but I know she has a kind and loving heart. Somehow, I don't know how, but I do know, I want her for my wife!*

Alford was silent as they rode back and over the rocky brook, except for an occasional longing glace toward Rose.

They galloped the horses in silence across the open field that led to the crossing of the narrow pathway.

As they neared the other side of the field, Rose and Snowflake out ahead, Snow became even more fidgety and Rose heard Jo behind her with a restless nicker.

Rose thought, *Maybe it was the rocky pathway with its deep ravine they knew was coming and it was making them nervous -- the narrow path had excited them before.*

The cougar had been drinking from the brook just a short time before Rose and Alford had arrived, and had been stalking them every since. Snowflake and Jo had sensed his presence.

On the south side of the pathway were high rocks; on the north was a deep drop-off. The cat was crouched on one of the rocks to the south, and as Snowflake and Rose came close, the cougar let out a blood-curdling scream!

Snowflake squealed. Her eyes wild with fright, she bolted back and then reared up, and Rose went tumbling down the ravine. Alford on Jo, close behind, pulled the rifle from the scabbard on the side of the saddle and fired in the direction of the scream! Out of the corner of his eye he saw the cougar run down the side of the boulder and off into the south woods.

Quickly he dismounted and ran to find Rose! When he came to the edge of the cliff he could see she had rolled into a patch of brush that had stayed her fall and kept her from slipping farther down into the chasm.

Alford called, "Rose, are you all right!? Don't move -- I'm coming down to get you!"

As he steadily made his way down the steep incline, he prayed, "Oh please God I plead with You that she not be injured!"

When he reached Rose he said, "Are you all right!"

"I think so, except my ankle does hurt."

"See if you can stand up, and I'll help you back to the top."

Rose tried to stand, but she said, "Oh, no -- Alford, I can't put my weight on it. Do you think it's broken?"

"I don't know, Rose -- but we just need to get you up this hill and home, and I'll ride for the doc."

Alford put his arms under Rose's arms and legs and picked her up.

"No, Alford -- it's too steep for you to carry me!"

Alford tightened his grip and swung her a little this way and that. He looked into her eyes and said with a wink and a smile, "No it's not, Miss Rose -- you're as light as a feather." But under his breath he prayed, "Please, God -- give me the strength to get her up this hill and to safety!"

Alford managed to climb to the top, and he took Rose and gently set her on a grassy nook where she could lean back onto a rock that was cushioned with soft gray moss. He removed Rose's boot, took his handkerchief from his back pocket, and wrapped it around her ankle for support as he said to her, "If we leave your boot on and your ankle swells…well, that just wouldn't be a good thing. This is better until I get you home and put some ice on it."

"That's all right, Alford -- whatever you think best."

Snow had run down the pathway from the fright of the cougar's scream, but was back now and waiting next to Jo.

Alford lifted Rose onto her horse and they headed across the last field and down the road to the farm. When they arrived, Alford climbed off Jo and walked over to Rose. She slid into his arms and he carried her into the parlor and lowered her onto the soft couch.

Jessie had seen them arrive, and seeing Alford carrying Rose, he knew something was wrong. He came to the front door and knocked. "Miss Rose," he called, "is everything all right?"

"Come on in, Jessie, we can use your help. Miss Rose has hurt her ankle and I need to go get Doc Davis. Can you chop some ice and wrap it in a cloth for her ankle?"

"Sure can, Mr. Alford. What in the world happened, Miss Rose?"

"That cougar that you warned me about…please, Jessie, go on and get the ice and I'll tell you all about it while Mr. Alford goes after the doctor."

Jessie wrapped the ice pack around Rose's ankle and set Storm in her lap, and Rose told him the whole frightening story.

Doc Davis arrived and examined Rose's ankle. He said, "It's not broken; just a bad sprain. Rosie, you need to stay off that ankle and you need to come to the office in a couple of days and let me check it again.

"Oh by the way, Alford asked me to stop by the mercantile and tell him my findings -- is there some romance brewing there, Rosie?"

"That's just none of your business, Doc," she said with playfulness in her voice. "Jessie and I are coming to town Thursday to hear Papa's will read. I'll stop at your office then."

As the doc was leaving he said, "See that you do -- and remember to stay off that ankle!"

"Oh, Doc; you don't have to be so crotchety. I don't always have to mind what you say," Rose said with a chuckle in her voice.

"Yes you do, Rosie Ann -- if you know what's good for you, you'll mind what I say!" Doc answered back with a twinkle in his eye.

Chapter 7

It was Thursday afternoon and Jessie hitched up one of the farm horses to the buckboard. He was anticipating what Jeremiah would have left him in his will. He just couldn't imagine what it could be, but he was certainly anxious to find out.

He walked up to the front door of the farmhouse and called, "Miss Rose, are you about ready to leave? It's time to go, Miss Rose!"

"All right, Jessie, I'm coming -- why are you in such a hurry?"

"I'm sorry, I jest want to find out what's in that will!"

"You'll find out soon enough. Let's go; I'm anxious too," Rose said with a smile.

They walked into the lawyer's office and Mr. Smith asked them to take a seat.

Jessie waited until Rose was seated; then he took off his hat and sat down.

With a formal, somber voice, Mr. Smith read the beginning of the will:

"I, Jeremiah Collins, being of sound mind, do bequeath all my worldly goods to my daughter Rose Ann Collins, with the exception of the log cabin which is situated on the fifty- acre plot in the northwest corner of the property. This cabin and the fifty acres I leave to Jessie Adams with the stipulation that he will not receive ownership until Rose Ann has sold the remaining three hundred acres of land, homestead, and farm animals and is ready to vacate the property."

Jessie was ecstatic. He said, "I can't believe it, the house and fifty acres! Why, Miss Rose, did you know about this?"

"Yes I did, Jessie; Papa said he wanted to know that you and your little family would always have a home on the property that you worked so many years. He said for me to tell you that you had earned this inheritance with your honesty, loyalty, and hard work."

"Well, I'll be -- that papa of yours was quite a man. Can't wait to tell Lucy and the young'uns that we actually will own the house and the fifty acres that we're livin' on!"

"Right now, Jessie, would you drop me off at Doc's office while you load the buckboard with the feed?"

"Sure will, Miss Rose."

On the ride home, Rose asked Jessie if he would tell Lucy to come see her, and they could plan the Thanksgiving dinner. "Tell her Doc and his wife, Susan and Eddy, and Alford Claybrook and his children are going to join us this year."

"It's going to be hard for you this Thanksgiving without your papa, isn't it Miss Rose?"

"Yes it is, Jessie, but Papa would want us all to enjoy the special day of thanksgiving, celebrating all our blessings and this wonderful land of freedom that God has so graciously given us where we can worship Him without fear of persecution."

Lucy and Rose planned the dinner of roasted turkey with all the trimmings, pumpkin and fruit pies, and cranberries.

Rose woke up early Thanksgiving morning, hurried and dressed in a beautiful bronze- colored blouse that made the glow of her cheeks even more outstanding, and complemented her auburn hair. She slipped into her long gathered black skirt and wrapped the wide black patent-leather belt around her small waist.

When she arrived in the kitchen she put on her long cotton apron, started a fire in the cook stove, and got the turkey ready to bake. She placed the stuffed bird in the roaster and placed it in the oven, breathed a sigh of relief, and walked out onto the veranda to greet the morning, Storm scampering at her feet, ready to be fed.

The sun was just coming up over the eastern horizon and casting its warming rays and diminishing the foggy mist that was still clinging to the tops of the trees and down into the hollows.

Lucy and Jessie and their children arrived and began to unload the pies and other goodies from the buckboard.

Kip jumped down and ran over and picked up Storm; Bell skipped over to Rose and said, "Miss Rose, what can I do to help? Momma let me help with the pies, and I know how to make biscuits."

"That's fine, Bell -- I'm sure there will be much that you can help with."

Lucy said to Bell, "For right now you can watch Janie and keep her out of trouble until we can get all this unloaded—she's already out there chasing the chickens!"

Bell ran after her, calling, "You come back here right now and leave those chickens alone, you hear me? Come here right now! That old rooster will flog you, little sister!"

That Thanksgiving Day was one to remember. All had a glorious time. After dinner, Bell, Janie, and all the other children went outside to play. They took Storm and he scampered and played with them.

As the evening came upon them, Doc Davis and his wife, Susan and Eddy, and all the rest said their goodbyes and headed for home.

Rose noticed that Danny, Jenny, and Alice left with the doc and his wife.

"I asked them to take my children with them so that I could talk to you alone, Rose. Can we sit down? I have something to say to you."

"Well of course we can, Alford; let's sit here in the parlor. What is it that you have to tell me that's so important?"

Alford and Rose were seated together on the couch. Alford turned toward Rose and said, "I have to confess that I have admired you for some time now...admire and even more... it's more like a beautiful attraction that has flourished into a deep love.

"Every since that day in your kitchen when I delivered your and your papa's groceries, I have been spellbound by your loveliness -- not only your outside beauty, but I know you have a generous heart...the way you took such good care of your papa told me that.

"I love you, Rose, and I want you to be my wife. But that's not all -- I received a letter from my sister Lucinda in Indian Territory. She and her husband Charles want me and the children and my sister Alice to come and live there. Since our parents died we have no other relatives here in Oregon Territory, and Lucinda is very lonely for her family.

"I know this is a lot to take in all at once, but I thought if we married we could go there together. It would be closer to your family in Missouri and we could visit them often."

"Oh, Alford -- it is a lot to take in, but yes, I will marry you.

I love you too, and I will be happy to become your wife."

Alford turned, took Rose into his arms, kissed her ever so gently and said, "You have made me the happiest man on earth."

Chapter 8

Fifteen years earlier, 1847

It had been nineteen years since the horrific, grueling and punishing removal of the Cherokee Indian tribes from their homeland where they were forced to move west of the Mississippi River to Indian Territory.

Although the move from their homeland had been a devastating experience for the Cherokees as well as other Indian tribes, the Indians that survived did learn to prosper in this rich land.

The Five Civilized Tribes -- the Cherokee, Choctaw, Chickasaw, Creek, and Seminole -- had become quite productive within this nineteen-year period. Some had even become quite wealthy, possessing large farms and many slaves, and having extensive trade in the Southern cities.

The Territory was well watered and wooded, and had much fertile land suitable for raising cereals and cottons, while the climate was mild and salubrious.

They produced large quantities of maple sugar, wild rice, cord wood, hemlock bark, and wool. They also possessed large herds of livestock.

The white settlers had begun to move into the Territory --

not only settlers who were looking for new land to raise their families, but also renegades that had come there to defraud and to pillage.

Because of the desperadoes, most of the inhabitants in Indian Territory wore firearms strapped to their hips or concealed on their bodies in some way or fashion, and they kept the shotgun loaded and handy in their homes.

With the Indians and the white settlers moving into the territory, there was more and more need for the addition of rural schools and teachers to fill the void.

The Federal Government put advertisements in newspapers across the land asking for teachers. They were offering a good salary and payment for passage.

Lucinda Claybrook, the older sister of Alford, came in from the living room and said to her momma, "I found an ad in the newspaper that says they are looking for teachers in Indian Territory."

Her momma replied, "What's your interest in the ad, daughter? You have a good teaching job here."

"I know, Momma, but they really need good teachers and the salary is much more than I am receiving now, and think of the adventure! Momma, I want to see more than this land I grew up in. I need a change and I'm thinking seriously about going!"

"Lucinda, I don't think your papa will allow you to go."

"Momma, I'm almost twenty-four and I don't need Papa's permission -- besides, the people around here are beginning to call me a spinster. Maybe I'll find someone if I widen my horizons and go east."

Later that evening when Joseph Claybrook returned home, his daughter presented her plans to him.

"Luc, I won't hear of such a thing! You are not traipsing off across the country to go to a strange land full of wild Indians! I won't hear of it! Do you hear me!?"

"Yes, Papa; I hear you, but you need to calm down. You know I can take care of myself; you've taught me well. I can ride as well as any man and I'm an excellent shot with a rifle -- you know that; we've gone hunting enough, and I got that big buck last year…remember?"

"You're still a girl, and you need to be taken care of."

"Now, Papa -- I'm a woman, not your little girl anymore, and it's your fault that I'm so independent…you know, you always insisted that I help you on the farm with the stock and the planting when I could have been here learning how to be a good cook, like Momma's teaching Alice."

Rachel, Lucinda's momma, spoke up and said, "You know she's right, Joseph -- you made her into a tomboy; that's one of the reasons that she's not married yet. It's gonna take a real strong, audacious man to get her out of those britches and walk her down the aisle."

Joseph's heart softened. He walked over to his daughter, put his arms around her, and said, "Luc, you are my little girl, and you always will be -- no matter how old you are."

"I know, Papa, and I know how much you love me -- and I love you, too, but I need to look into this and make up my own mind. If I decide it's what I want to do, I will need you and Momma to trust my decision and let me live my own life. I don't need your permission, but I would hope for your blessing."

The next day Lucinda sent a telegram to the educational administration agency in the advertisement and received an answer back that afternoon.

They said they would provide safe passage for all those in the area who qualified, and they had already received telegrams from several others in Oregon Territory and California who were interested in making the trip. It also stated in the telegram that they would provide temporary housing for the teachers when they arrived in Indian Territory.

Lucinda had been teaching ever since she finished school. She had graduated at the top of her class and taught at a little country school close to Sand Creek, only a couple of miles from her family's farm.

In the evenings, she helped her papa with the outside chores while her little sister Alice helped Momma with the housework.

This kind of outside labor had made Lucinda stronger than most women, and had assisted with her authority in the classroom. The older boys thought twice before acting up in her class.

Although Lucinda was stronger than the average woman, she was still quite attractive. She had a slender, good figure; her hair was long and black as a moonless night; and she had soft hazel eyes.

Most of the time, when she was working with her papa or riding her horse Jack across the fields, she wore her hair in braids tied with strips of leather -- but when she was teaching her students, it was in one braid and coiled into a tight bun on the back of her head.

She didn't resemble the average schoolmarm. She wore long full skirts down to her ankles, with a wide leather belt around her waist, and Western boots. Her blouses were made from fabrics loomed by the Wasco Indians.

Because of the Indians' dark features they dyed their fabrics with brilliant colors, such as bright blues and turquoise and scarlet. With Lucinda's black hair and olive complexion, she was also drawn to these vivid shades of color.

Lucinda had befriended some of the Indian women, especially Morning Star and Shining Lady. The three of them had become good friends, and they taught her much about the Indian ways. They also helped her stitch her brightly colored blouses with small ribbons and beads sewn into the bodice and cuffs, Wasco Indian style.

In a few days, a man came to the Claybrooks' door and asked to speak with Lucinda.

Rachel said, "Come in, sir, and I'll call her. Has this to do with the teaching in Indian Territory?"

"Yes, ma'am -- I have been authorized to substantiate her qualifications to teach."

Lucinda's momma called to her and they all sat down in the living room. Lucinda showed her diploma and a record of her grades, and gave him character references.

He said she definitely qualified, and he gave them more details concerning the trip to Indian Territory.

He also told her, "We have ten teachers that have qualified -- seven men and, counting you, miss, three women.

"Mr. and Mrs. Troy Elis are both teachers from California, and they have two small children. Mary Allen is a friend and teaching associate of the Elises, and will be traveling with them.

"We will expect you to share a wagon with Helen Wyman and her son and daughter.

"We will provide three more wagons for the men to share, and a hired man to drive the chuck wagon carrying provisions. Mr. Bob Williamson has been hired as the wagon master. He has made this trip over the Oregon Trail several times, and is well-qualified to get all of you to your destination. All of this will be provided by the Education Department of Indian Territory.

"Some of the men will be bringing their own horses, which they will be responsible for."

Lucinda spoke up and said, "I'll be bring my horse, Jack, and I will be responsible for him."

"That's fine, miss."

"We have contacted the United States Calvary at Fort Boise, and they will give an escort to Fort Hall. There will be a stopover for a few days and then an escort on to Fort Laramie. At Fort Kearny, you will leave the Oregon Trail and head directly south to Indian Territory.

"If everything goes well, the entire trip should take about six months. This is the first of February -- the trip should begin the first part of March for the group to make it to its destination and settle in before winter, which gives everyone a good month to get their affairs in order and be ready to travel."

Lucinda said, "Mr. Rifkin, that is not a lot of time to get ready!"

"Well, miss, most of the rest of the teachers answered the ad before you and have been preparing for the trip for some time. The Elises are already on their way here from California."

Despite the sadness of the Claybrook family, they did give their blessing to their daughter.

Lucinda's older brother Alford had volunteered to take his sister to the designated meeting place from where the trek to Indian Territory would begin.

It was a two-day trip by buckboard to the east side of Malheur Lake, and Lucinda didn't want to make the trip with her papa. He was still adamantly against her leaving, but out of respect for her, he had given his blessing. Alford, on the other hand, understood her independence and determination; although he was concerned for her safety on such a long trip after hearing the special protection of the cavalry, he had given his blessing.

Chapter 9

They left early Monday morning, with Jack tied to the back of the buckboard, and arrived at Malheur Lake Wednesday morning just as the sun was peeking up over the horizon.

Alford went with his sister to meet all that were gathered there. The wagon master was very friendly, and reassured Alford that his sister would be well taken care of.

Alford looked over the six covered wagons, including the chuck wagon, and could see that they were in excellent condition and all six would be pulled by sturdy mules that all seemed to be in good shape.

Alford wanted to be able to go back to the family and give as comforting a report as possible. He stayed until early afternoon and then kissed his sister, and they said their goodbyes, each promising to write to one another.

Lucinda loaded her belongings into the wagon that she would travel in with Helen Wyman and her two children.

After getting acquainted, Lucinda found out that Helen's husband had died a few years before, and it had been very difficult to support herself and her children, so she had jumped at the chance to make a new start in Indian Territory. Her son Tommy was now twelve years of age, and a big help to his momma with the chores, and taking care of his little sister Maggie.

As the day diminished and the western sky became tinted with yellows and golds, the sun slipped behind the horizon until only winks of light could be seen on the far skyline. The trail master asked everyone to gather round the large campfire to get better acquainted, and also for instructions and rules for the trip.

There was excitement in the air and everyone was discussing what the trip would be like, but also what they would encounter once they arrived in Indian Territory. Many of their questions were answered by the trail master, for he had come from that part of the midwest and was familiar with the activities there. The meeting broke up and they were all instructed to bed down early, for they would start out at first dawn.

Lucinda left the meeting and walked to where Jack was tethered in a line with the other horses. Jack caught her scent even before he saw her darkened form coming toward him in the blue-black night. He whinnied a gentle call for her, and as she approached, she called back at him, "Hey, boy -- how you doin'?" As she came close to him he raised his nose up in the air, and shook his head.

As she stroked his soft muzzle and ran her hand over his neck and down under his belly, she said, "It's all right, Jack -- you settle down, now. We've got a lot of riding to do tomorrow."

Jack was gilded buckskin, a beautiful muscular horse with fine lines. He was the smartest and most alert horse she had ever been around. Lucinda had raised him from a colt, and as soon as he was born she recognized how special he was, and she knew he would be hers. With those big black eyes and long lanky spindly legs, how could she not love that perky little fellow?

Lucinda spread her quilt in her end of the wagon and said

good night to Helen and the children.

In the far distance, they could hear the yapping howl of the coyote and the muffled voices of the other folks as they gathered their belongings and disappeared into the wagons.

Mr. Williamson, the wagon master, would be the first to keep watch, with his rifle in hand. He had appointed another man to spell him off at midnight, and then another would replace him at three.

Most of the Indian tribes in Oregon Territory were friendly, but they had heard of a band of Paiute renegades in this part of the territory, and they weren't taking any chances. Of course there would always be sentries posted through the night; this was one of the stipulations in the agreement of safe passage.

The morning dawned and the camp began to come to life. The mules were being hitched to the wagons, and everyone was scurrying this way and that.

Lucinda jumped up, folded her blanket, and quickly dressed. She told Helen, "I'm going to ride my horse part of the time, but I will spell you driving the wagon when you want me to."

"That's fine," replied Helen. "Some of the men have also volunteered to help us drive our wagon."

Lucinda saddled Jack, brought him into camp, and tied him to the back of the wagon.

Scraper, the chuck wagon cook, rang the bell to let everyone know that breakfast was ready.

Scraper was a jolly old man with a wiry rumpled beard and baggy pants, but he was one of the best chuck wagon cooks around. Everyone enjoyed his cooking; he could make a meal as simple as beans and cornpone into a delectable banquet.

After all were fed, the wagon master called everyone together and explained to them, "We should be in Fort Boise in three days, and when we arrive we will be provided a military escort, but until then we all need to keep a watchful eye out for danger. Above all, we need to beseech God's protection on this long journey, so if everyone will bow their heads, we will ask His blessings."

Within the next couple of days, Lucinda got well-acquainted with Helen and her children, as well as most of the others in the wagon train.

Tommy wanted to ride Jack, and Lucinda, finding that he was not a well-seasoned rider, wouldn't let him ride her horse.

"Sorry, Tommy -- but Jack's just too frisky for you to ride. I'll let you ride with me sometimes, and maybe after some training you well be ready to ride him by yourself."

Lucinda tied Jack to the back of their wagon, rode on the wagon seat, and conversed with Helen. They quickly became friends.

The second day out, they saw a group of Indians in the distance, but they didn't come close. The wagon master said, "It is probably a hunting party; nothing to worry about," but when he spoke to them his words didn't match the tone in his voice—his voice said that he was worried, and when night came, extra sentries were posted.

It was the wee hours of that dark moonless night, the only light being the flickering of the dying campfires. The two sentries were at their posts, but the darkness and quiet night had drawn them both into inertness near slumber.

The Paiute Indians had been trailing the wagon train and had seen the fine horses that the men had brought with them, and which they were waiting for a chance to steal. One brave especially was taken with Lucinda's sturdy buckskin, with his showy black flowing mane.

Four of the Indians moved slowly on their bellies through the thick underbrush, with only the muffled sound of crackling twigs as they made their way close to the tethered horses.

They began loosening the reins of the docile, halfway slumbering horses, but when they came to Jack, he protested with a loud whinny! The Indian grabbed him by his halter and Jack jumped back, pulling free with a loud scream!

The sentries came to fast attention, cocked their rifles, and headed toward the horses. Jim Clay, with his heart pounding, began firing in the air as he was running toward where he heard the scream. The Indians, hearing the rifle shots, dropped the horses' reins and disappeared into the thick dark brush!

The whole camp was up! Lucinda came running to see what all the commotion was about. Someone told her that Indians had tried to steal the horses, but one of the mounts had protested and warned the camp.

"I know it was Jack! He wouldn't let anyone take him! He's a fighter; my Jack's a fighter!" Lucinda said excitedly.

She ran to where the horses were, and there was Jack, safe and sound. She went over to him and rubbed his neck, kissed his muzzle, and said, "It's all right, boy -- I know you're the one who warned them. Even if they don't know, I know it was you!"

In the eastern sky a faint light began to appear, and there was no reason for anyone to return to their beds, for it was apparent that a new day had begun to dawn.

The last day before they reached Fort Boise was uneventful until they reached Three Island Crossing to ford Snake River on Glenn's Ferry. The bountiful spring rains had swollen the river to its banks, and the water was swift and treacherous -- even for crossing on the ferry, it was dangerous.

It took several men to work the ferry, but Allen Young was

the owner and the man in charge. He told them that he had six mules on the west side of the river and six on the east, to pull the ferry across.

He explained that the ropes and the mules were strong, but with the raging waters it would be safe to take only two wagons and their teams at a time.

"When the river was calm, a few more horses could be loaded -- but not in these waters," he said.

It took the remainder of the day to get the wagons and horses across. But they forded the river without any calamities. They made camp on the other side, in Idaho Territory.

Tomorrow it would be only a few more miles until they would reach the fort, and they could breathe easier when they left there with a cavalry escort.

The setting sun cast a pale pink shadow over the grassland. Lucinda and Helen settled down around their campfire, Tommy and Maggie running and playing with some of the other children.

Henry Shelton, Timothy Elis, and his wife Elaine stopped by their camp to visit. Henry was a tall husky man with a good-sized mustache and a glint in his eye for Lucinda. He wasn't a good-looking man but he wasn't homely, either; somewhere in-between.

They talked about what their plans were when they reached Indian Territory.

Henry said, "I want to teach, but I also want to find me a wife, settle down, and raise a family."

As Henry spoke, he couldn't seem to keep his eyes off Lucinda, although she didn't give him any encouragement.

After everyone left and it was just Lucinda and Helen, Helen said to Lucinda, "You know Henry is interested in you."

"I know, but I'm not at all attracted to him. What about you, Helen? Are you interested in him?"

"Lucy -- do you mind if I call you Lucy?"

"It's all right; I don't mind."

"It will really take a special fellow for me with my two young'uns; someone who could love them as much as if they were his children."

"It is true though, Helen, you do need a husband. If you pray and ask God, He will provide a good man to love you and your children."

"Do you really believe that, Lucy?"

"I do, and I'm sure there is a right mister out there for me. God knows who he is…I just have to wait until he comes into my life, and I'll know when he does."

"How can you be so sure that you'll know him?"

"Helen, I just know…and Henry isn't him!"

Helen was a pretty woman with blonde hair and blue eyes; she was very petite, a little plump, but with very sweet and feminine ways.

The next morning there was excitement in the air because everyone knew they would be arriving at Fort Boise before the day was over.

Henry Shelton came by and asked if he could drive Lucinda and Helen's wagon. Helen accepted and Lucinda thought to herself, *That will give me more freedom to ride Jack and explore some of the countryside up ahead.*

Chapter 10

That morning Lucinda wore her high boots and leather riding skirt for protection from the brush and high weeds. She was also adorned in her bright turquoise shirt with white beads and ribbons that the Wasco Indians had aided her in making. She wore her hair in braids, as always.

As the five wagons pulled out, Mr. Williamson, the trail master, rode his large bay up next to Lucinda and Jack.

"I have been watching you Miss Claybrook, and I've noticed that you are an excellent rider -- most women wouldn't bring their own horse on such a long journey."

"I would be lost without Jack. I raised him from a colt -- and besides that, I've been riding all my life. I can't even remember when I first sat on a horse. My papa taught me well."

"I can see that he did, miss."

"You don't have to be so formal, Mr. Williamson; it's a long journey for formalities. If you wish, you can call me Lucinda."

"All right, Miss Lucinda," Williamson said with a receptive smile as he kicked his bay and galloped on ahead.

Lucinda noticed Sam Casey and Ronny McMahan, who had also brought their own horses, riding out across the grass land, and she turned Jack and headed off to join them.

Sam and Ronny saw her riding toward them and Sam said,

"Hey, Ron -- watch how that woman rides -- like an expert, like she was born on a horse."

"Yeah, and she cuts quite a figure, too … but it's gonna take a strong man to tame that female!"

"Well, then -- it's not gonna be the likes of you, cowboy!"

"It's not gonna be you, neither, you old mule skinner!"

"Mule skinner? Who you callin' a mule skinner?!"

Lucinda rode up and said, "What are you two arguing about this time?"

Ronny spoke up and said, "Oh, Lucinda, it's not an argument -- just funnin'. Come on; let's ride."

They galloped their horses over the grassland that rippled like a vast green sea, but the looming mountain range could be seen in the far distance.

Sam said, "We'll reach the fort before we reach the mountains. Taking these wagons over those mountains is a fearsome thing to think about, but the trail boss says it's not as bad as it looks if we go the southern pass, and that's the way he's planning on taking us."

Lucinda said, "Thanks for that bit of encouragement, Sam; I think we're all going to need a lot of that kind of reassurance before we reach our destination. Come on; let's head back to the wagon train."

As they approached the wagons, they saw the wagon master out ahead; he raised his arm in the air, waved his hand, and yelled, "Fort Boise direct ahead! I can see the fort!"

Everyone cheered with excitement and hurried the mules to a trot. Mr. Williamson rode back to the wagons and said, "Ho! Slow those wagons down -- we don't want to overtax the mules -- they still have a lot of land to cover. We'll get to the fort soon enough!"

As the wagon train pulled into Fort Boise they were greeted by a barrage of soldiers, their wives and children running after the wagons, dogs barking, all excited to see new faces coming into their domain.

Major George Baker and Lieutenant Mark Smith came to the first wagon, where the wagon master had ridden his bay.

Major Baker introduced himself and then Lieutenant Smith. Mr. Williamson introduced himself and some of the others that were close by.

"Welcome to Fort Boise," the major said. "We hope you will be staying a couple of days. We planned on having a celebration of your arrival tonight with a get-acquainted dance. We hope this is something that is pleasing to you all. The ladies will have prepared a feast -- so bring your appetites with you."

"Thank you, major; that sounds great, I would like to talk to you concerning the soldiers who will be going with us when we leave. How many can you spare?" the wagon master asked.

"Yes, yes," he said abruptly as he turned on his heel and waved to his lieutenant. "We'll talk about that later -- right now, follow my lieutenant, and he will show you where to pull your wagons and get settled."

Fort Boise was a large fort, thorough in its surrounding walls. The walls encompassed a row of army barracks on the south for the soldiers without wives or family, and on the north living quarters of those with families. On the west end of the fort were the officers' quarters, with the major's office, and a large meeting hall in the center. In the south corner were the large barn and the corrals for the stock.

The complete complex covered a four-acre plot of land with a Shoshone Indian settlement on the south close, to the White Water Creek.

The Indian settlement was as close to the fort as the army would allow, for protection from the Shoshones' enemies, the Paiutes.

The Shoshone village had been close to the fort for many years. They raised corn and other vegetables, made jewelry and pottery, and traded with the white man. The army shipped some of the corn off to be sold, and saved some to feed their stock. They also shipped the pottery and jewelry to towns and settlements farther east, making a good profit for the fort and the Indians, as well as helping the white man and the Shoshone to live with a mutual peaceful understanding. This had not always been the case. The Indian settlement hadn't always been this close to the fort.

Chapter 11

Over Thirty Years Before

Over thirty years before, when Fort Boise was a relatively new fort, a young lieutenant named Jim Clancy, set on making a name for himself, slaughtered as many Indians as he could find.

When he was sent to Fort Boise by some in authorities to do the same against the Shoshones, he was told by those in charge of the fort that the Shoshones were a peaceful, cooperative tribe, and when he persisted in his vicious dialogue of "The only good Indian is a dead Indian," he found himself in bristling opposition.

Clancy and his army of butchering troops backed off and acted as though they were in agreement with the fort authorities; if the Shoshones weren't causing any trouble, they could be left alone. All the while, they were secretly planning to attack the Indian village.

A few months before, the merciless slaughter of the red man by this lieutenant and his followers had gotten back to some in Washington, who were adamantly against the cold-blooded slaughter of the Indians. They sent word that this Jim Clancy was to be stopped!

Lt. Colonel Scott McCord, with his platoon of troops, was hot on Clancy's trail and was only a short distance from the fort when Clancy and his troops pulled out and headed to the unknowing Shoshone village.

As Lt. Colonel McCord and his troops pulled into the fort and dismounted from their horses, they enquired after Lieutenant Clancy.

The major said, "They rode out just a short time before, their destination being Fort Hall."

Lt. Colonel McCord asked, "Is there an Indian village close by, and did the lieutenant ask about it?"

"He did, and they acted in the beginning as if they were going to wipe out the tribe, but after they were informed that the Shoshones were a peaceful people, their tyrannical attitude changed and they said they were leaving to head for Fort Hall."

Lt. Colonel McCord scowled, and shouted, "Hurry! Sound the alarm, muster your troops, and mount your horses! They're on their way to slaughter all in the village -- call a guide now, who can lead us to the Indian camp!"

The major grabbed the closest trooper and gave him instructions to lead McCord and his troops to the Indian village with no delay. It was imperative to not waste a second of time in leading them to this destination.

The trooper grabbed the nearest mount, slung himself up in the saddle, and headed out the front gate with McCord and his troops close behind.

The villagers were busy with their everyday work, the women either tending to the tedious job of scraping buffalo hides to make them soft and supple, or fashioning pottery or jewelry; the men planning their next hunting party; the children running and playing, with no concept of the approaching peril just a few miles away.

Clancy and his troopers were in no hurry to get to the village, making their hideous plans as they sauntered the horses toward the camp.

Lt. Colonel McCord and his troopers were riding hard, the horses breathing heavy as they galloped in a hard run.

As Clancy and his men came close to the camp, they separated into four divisions to surround the unsuspecting Shoshones.

Two children down by the creek, Little Bear and Yellow Bird, saw the soldiers circling around, and ducked behind some bushes. They heard gunfire coming from the other side of the village and they lay still and quiet, afraid even to breathe.

The barrage of bullets continued -- women and children began to run out of the village toward the heavy trees and bushes for cover!

The braves were running for the few rifles they possessed, and any weapons they could gather…but they weren't prepared and the whirl of bluecoats was upon them, cutting them down -- old men, women, and children were falling!

All of a sudden the air was filled with the blast of a bugle: the long, ear-piercing call to retreat!

Clancy and his butchering bluecoats pulled up their mounts and stopped firing with surprise and confusion, their heads turning this way and that. Clancy yelled, "Who's sounding retreat? Who blew that bugle?"

The men began to back off; they had been trained to retreat at that sound, and in their confusion they knew nothing else to do!

McCord said to the bugler, "Keep sounding --don't stop!"

As Clancy's men in their retreat began to leave the camp, the Shoshone braves gathered their rifles, lances, and bows and fired upon them with all their strength, cutting a few of them down!

Lt. Colonel McCord and his men couldn't ride in and help the Shoshones; the Indians wouldn't know them from Clancy's men.

While the braves had turned away from the village and toward the retreating soldiers, Clancy had not left; in his depraved, bloodthirsty mind, he turned on a group of women and children who were hunkered down close to a tepee.

Scott didn't see Clancy; he had a sick feeling in the pit of his stomach that told him to ride into the camp and find him. He and two of his troopers circled around on the east and came into the camp just as Clancy aimed his rifle at the frightened vulnerable group of children and women!

There wasn't a second to spare, no time to call him down a warning; all McCord could do was raise his rifle and fire!

Clancy fell from his horse and lay dead on the ground, his blood mingled with that of a young wounded Shoshone brave who lay only a foot away.

Some of the soldiers from the fort, whom the Shoshones recognized, rode up and called for Clancy's men to lower their weapons. They held their hands up for the Indians to stop their attack!

After McCord shot Clancy, he dismounted his large stallion and ran over to look after the women and children that Clancy had aimed to kill. He took the hand of a young Indian maiden and lifted her up to her feet, her head bowed down to the ground. As she rose, she lifted her head and looked into the eyes of the one who assisted her.

For one instant, McCord was spellbound. He thought, *Such loveliness, those beautiful, gentle dove eyes ...* he had never seen a female with such an exquisite form as this little sweet Indian maiden, and just observing her that instant, his heart was pounding with excitement.

Her name was White Willow, the daughter of Chief Pocatello. She was considered a princess by the tribe. All the braves wanted to win her for their own, but White Willow hadn't accepted any of the braves as yet.

McCord, regaining his composure, ever so gently let go of White Willow's hand, and taking hold of the bill of his hat, he gave his head a forward dip, turned back toward his mount, and rode out toward the other soldiers.

He spoke sharply to Clancy's men. "Your leader is dead, his blood mingled with the blood of a Shoshone brave. Your cruel bloodletting is also over, and if I have anything to say about it, you will all be court-martialed!"

He yelled, "Now pick up your wounded and your dead, and get back to the fort on the double!"

He said to the soldiers from the fort, "Make sure that's where they go!"

McCord went back into the Indian village to help with the casualties. Chief Pocatello came to him, and with an interpreter from the fort, thanked him for saving his daughter and others.

Scott saw Pocatello's daughter across the camp, and it was though she felt his gaze -- for in an instant she turned, and their eyes met.

Chapter 12

Lt. Colonel Scott McCord was a man in his early thirties, a tall well-built fellow with sandy red hair and steel-gray eyes. He wore his army blues well, with high black boots, a yellow kerchief around his neck, and a long saber at his side.

McCord sent a wire to his superiors and explained the situation. He asked for permission to stay at Fort Boise until things had quieted down.

He received word back that he was given permission to remain in that area as long as necessary. The bad news was that Lieutenant Clancy's men were not to be reprimanded, for they were only following orders from those in Washington who wanted to wipe out the Indians.

McCord knew there were conflicting views in Washington and there wasn't anything he could do about it -- except he vowed to save the innocent in any way that he was able. He had begun here at Fort Boise, and he intended to help this Shoshone village while he was here at fort Boise.

In a few days McCord and the interpreter, Captain Harry Martin, and Major George Baker rode to the Shoshone village. They were informed that they had lost many of their young braves -- four women and three children had been slaughtered.

Major Baker explained to Chief Pocatello and the other

council members that he and the other officers thought it wise for the remainder of their village to move close to the fort, especially now that so many of the young braves had been killed.

Major Baker said, "With your village close to the fort, we can better protect your people from your enemies the Paiutes, or any other crazed soldiers that may come into our midst."

The Chief of the Shoshones and the council agreed that they would move close to the fort, and within a few weeks the move was complete.

Lt. Colonel Scott McCord couldn't forget the beautiful Indian princess with the dark dove eyes and sweet shy smile. He knew that in the early morning hours, the Shoshone women spent time at the stream to fill their water skins and wash their garments.

He asked Harry Martin to help him learn to speak Shoshone, at least a few words, like "hello" or "you are very beautiful."

Scott decided it was time to try and get to know this maiden, this lovely girl called White Willow.

It was early morning, and the sun just up above the horizon cast its iridescent light over the trees; the meadow flowers sparkled with shimmering diamonds from the drops of dew that had formed on their soft, supple petals.

McCord left the fort and strolled over the meadow, bent down and selected a handful of daisies and other wildflowers, and tied them together with a limber green stem.

He was so hoping that White Willow would be at the flowing brook, and as he came closer he saw her bending over the stream filling a clay pitcher. When she rose to her feet and turned, Scott was standing there looking at her, and she backed away startled and frightened.

Scott said, "Oh, I didn't mean to frighten you." And then

he thought, *She doesn't know what I'm saying.* He held out his hand with the wildflowers and said in Shoshone, as Harry had taught him, "Hello, White Willow. I come in friendship."

She cautiously took a step forward and procured the flowers from Scott's hand. She brought them to her nose and smelled their fragrance.

Scott thought, *How lovely she looks with the morning light dancing on her hair—hair that is as black as midnight.* Her thick braided tresses, intertwined with tiny strands of doe hide, hung down her back past her small waist.

White Willow made her way to a large boulder and sat down. She patted the rock with her hand and motioned for Scott to sit by her.

Scott planted himself on the rock and said to her in Shoshone, "White Willow, you are very beautiful."

He knew her name but she didn't know what to call him, so she gestured by bring her small hand to her mouth, and then brought it toward his.

Scott said, "Oh, you want to know what I'm called. I'm called Scott. My name is Scott."

Willow said, "Scott."

He nodded his head and said, "Yes, that's it! Scott!"

Willow smiled and said his name again.

Willow was as taken with Scott as he was with her, and with the permission of her father Pocatello, they spent much time together. Harry taught more of her language to Scott, and he and Willow began to understand one another, she learning English and he learning Shoshone.

Major George Baker and some of the other officers at the fort had warned Scott that he couldn't marry Willow and bring her to live at the fort. Such a union wasn't allowed and wouldn't be tolerated -- but Scott didn't care; he loved Willow, and she loved him.

Scott came to the decision that he would resign his commission as soon as he was allowed and he would make a life with Willow, but for now he would marry her the Shoshone way.

He planned on saving his pay and adding it to the nest egg that he had already accumulated until he could purchase a plot of land for their home, and then he would resign. Until then, Willow would live in the Indian camp and he at the fort, but he would be with her as much as he could.

As was the tradition of the Shoshones, Scott brought five fine horses to Pocatello in payment for his daughter's hand in marriage.

When this gift was accepted by the chief, a special wedding lodge was built.

The Shoshones had no formal ceremony. The wedding lodge was built and on the day of its completion, Willow was given to Scott.

Willow came from her parents' lodge dressed in a white buckskin wedding garment covered with turquoise beading and long flowing fringe that hung down over her white buckskin moccasins.

When Scott saw her she almost took his breath, she was so beautiful.

Scott was dressed in his finest formal army uniform. His pants were creased to an edge and his high black boots shined to a shimmer.

Scott was handed a large colorful Indian blanket by Willow's mother. Scott had been informed that he was to hold the blanket behind him, holding on to the corner over his left shoulder and the other corner with his right hand, his arm straight out to receive his bride.

When White Willow stepped into the blanket he was to close it around her, and the two were to enter the wedding lodge together wrapped in the wedding blanket.

They were married now, and their honeymoon consisted of everyone staying away from their lodge except when food was left at the entryway. There was also a special place in the timbers that was designated just for them; any intrusions were strictly forbidden. It was a charming secluded place by a beautiful flowing waterfall that gushed into the sparkling Sweet Water Brook.

McCord's superiors gave him a two-week leave; although they didn't approve of him marrying an Indian, they respected his right to marry White Willow.

They had a wondrous, joyful two weeks together before Scott had to return to his regiment. When he returned to the fort he was given his orders; he and his troops were ordered to fort Hall for a month.

Scott and Willow were very saddened to find out the news, and it was a very difficult parting.

"My sweet lovely Willow, the time will pass quickly and I'll be back in your arms, I promise."

"Oh my Scotty, how I love you -- come back to me soon. I will count each setting of the sun and each lonely night until you return."

Chapter 13

Scott was gone much longer than the month he had been assigned, for it was over two hundred and fifty miles to Fort Hall, and it would take the regiment a good ten days, with good weather, to arrive and also at least that long to return. Scott found out the travel time wasn't included in the month's assignment.

While they were on duty, trouble broke out with some of the renegade Indians, with much unrest and fighting. The authorities at Fort Hall expected Lt. Colonel McCord and his troops to remain until things had settled down.

Scott sent telegrams to Harry Martin and asked him to interpret them to Willow.

It was a good three months before Scott returned, and when he did, he found Willow was carrying his child. They weren't planning a family this soon, but Scott was joyful that she was going to have his baby. He thought to himself, *I can't wait any longer; I have to start looking for land where I can move my family after this child is born.*

He let his superiors know that he was resigning his commission before the year was out.

Scott found a beautiful spot just north of the fort, about two miles from Snake River. The cleared land had an abandoned two-room log cabin on it and the Sweet Water Brook was only a few yards from the cabin. There was no claim to the land, for it had been abandoned by squatters; no claim was ever registered.

Scott claimed the land, and he and Willow began to make plans to move there after the baby was born.

Willow was now heavy with child, and Scott spent more and more time in the Indian village close to his sweet Willow.

The night came for White Willow to deliver. Her mother, Morning Flower, and Scott were by her side, the two midwives, Forest Water and Returning Moon told them both to leave the lodge until the baby came.

They waited in anticipation for the new arrival, but hours passed and there was no news from the lodge -- only agonizing cries from Willow.

Forest Water came out of the lodge and called for the tribal medicine man Wild Wind. He hurried into the lodge.

Scott grabbed Forest Water by the arm and said, "What's going on in there? You tell me now, or I'm coming in to see for myself. You tell me now -- is Willow all right?"

A baby's cry came from the lodge and the Indian woman came to the door of the lodge and said, "It's a boy. You better come in, Scott; Willow wants to see you."

As Scott approached where Willow lay on a buffalo pelt, the medicine man shook his head at Scott and said in his native tongue, "There's little time."

Willow's rosy cheeks had gone pale and drawn and she was very weak, but she was able to hold within the bend of her arm their tiny baby boy.

"Oh, my Scotty, come close and see your boy. You must raise him well. His name is to be Strong Eagle, for our love has been as strong as the flight of the eagle that soars in the luminous sky!"

Willows voice rose with emotion. "Tell me, Scotty! Tell me you'll give him the name Strong Eagle!"

Scott was down on his knees, gently stroking Willow's forehead. "My sweet Willow, we will name him Strong Eagle, and we'll raise him together."

Willow's eyes closed; her breath left her, and she was gone.

Scott called with a loud cry, "Oh no, Willow! Please don't leave me, my sweet Willow, my darling, sweet Willow -- don't leave me!"

Wild Wind came and took Scott by the shoulders, raised him up and said, "She's gone now; you must think about your son. Fawn Shadow's baby was stillborn only a few days ago -- she can nurse him."

Returning Moon ever so gently took the baby from his mother's arm, and she and Willow's mother, Morning Flower, took him to the young Indian maiden who had lost her infant. She was still heavy with milk, and was glad to nurse this tiny baby boy.

Scott mourned Willow for many months. He lamented by her grave and meandered in the woods where they first began to get acquainted by that special rock where she had ask him to sit by her side.

The months passed, and Strong Eagle was old enough to be weaned from his nursemaid, Fawn Shadow.

When it was time for Scott to take his son to the fort to live with him, he explained to Fawn Shadow that he would bring him to visit often. It was very difficult for her to lose the child she had nurtured for these long months, but she had discovered that she was again with child, and this eased the grief of losing this little one named Strong Eagle.

Scott also assured Chief Pocatello and Morning Flower that their grandson would spend time with them as he grew up.

The child's Indian name would always be Strong Eagle, as Scott had promised Willow, but Scott gave him the Christian name Charles Edward McCord after his father and grandfather.

Charles attended the school at the fort and was a good student—quick to learn, and strong in body and mind. He became well-educated in the white man's ways, but he also spent many hours with his grandfather Pocatello in learning the Shoshones' ways.

When Strong Eagle was of age, the age when a boy became a warrior among the Shoshones, Pocatello presented him with a special necklace. It was an eagle carved from a buffalo bone, set together by long hair pipe and other beads. Pocatello explained to his grandson the great meaning of the eagle among the Shoshones.

"The eagle is the master of the sky and a carrier of prayers to the great creator in the heavens.

"Strong Eagle, wear this necklace well, for it gives you a special connection to that great creator.

"Your mother White Willow, before she died, saw in a vision that your name was to be connected to the eagle and you would have to be strong because of your divided heritage. Your mother's prayer for you, Strong Eagle, was that you would use that divided heritage to help make peace between the two nations in any way you were able."

From that time on, Strong Eagle was never without the eagle around his neck, and when he held it in his hand he remembered his mother's vision.

Chuck, as he was called by his friends at the fort, had a special gift with horses. He rode and trained the Indian ponies as well as the cavalry's stock.

Chuck had no desire to join the army. He told his father that he would remain a civilian. He never wanted to be in a position where he would be ordered to kill any of his people, white man or Indian.

He did become a civilian scout for the army. Trained by his grandfather and other Shoshone braves, he was very proficient in tracking and scouting.

It had been thirty years since the Shoshones had moved their camp close to Fort Boise.

Chapter 14

Lieutenant Mark Smith guided the trail master Mr. Williamson and the five wagons to their camping area within the fort.

Lucinda and Helen unloaded what was needed out of their wagon. Henry Shelton unharnessed the mules and took them to feed.

Everyone was excited about the night's festivities; the evening was nearing and everyone was busily bathing and putting on their finest attire.

Helen scrubbed and dressed Tommy and Maggie and then, dressing herself in a lovely burgundy gown, she asked Lucinda, "What are you going to wear tonight, Lucy?"

"I have only one choice, Helen -- I brought just one dress besides my riding skirts and my Indian blouses. Wait a minute and I'll show it to you."

"Go ahead and try it on and then let me see, Lucy."

Lucinda climbed into the wagon and opened her valise, gently unfolded a white cotton dress, and slipped it over her head.

The long full skirt fell down around her ankles and the bodice fit snug around her midriff. The sleeves were long and close-fitting on her arms and a small turned-up band around her wrists fastened with single turquoise buttons. The dress had a square neckline that fell just above her bust; the border around the neck was embellished with clusters of tiny white and turquoise beads.

Lucinda stepped down from the wagon and Helen was surprised to see her friend in such a lovely gown.

"Lucy, that dress is just beautiful on you -- it fits you so perfectly, and the beading is so unique. Where did you ever get such a dress?

"My Wasco Indian friends Morning Star and Shining Lady helped me make the dress, and they sewed the beads onto the border of the neckline. We had such a wonderful friendship, and I'm going to miss them both so very much. They were sad to see me leave, and they gave me a going-away gift that I will always cherish."

Lucinda handed Helen the Indian necklace that her two friends had fashioned for her, and asked her to fasten it around her neck.

The necklace consisted of white pearls and teardrop turquoise beads, delicately strung together.

Helen stood back and looked at Lucinda and said, "The necklace is just perfect with the dress. Now come over here and let me see what I can do with that long hair of yours."

Helen unbraided Lucinda's black hair and brushed it into a lustrous sheen down her back. She brushed the sides back into a lovely swirl and held them with a silver clip.

Helen said, "I am so excited about tonight, and even though I had told you I wasn't interested in Henry, these last few days that he drove our wagon for us I have found him gentle and caring. I think he really likes Tommy and Maggie, and they seem to like him. I hope he asks me to dance tonight, Lucinda -- do you think he will?"

"Now Helen, I've seen the way he looks at you; I'm sure he will ask you to dance ... if he can dance -- you know some men can't. Even if he doesn't ask you to dance, I'm sure he will pay some attention to you, just wait and see. He can't help but notice you in that burgundy dress. You really do look lovely!"

Mr. Williamson, Troy Elis, and Henry Shelton were seated at one of the tables surrounding a large center dance floor.

Major Baker and Lieutenant Smith came in from the office of Colonel Scott McCord, Scott McCord with them. They all three walked up to the wagon master's table. All three seated at the table rose to their feet.

"I'd like to introduce the man in charge of this fort -- this is Colonel Scott McCord," Major Baker said.

"Colonel, this is the wagon master, Mr. Bob Williamson, and this is Troy Elis and Henry Shelton."

There were handshakes, and all were seated around the table.

Colonel McCord was in his sixties now, his sandy red hair salted with gray. He now wore eagle bars on his shoulders, which signified the rank of a colonel, and the highest rank at Fort Boise.

A few years after he lost Willow, Scott had married the young daughter of an officer at Fort Boise and he pledged his love to her, but he never forgot his sweet little Indian princess, Willow.

Colonel McCord spoke to them, saying, "Gentlemen, we have had to send some of our soldiers to Fort Bridger -- some trouble with a group called Mormons. A war with these people may break out at any time; this has left us a little shorthanded. We are going to be able to provide only about fifteen soldiers as escorts to Fort Hall, but after you arrive there, a greater number of the troops stationed at that garrison will escort you on to Fort Laramie."

Charles McCord walked through the hall's entryway. His father noticed his entering and raised to his feet. Scott motioned to his son to join them.

The colonel said, "I want you all to meet Charles McCord. Charles works for the army as a civilian scout, and he is also my son. He will be your scout on the trip, going with you when you leave for Fort Hall."

Charles was very dashing in his fringed buckskin jacket, which had been made by some of the Shoshone women especially for Strong Eagle. They had sewn rows of hair-pipe beads diagonally just under the collar and down the front a few inches. From his shoulders downward was a beaded strip with a display of an eagle on a background of blue sky.

Under his open jacket could be seen a blue chambray shirt, and his eagle necklace hanging free. He wore his breeches tucked inside his tall moccasin boots that extended up just below his knees, turned down at the top with fringes.

Even though Charles was half Shoshone Indian and exhibited it with his high cheekbones and dark skin tone, his hair had a reddish tint inherited from his Scots ancestry.

Charles said, "I'm glad to meet all of you, and look forward to getting to know you on the trip. All my friends call me Chuck." He said with a smile and a glint in his eye, "If you're obliged to call me by that name, I'll answer."

Henry Shelton was quite taken with Helen, and he was keeping a close eye for her entering the hall.

Lucinda and Helen came through the open door, walked into the room, and stood for a moment deciding where they should be seated. Henry immediately rose to his feet and walked toward the two ladies.

"Helen, Lucinda -- I've been waiting for you. Come over here and sit with us."

Henry escorted Helen and Lucinda, one on each arm, over to the table. All the men rose from their seats with gentlemen's grace. Henry introduced the ladies to all the men and then held a chair for Helen, and Troy helped Lucinda.

Chuck, who hadn't sat with the rest of the men but was mingling among the crowd, also saw the two ladies enter.

Lucinda was especially striking in the white dress—the bright white brought out the beautiful dark olive tones of her complexion.

Chuck noticed the native bead work and the Indian necklace, and that long black shimmering hair. He thought, *What a beautiful woman -- dark and mysterious. I would say she must have some native blood; look at that jewelry and the native bead work.*

Chuck also noticed a man escorting them to his father's table; he waited until they were all seated, and then he walked over to the group and requested, "Father, would you please introduce me to these two beautiful ladies?" But Chuck's steel-gray eyes were on Lucinda as he asked this.

"Ladies, this is my son Charles Edward McCord -- better known by the Shoshone Indians as Strong Eagle. Son, this is Lucinda Claybrook and Helen Wyman."

"I'm very glad to meet you both."

There was a vacant seat across the table from Lucinda. Chuck walked over and took it.

Henry asked Helen if she would like to dance; she turned to Lucinda, cupped her hand at the side of her mouth, and whispered, "He dances."

Lucinda looked at her and grinned, and nodded her head in recognition.

Helen discovered not only could he dance, but he was an excellent dancer at that!

Chuck, with his elbows on the table and leaning over toward Lucinda, inquired, "Miss Claybrook, why have you left Oregon Territory to travel such a long journey to Indian Territory?"

"To teach school -- all of us are being paid to come to Indian Territory and teach."

Chuck observed, "I've heard it's still an unsettled part of the country, with many Indian tribes. Some are thriving on their reservations and some are now being allowed to move wherever they wish, as long as they stay in what the government considers Indian Territory. I have heard there are more white settlers moving to the land also. It is a land with much potential, much game, and good rich farm land, and an abundance of wild horses -- that's what I've heard, anyway."

Lucinda said, "Yes, I've heard that too. I'm really looking forward to seeing this Indian Territory, and I've heard they are petitioning to become a state."

"Miss Claybrook...."

Lucinda interrupted, "I hope you don't think I'm being too forward; I'm not much on formalities, so if you want, you can call me Lucinda."

"No...not too forward at all, and I will call you by your given name if you will call me Chuck."

Lucinda smiled and said, "That's fine with me, Chuck."

"I'm sorry that I interrupted you -- what were you about to say?"

"Well, Lucinda, now I hope I'm not being too forward -- I was just going to ask you about your native-made necklace, but now can I be so bold as to ask you if you are part Indian?"

"Yes, Chuck, my great-grandfather was married to an Indian woman; my great- grandmother was Wasco Indian, which gives Wasco Indian blood running through my veins. Do you have a problem with that, as some people do?"

"No…no, Lucinda; as you heard, I'm part Indian also, my mother was a Shoshone Indian princess, the daughter of Pocatello, the chief of the Shoshones. My father loved her very much and married her the Shoshone way, but she died giving birth to me."

"Oh, Chuck -- I'm so sorry…not that you're half Indian, but that you never got to know your mother. I'm so sorry…and she was a princess?"

"Yes, and they say she was very beautiful and as lovely in spirit as she was in beauty. Her name was White Willow, and before she died she had a vision, and in the vision she was told to give me the name Strong Eagle."

"Strong Eagle. I had noticed the eagle on your jacket, and the necklace with the eagle."

"Yes, Lucinda, and I'll tell you more later if you're interested -- but now I would like to ask you to dance…or would you rather go to the serving table and get some food?"

Lucinda smiled and said, "I had rather dance, if you don't mind."

Chuck rose from his chair and said with a smile and a wink, "I don't mind at all." And he took her hand and led her to the dance floor and took her in his arms ever so gently, and they danced and talked even more.

Lucinda told Chuck the way she was raised, how she spent so much time with her papa.

She conveyed to him, "My papa taught me how to ride, and

they say I'm a good rider. I loved riding Jack across the fields and through the woods."

"Jack -- that was your horse. I bet you hated leaving him behind?"

"But I didn't leave him behind. He came with me; I brought my own horse. I raised Jack from a colt -- I would never even think of not taking him with me!"

"I understand, Lucinda; I love horses too. My dream is to have my own horse ranch someday."

It was as though each had met their soul mate. The more they talked, the more they realized how much they had in common, and it was like the old saying, "birds of a feather," or "kindred spirits." The more they conversed, it was as though they had known one another longer than just this one evening. It seemed that they had been destined to meet—and into the future, they would find this was true.

Chapter 15

The wagon train pulled out in the early morning after two days rest for the mules and the travelers. The unforeseen trial stretched out before them, and the wild beauty of the land with the verdant hills was as far as the eye could see.

Henry Shelton was driving Helen and Lucinda's wagon, and he was now even more welcome than he had been before. Helen was glad he was with them, and Tommy and Maggie were too.

Chuck, on his black and white mustang, rode out ahead of the wagons and the soldiers. A few of the troopers took up the rear of the train; some rode close to the wagons and some out in the front. This way the wagon train was completely surrounded by the fifteen troopers. Bob Williamson and the other men who had brought their own horses helped to fill in the gap, and of course Lucinda was riding Jack.

All of them kept their rifles handy and their revolvers fully loaded.

Colonel Scott McCord had warned them that he'd heard some of the renegade Indians had been seen a few miles from the fort.

Bob Williamson rode close to Lucinda and said, "Lucinda, I know you like to ride off by yourself, but I don't want you moseying too far from the wagon train. Stay well within sight of the soldiers."

"Does that mean you're expecting trouble, Mr. Williamson?"

"Not necessarily, but we have been warned of renegades in the area, so we need to all be watchful."

With this warning, Lucinda stayed close to the wagons and she thought to herself that this would be a good time to let Tommy ride with her, so she could give him some more pointers on handling a horse.

She rode up close to their wagon. "Hey, Tommy -- you want to ride with me today?"

"Sure do, Miss Lucinda!"

Lucinda pushed herself back and onto the saddle blanket, and pulled Tommy up and into the saddle and handed him the reins.

Tommy was twelve, but not very big for his age. If he had had a papa these last few years he would have been a more accomplished rider, but now he had much to learn before he could handle a spirited horse like Jack by himself.

Lucinda told him, "Young man, before this trip is over you'll be riding Jack by yourself. Now turn Jack to the right by holding the reins taut and pulling them against his neck. That's right -- we're turning; you're doing well."

Lucinda and Tommy rode together for much of the day, and then evening came, and the wagons circled and made camp.

Scraper had cooked up a venison stew, but with the extra mouths to feed, Lucinda and Helen decided it would be better if they prepared their own supper as some of the other travelers were doing who had wives to prepare their food.

Helen, Lucinda, and the children gathered around the campfire after supper, Maggie leaned back on her momma, almost asleep, her blonde hair tickling Helen's face. Henry came over and sat by Helen, and they began to talk heart-to-heart, at first in whispers, and then laughing and conversing about some of the things that had happened that day.

Lucinda decided this would be a good time for her to take a walk, and she was in doubt that they would even know she was gone.

She walked over to the Elises' wagon and talked to Mary and Elaine. They were just finishing the dishes, and as Lucinda walked up Mary threw the dishwater out, hung the granite pan on the side of the wagon, and said, "Lucinda, come over here and set a spell. Can I get you a cup of coffee? It's still hot on the fire."

"Yes, thank you -- that sounds fine."

Mary came over and sat down by Lucinda and said, "Lucinda, have you noticed that Sergeant Sam Cummings? He's really nice- looking, and he smiles and speaks to me every time he passes our wagon."

"No, Mary; not really. I hadn't paid that much attention to the soldiers."

"I hear you only have eyes for one fellow, that Chuck McCord."

"Now, Mary -- who told you that? Some people need to mind their own business."

"Oh now, Lucinda, you know how people talk -- and it is true, isn't it?"

Lucinda rose to her feet and as she turned to walk away she turned back around and said with a smile and a twinkle in her eye, "Mary, I'm just not going to answer that question, but he is awfully good-looking, and I find there's strength about him...an inner air of confidence and assurance that is exceptionally attractive."

From Lucinda and Chuck's first meeting at Fort Boise, there was hardly a day that they didn't spend some time together, walking and talking, or gathered around the campfire with Helen and Henry.

As Lucinda continued her walk through the camp, she passed by the chuck wagon, where Scraper was busy cleaning his pots and cooking utensils. He guffawed as he scratched his scruffy beard.

"Here comes Miss Lucinda walkin' by; how come yar ain't come by hare sooner ta sample some of my venison stew? Mind you, girl, I ain't a-carin', but you don't know what yarn a missin'."

Scraper grimaced at Lucinda and said, "What you gotta say about that, huh? What you gotta say, you perty little thang?"

"Now Scraper, you're gonna turn my head if you keep talkin' like that -- besides, I was thinkin' the soldiers had first dibs on that stew."

"No sir, there are plenty of stew for Miss Lucinda. Yar come and eat next time, you hear!"

"I will, Scraper; I'll be here next time."

As Lucinda left Scraper and started back to her wagon, Chuck walked out of the darkness and said, "Hey there, Lucinda -- is that you? What are you doing out here by yourself on this black moonless night? Let me walk you back to your wagon."

"All right, kind sir, I will let you." Lucinda slipped her arm in his and they walked slowly back to her wagon. It was getting late and they had to be up at the crack of dawn—Helen and the children had already turned in.

Lucinda said, "Chuck, stay awhile and talk."

"Not very long, Lucinda; you need your rest."

Chuck added some more wood to the campfire and stoked

up the coals, and they sat for a while and just listened to the night sounds. In the far distance they could hear the lonesome call of the whippoorwill, and the coyote yapping on the hillside.

"I love to just lie in my bed at night and listen to all the night birds, but the sounds are so lonesome."

"Listen, the whippoorwill's calling for his mate," Chuck remarked.

"Chuck, is she answering his call?"

Looking intently into her eyes, he said, "What do you think, Lucinda -- is she answering his call?"

Lucinda moved closer to him, reached over and pushed the mop of auburn hair from off his brow and said,

"Yes, Strong Eagle, she is answering his call -- do you mind if I call you Strong Eagle?"

"Of course not, Lucinda; why would you think I would mind?"

"I suppose because the name is so intimate."

"I want you to understand something right now; I want you for my woman. I have had eyes for no other from the first time we met."

"Oh, Strong Eagle -- I feel the same!"

He took her in his arms and kissed her gently, then rose to his feet and said, "Will you ride with me tomorrow, sweetheart?"

"Yes, I will, Strong Eagle; I will joyfully ride with you."

The sun rose above the horizon and stood at bold attention in the clear blue morning sky. The camp was in a buzz preparing for the day. Scraper had fed the soldiers on soda biscuits, bacon, and red-eye gravy.

Lucinda combed and braided her hair and tied the ends with turquoise ribbons, and pulled on her high boots and her riding skirt. She wore her prettiest turquoise shirt with full blousy long sleeves, and her tan leather vest.

This was such a wonderful exciting day for Lucinda to ride with Strong Eagle. He really cared for her, as she did for him! But Lucinda thought, *My destination is Indian Territory, and Strong Eagle is a scout for the army. How can we make a life together under those circumstances? I truly do believe he is the man I have been waiting for all my life, the mate God has chosen – if we are destined to be together, then God will make a way for it to be.*

Lucinda hurried out to where Jack was tethered, and found that Chuck was saddling Jack for her with Star, his large mustang, already saddled and ready to ride.

He said, "Hey, sweetheart -- are you ready to ride? I hope you don't mind my taking care of Jack."

Lucinda said with a chuckle, "It all right with me if it's all right with Jack."

Chuck said as he tightened the horse's cinch, "Nope, he don't mind -- do you Jack?"

Chuck gave Lucinda a boost up and into the saddle; although she really didn't need any help she allowed him to do so. She thought to herself, *Momma and now Helen have told me that I need to act more feminine, and with Strong Eagle—well, I just feel more feminine with him because he is so self-assured and masculine. I admire him even in the mannish way he sits his horse, his strong jaw and high cheekbones…and oh, that generous mouth!*

Chuck broke her thoughts as he said, "Let's go, Lucinda -- we've gotta find a suitable crossing on Snake River." They cantered their horse out in front of the wagons and disappeared from sight as they rode across the wide open prairie.

As they rode together, Chuck took even more notice of what an exceptional rider Lucinda was. He thought, *My initial attraction for her has grown into admiration over the days since we left Fort Boise. From everything I've seen, she is spirited and hardworking ... not to mention such a lovely young woman, who has stolen my heart.*

They rode for several miles until they could see a wooded area.

"That's the Snake River up ahead," Chuck said.

As they approached the thick willows concealing the slow-moving ribbon of shimmering indigo water, Chuck concluded that they wouldn't be able to cross in this area— the trees were too thick for the wagons to get through.

"Lucinda, we'll have to head on downstream for a better crossing, but let's rest awhile under the shade of the willows, and the horses can quench their thirst."

"That sounds good to me Strong Eagle"

Chuck dismounted Star and dropped the reins to let him drink from the refreshing stream.

He removed his wide-brimmed felt hat which an eagle feather stuck jauntily in the beaded band, took his bandana from his back pocket, and wiped the sweat from the inside.

Lucinda slid off of Jack and let the reins fall to the ground. Jack joined Star at the edge of the water.

Lucinda found a shady spot next to a bulky old moss-covered tree trunk. She lowered herself down on the cool green grass and lay back against the tree. The flicker of the sun through the thick overhang of the high, leaf-covered limbs sent sprinkles of golden light onto Lucinda's cold black hair, and down onto her clothing and all around her. Chuck turned to speak to her, but instead he just stood a moment to take in the tranquil picture, and then he said, "You look so beautiful sitting there, Lucinda -- you are my sweetheart, aren't you?"

Chuck dropped down on his knees in front of her and said,

"I want to spend the rest of my life making you happy—I do truly adore you, Lucinda; I love you with all my heart and I want you to become my wife."

"Oh yes, Strong Eagle -- I'll marry you, for I also love you with a deep abiding love."

Chuck turned and set down beside Lucinda and took her in his arms and kissed her—they clung to one another in a moment of passion, but then Chuck pulled away and said, "My darling, I want to make love to you, but not this way—not until I've made you my wife. You're sweet and pure and precious to me, and I love you too much."

"Yes, Strong Eagle, that's what I want too, my darling but how will we make a life together? I've given my word to go to Indian Territory and teach, and I can't turn back now."

"I know, and I've been thinking about that. I've been saving my money for quite some time now. As I told you before, my dream is to start my own horse ranch. I was thinking about Wyoming, but after hearing there are a lot of wild horses in Indian Territory, we can go there and make our life together."

"Oh, Strong Eagle -- we are truly meant to be with one another. God has brought us this far, and I'm sure He'll bless us in Indian Territory."

"Lucinda, we can be married when we reach Fort Laramie, if that's all right with you. My uncle is stationed there, Captain JR McCord. He would want to be at our wedding."

"Yes, Strong Eagle; when we reach Fort Laramie, I will become your wife."

Strong Eagle and Lucinda rode on down the river until they found where other wagons had crossed on the Oregon Trail. The current was slow and the water was shallow enough to accommodate the crossing of the five wagons.

When they returned to the wagon train, Lucinda told Helen the good news.

That evening around the train's campfire, Chuck and Lucinda together announced their engagement and that the wedding would take place when they arrived at Fort Laramie.

The whole camp was full of congratulations; Old Scraper, shaking Chuck's hand, said with a wry smile, "Yaw better treat this little missy right or I'll come a lookin' fer you, Mr. Chuck!"

"Hey, old-timer, you don't have to worry about that -- I plan on takin' good care of her," Chuck exclaimed with a wink and a hint of a smile.

Chapter 16

Black Moon, a Paiute brave, the leader of those who had tried to steal Jack that moonless night before the train reached Fort Boise, was still following the wagon train.

They were a band of young braves that spent their time steeling horses and raiding any unprotected homestead.

In times past, Chuck McCord had had dealings with Black Moon. He was a troublemaker, always stirring up the Paiutes against the Shoshones. Chuck had warned him in no uncertain terms that if he came against the Shoshone settlement, he would answer to him.

Chuck had the reputation of a man who wasn't to be taken lightly, by either white man or Indian, so with this warning Black Moon and his followers stayed away from the Shoshone village and did their raiding elsewhere.

Now Black Moon knew Strong Eagle was scouting for this wagon train, and ordinarily would have avoided it all altogether, but the Indian had an obsession with that stout buckskin with the beautiful flowing back mane and tail. In watching the horse he was also infatuated with the horse's rider and he wanted her, too.

When Lucinda and Chuck were down by the river Lucinda noticed a lot of wild onions growing in the rich soil near the river bank. As the wagon train drew closer to the river, only a few miles away, Lucinda decided to ride ahead and pick some of the onions. Tommy asked if he could go with her, and Helen said it was all right with her.

It was a beautiful afternoon; the sun had burned away the clouds and beat down on Lucinda and Tommy. When they arrived at the river, the damp cool shade of the willow trees felt refreshing.

Unbeknownst to either of them, Black Moon had seen the two leave the wagon train and head in the direction of the river, and he felt this would be his chance to steal the horse and Lucinda.

Black Moon had the other Indian that had come with him hold his horse a ways back, and he hid in the bushes and willows close to where they were picking, and watched as Lucinda and Tommy gathering the onions.

After the onions were harvested, Lucinda wrapped them in a tow sack and tied them to the back of the saddle. She mounted Jack and pulled Tommy up in front of her. This was what the Indian was waiting for—he ran out of the bush, jumped behind Lucinda, grabbed Tommy by the arm and viciously threw him to the ground, grabbed the reins with one hand, and wrapped his steel-strong arm around Lucinda's waist with the other.

Lucinda screamed, "Tommy, run -- tell Chuck!"

This was all she was able to say, because Black Moon fiercely tightened his grip on her stomach, turned Jack, and headed out of sight!

Tommy scrambled to his feet and began to run toward the wagon train. When he and Lucinda had left, they were about three miles from the river. Now Tommy thought they would be much closer.

Tommy stumbled over rocks and scrub brush, but he lifted himself up and was on his way again -- but what was the way? Was he sure he was headed toward the wagon train? Yes, he was sure ... he looked up at the sun, which was dropping lower into the west. The wagon train was east, he was certain!

Tommy ran hard, until he thought his lungs would burst! He stopped and rested and then ran some more until he saw several men on horseback up ahead.

It was Chuck McCord and two of the troopers riding out ahead of the wagon train. Tommy waved his arms and yelled, "Help, over here, over here, I'm over here!"

They wheeled their horses toward the boy. Chuck galloped Star up to the boy and dismounted even before Star was at a complete halt.

"Tommy, are you all right? You're supposed to be with Lucinda -- where is she, boy?!"

"Oh, Mr. Chuck, an Indian came and jumped on behind Miss Lucinda, threw me off, and hightailed it off with her! I was so scared -- Miss Lucinda told me to go tell Chuck, that's all she got to say before that Indian took off with her!"

"Tommy, did you get a good look at that Indian? What did he look like?

"He was scary-lookin', half of his face was painted coal black, from just over his nose and up through his hair was black, and he had fierce-lookin' eyes!"

Chuck said to the troopers, "That sounds like Black Moon, a Paiute I know of. One of you troopers take Tommy back to his momma and come back with a couple more troopers to follow us. Don't send any more men than that; this may be an Indian trick to get the men away from the wagon train, so tell them to circle the wagons and be on guard until I return. Every minute counts, so we're riding on, but I'll try to leave a trail for you and the other troopers to follow."

Lucinda squirmed against the Indian's arm, but he only tightened his grip. Black Moon dug his heels in Jack's sides and tore on over increasingly broken ground, dodging rocks and hollows.

Lucinda could feel Black Moon's hot breath on her neck and could smell his nauseating sweaty body, so close to hers.

As she stared into the open land, she could see another garishly painted Indian up ahead on horseback, holding the reins of a spotted mustang.

Lucinda prayed, "Oh please Lord, protect me from these savages; please spare my life Lord and my honor, and guide Strong Eagle to find us!"

As they rode up to the other Indian, Black Moon pulled Jack to an abrupt stop and Jack heaved heavily for breath. Black Moon dismounted and roughly pulled Lucinda off the horse, tied her hands with rawhide, and set her in front of the other Indian.

Black Moon wanted to be rid of her for now. He wanted to bask in his trophy, this buckskin beauty that he had so desired; now the mount was his to show off to the other braves -- this strong beautiful horse that they would all be envious of -- but he wasn't forgetting his other prize; he would see to her when Yellow Hawk got her to their Indian camp.

Black Moon took the reins of the buckskin and rode ahead, anxious to get to the camp and show his trophy.

Yellow Hawk was a young Indian, not much more than a boy, but strong enough to hold Lucinda around her waist the same as Black Moon had held her, and just as rough. She thought, *The stench is horrid – even worse than the other Indian.*

She entangled her fingers in the horse's mane and held on as tight as she could, but this was an Indian horse that had no saddle, and he lunged the horse into a rough canter.

The sun was dipping low in the western sky and Lucinda wondered how soon Tommy had made it back to the wagon train, or even if he had found his way back. It would be dark soon and the trail would be hard to follow in the dead of night.

Could Tommy have gotten lost? Oh, I pray he didn't lose his way and he was able to tell Strong Eagle what happened...if only I could leave Strong Eagle something to mark the trail...but how, with my hands tied and this Indian knowing every move I make?

But then she thought of the necklace Strong Eagle had made for her -- if she dropped it, would it be seen by him? It was worth a try.

The Indian was behind her; maybe he wouldn't notice. She leaned forward with a groan as if she were in pain, and wrapped her fingers around the necklace; when the Indian roughly pulled her back, her necklace broke loose and fell to the ground without the Indian noticing.

Strong Eagle and Trooper Jones were riding hard!

They had found where Lucinda had been abducted and where they rode out with the other Indian.

Strong Eagle recognized Jack's shod hoofprints and he knew when he and the other Indian left that Lucinda was no longer riding with Black Moon, but with the other Indian be-cause of the deeper tracks.

As they followed the hoofprints, he determined that Black Moon on Jack was riding fast and leaving Lucinda and the oth-er Indian farther behind. Chuck thought, *That scoundrel, that crazy Indian – he's in a hurry to show off that horse of Lucinda's! I'll worry about Jack later, but right now I've got to get to Lucinda.*

Lucinda began to hear steady hoofbeats coming fast from behind. She prayed, *"Oh please let that be Strong Eagle!"*

Chuck pulled Star to a sudden halt; he had seen something on the ground. He jumped from his horse and ran over to the object. It was Lucinda's necklace -- he hoped that she had managed to leave it for a sign, and not that she had been so roughly treated that it was broken from her neck.

Chuck yelled to Jones, "We're on the right track -- this is Lucinda's necklace!"

Chuck mounted Star and said to Jones, "They can't be far ahead -- we have to catch them before the night overtakes us!"

They rode their horses in a hard gallop over dry prairie. The sun had long disappeared behind the hills, and only a faint amber glow was visible now on the westward skyline.

Lucinda was sure now that she heard the hoofbeats and the Indian heard them too. The Indian's horse was sucking air hard from carrying double weight. Yellow Hawk knew it was still too far before he would reach the Indian camp; he knew of a cave in the rocks up ahead. If he could reach the cave, the pursuers would pass them by in the dusky dark.

Yellow Hawk turned the horse off the trail and began to climb a rocky incline.

Lucinda slipped back against the Indian and felt the bear claw hanging from his neck cut into her back. His body heat, sending a nauseating stench, was overwhelming -- she heaved herself forward, pulling on the horse's mane for relief!

They climbed higher over the craggy rocks until they reached a dark cave with humungous overhanging boulders.

Yellow Hawk dismounted and pulled Lucinda off the horse, and pushed her in ahead of him, and brought the horse in out of sight.

The Indian could hear Chuck and the trooper coming closer, and knew they would soon pass by in the dusky faded light.

The Indian grabbed the rawhide between Lucinda's hands and roughly threw her down to a sitting position while he crouched down behind her, close to the front of the cave. He planted his hand firmly over Lucinda's mouth to keep her quiet until they passed.

Lucinda could hear the horses and riders almost to the path that the Indian took at the bottom of the hill.

She thought, *This is my only chance; I have to do something to let them know I'm here!*

She violently threw her head back against the Indian; his hand slid down below her upper lip and she sank her teeth in with all her might. He slung his bleeding hand in pain, and Lucinda screamed for help -- he grabbed her up from the ground and hit her in the jaw with his fist, and threw her back in the cave.

Lucinda was addled but not unconscious; she lay still until the Indian turned his back.

The Indian grabbed his rifle and hunkered down behind one of the large boulders outside the cave, to watch as to whether the pursuers had heard her scream.

Lucinda silently rose from the floor of the cave and made her way to the edge of the opening, and behind a large boulder and out of the sight of the Indian.

Chapter 17

The dusky light had abated and pitch black had covered the land. Lucinda, trying to find her way, stumbled, lost her footing, and rolled down a rocky hill; she grabbed for whatever could stay her fall, and her hands found a small twisted clump of sagebrush protruding from between the rocks. She lay still, afraid to move. *I might go even farther onto the jagged rocks below, but I can't stay like this – I have to do something to climb up,* Lucinda thought.

She moved her feet to one side and then to the other; one foot found a jutting flat rock and she pushed herself up and onto a ledge. She was safe, for the moment anyway, unless the Indian found her. She lay still and prayed, *"Please, Lord -- don't let him find me!"*

She heard small rocks tumbling down the incline.

"Oh no, it's that savage coming for me!"

She lay still, afraid even to breathe! She heard the sound of someone getting closer and then she saw his form in the darkness and she knew it wasn't the Indian -- it was Strong Eagle! Lucinda called, "Strong Eagle -- over here, I'm over here!"

In a moment Strong Eagle was there, and he lifted her up and into his arms.

"Sweetheart, are you all right? I was so afraid I wouldn't

find you before…before the Indian took you to their camp. We heard your scream, but we weren't sure where it came from. Jones thought it came from above this rocky incline. We left the horses at the bottom and I circled around this way and Jones started up the other."

All of a sudden a rifle shot rang out! And then another, and then one more -- then it was quiet, to quiet.

Lucinda stammered, "In the cave, just a few yards up! That's where the Indian had me, and he's still there!"

The pitch darkness had diminished as a full moon rose from the eastern horizon.

"Stay here. Don't move from this place -- lie down so you won't be seen … I'll be back!" Chuck ordered as he stepped up and over the stones, and disappeared from Lucinda's sight.

As Chuck made his way up the incline toward, the cave he met Jones leading the Indian's pony.

Chuck said, "I found Lucinda and left her back a ways. We heard rifle shots, Jones -- what happened?"

"As I was coming up the hill, the Indian fired his rifle my way. I dove behind a boulder and he fired at me again.

"The last time he fired, I was ready for him; when I saw the blaze from his rifle blast, I aimed and fired. I heard him groanin', so I circled around and found him in the cave with a bullet in the shoulder. I took his rifle and horse and come lookin' for you."

"Get back up there, Jones; ya can't just leave him there bleedin' to death!"

"What'a you care, Chuck? He's just a red-skinned Indian, and he helped steal Miss Lucinda."

Jones saw Chuck's eyes blaze and he said,

"In case you hadn't noticed, Jones, I'm half red-skinned

Indian myself -- now get back up there! I'll be with you as soon as I can go back and get Lucinda."

When the three returned to the cave, they found the Indian leaning back against the wall.

Chuck remarked, "Why, he's just a young brave."

Chuck spoke to him in the Paiute language. "Let me see where you were shot." The Indian sat up and kicked at Chuck, and then fell back against the wall.

Chuck said, "Here, Jones -- help me bring him forward so I can examine his wound." Jones reluctantly helped, and Chuck could see that the bullet had gone straight through his shoulder and out the back.

"That's good news -- now all we have to do is stop the bleeding. Lucinda, help Jones gather some wood and start a fire. We have to cauterize the wound to stop the bleeding."

Chuck talked to the Indian and told him who he was, and he remembered Strong Eagle. "What do they call you?" Chuck asked the Indian.

"I am Yellow Hawk!" the Indian exclaimed.

"Well, Yellow Hawk, I'm going to have to cauterize your wound to stop the bleeding."

"Why you do this for me, Strong Eagle, when I help Black Moon steal the woman and her horse?"

"You were lucky, Yellow Hawk -- you could have been killed, but God spared you. I have no desire to see you dead; you're young, with many years ahead of you. Black Moon is a troublemaker. You need to go back to your village and not run with such rebels.:

"Yellow Hawk can't go back to Black Moon camp; he kill me for losing woman."

"We'll take care of your shoulder and you wait here while

we get the horse back from that scoundrel, and I'll help you get back to your village."

Chuck cauterized the wound and Lucinda tore the ruffle off the bottom of her pantaloons and covered the wound, and wrapped the remainder of the cloth under his armpit and tied it on the opposite side of his body.

They all heard the sound of horses approaching from the north, and they knew it must be some of the men from the wagon train.

Jones stepped out of the cave and, holding his pistol up in the air, fired several shots. When the men heard the shots and rode closer, they saw Chuck and Jones' horses at the bottom of the incline. They dismounted and cautiously started up the hill. As they got close, Jones walked toward them, identifying himself in the light of the full moon, and led them to the cave.

Chuck explained what had happened and told them they were still going after Lucinda's horse, but he said, "I want you to take Lucinda and this young Indian back to the wagon train and wait for Jones and me to return."

Lucinda spoke up and said, "No, you're not leaving me behind! I'm going with you; it's my horse, my Jack!"

"But Lucinda, I want you safe," Chuck said. "I'll bring Jack back to you."

"There is no need to argue, Strong Eagle; I'm going!"

Chuck said with a sigh, "All right -- you can ride with me, sweetheart."

Chuck explained to the men, "I want this Indian well taken care of until I return. He's just a young brave not far from boyhood. He is ready to go back to the Paiute village under the rule of Chief Winnemucca. The Paiutes under their chief are peaceful toward the white man; only the rebels following Black

Moon have been raiding and causing trouble.

"You'll have to make a litter to take him back on; he's not able to ride that distance," Chuck explained.

The men agreed to Chuck's suggestion and began to look for long limbs to use to make the litter.

Yellow Hawk revealed to Strong Eagle where the Indian camp was located, southeast of where they were. Chuck, Lucinda, and Jones headed off in that direction but it wasn't long before they heard ponies approaching. They turned their horses, hid behind high brush, and waited.

It was Black Moon riding Jack, and two other braves coming back to look for Yellow Hawk and the captured woman.

Lucinda said, "What are we going to do now, Strong Eagle?" Jones and Chuck agreed to let them pass and fall back and follow them until they were close to the incline where the other troopers were located.

Lucinda said to Chuck, "When we get close enough for Jack to hear me whistle for him, he'll more than likely buck that Indian off and come running to me."

"Okay," Chuck said. "When they get close to the incline, Lucinda, you began your whistling for Jack, and then I'll fire my pistol in the air.

"Jones, you leave now and hightail it up the incline and alert the troopers -- tell them to bring their horses up the hill and out of sight. Let them know when they hear my shot to start firing their rifles in the air. I don't want them to fire on the Indians unless they're fired upon -- just fire over the Indians' heads.

"We're not here to kill Indians, but to retrieve the stolen horse! You hear that, Jones? You tell them that—not to fire on the Indians unless they have no other choice!"

"Yes, yes, Chuck -- I'll be sure and tell them that, okay?"

"Okay, Jones -- now you better take off while you still have time to get there before the Indians, and get those horses out of sight."

Chuck and Lucinda kept enough distance behind the Indians not to be detected, but as Black Moon and the braves drew closer to the incline, they narrowed the distance between them.

Black Moon knew the whereabouts of the cave, and he and the other braves were planning on investigating the area, so when they arrived at the pathway, they hesitated before starting up the rocky hill.

Chuck told Lucinda, "All right, sweetheart – let's hear that whistle!"

Lucinda placed her two fingers in her mouth and whistled the familiar sound that Jack had responded to so many times before.

Jack's ears shot forward, and he spun on his hooves toward the sound!

Chuck raised his pistol and the gunshots pierced the air!

Loud rifle shots began to blast from up the incline!

Black Moon, panic-stricken from the blasts of the guns and the horse he was riding, turned toward the ear-piercing whistle! He pulled wildly on Jack's reins to bring him back; Jack began to buck, and Black Moon fell to the ground.

Jack ran to where the sound was coming from and he found Lucinda, who was still whistling with all her might!

She slid off Star's back and mounted Jack; he turned his head toward her and gave a low affectionate nicker. She rubbed the side of his neck and said, "Yes, boy, I'm glad to see you too."

The Indians were in a panic -- they didn't know how many

were firing! One of the braves pulled Black Moon up behind him as a rifle shot hit a dead scrub tree close to them—in mortal fright, the Indians ran back down the trail toward their camp as fast as their horses could carry them!

The litter was completed and the trek began back to the wagons. Lucinda said, "One thing I know: as soon as we get that Indian back to the wagon train, someone's going to have to get him in a tub or the creek and give him a bath!"

Scraper was the closest thing the train had to a doctor. He took a look at Yellow Hawk's shoulder, poured whisky on the wound as a disinfectant, smeared it with one of his own concoctions of herbs that he used for a healing poultice, and wrapped it up with a clean bandage.

Now Scraper told Chuck, "This herb pack has ta be changed ever day for this Injun ta heal proper. It'al be a good week befer he's able to travel ta that Injun village, but right now we're gonna need fer you to take him to the creek and give him a good soap'n and get him ta smellin' better."

Chuck said with a smile and a chuckle, "Yes sir, I'll just do that -- and while we're there I'll give myself a good soap'n too."

"Hey, that's a dad-gum good idea, Mr. Chuck. I was a-thinkin' you could use that soap as well as the Injun."

"All right, you old codger -- you could stand a good dip in the creek yourself, and if you don't watch it, I could do the dippin.'" Chuck chuckled and winked his eye.

Later that evening, sitting around the campfire, Bob Williamson, Chuck, and some of the other men discussed what to do about Yellow Hawk.

Bob Williamson said, "I don't think we should lose a week's travel time staying here waiting for that Indian to heal."

Henry Shelton spoke up and said, "Yaw, I agree, that's just

too much time to lose." Most of the men were of the same opinion.

Scraper spoke up and said, "That Injun needs ta have them healin' herbs fer those days."

"I know, Scraper; someone's just gonna have to stay with him for that time, but we're gonna have to move on—whoever stays will just have to catch up with the train later," Bob Williamson explained with a firm command.

Chuck said, expressing his solution, "What if you stay here for two days? The women could use the time to catch up on laundry, and the men could maybe get some fresh meat. It's only about three days' travel to Independence Rock -- you could rest there for a day. I'll stay with Yellow Hawk until he's well enough to go back to his village, and then I'll catch up."

The men talked it over and agreed to Chuck's terms.

Chapter 18

Lucinda and the other women had been silent, but after the decision was made, Lucinda spoke up and said, "I'm staying with Chuck and Yellow Hawk. Scraper, you can show me how to mix the herbs, and I'll see that he heals quickly."

Chuck stood up and took Lucinda by the arm, raised her to her feet, and said to her, "Come over here with me; I need to talk to you about this."

They walked over to a private place and Chuck expressed his feelings to her. "Now sweetheart, it's just not as safe for you staying with me and Yellow Hawk. Black Moon could show up again, and I may not be able to stop him next time. You'll be safer staying with the wagon train."

Lucinda, folding her arms in front of her and stomping her foot on the ground, said defiantly, "Jack and I are staying with you, Strong Eagle -- I'm not afraid of anything when I'm with you! Besides, we have the fastest horses of anyone in the train, and we'll be able to catch up with the rest of them in no time!"

Chuck didn't argue with her any longer; he knew she had made up her mind, and there was no changing it!

They went back to the gathering and Chuck explained that Lucinda was staying with him and would help take care of Yellow Hawk's wound, but he said, "I need someone else to stay with us -- if Jones can be spared, I'd like for it to be him."

The captain in charge of the troopers argued with Chuck, saying, "Our orders were to stay with the wagon train, and I can't go against those orders."

Chuck said, "It will just have to be one of you civilians, then. Who wants to volunteer? You have to be good with a rifle and have a fast horse."

Tom Casey spoke up and said, "I can fill that bill -- I'm a good shot, and Ned's a strong, fast horse."

Tom was in his early thirties and a rather quiet gent, but a man that everybody liked.

Chuck said, "Okay, then it's settled. Tom Casey will stay with us."

The morning came for the wagon train to pull out. Scraper changed the bandage early morning and reported to Chuck that the wound was healing faster than he had imagined, and it might be only a couple more days until Yellow Hawk would be fit to travel.

That was good news to Chuck; there would be less time away from the wagon train—less danger from the renegades. He was still uneasy about Lucinda staying with him and Tom; with Tom along, though, one of them -- he or Tom --could be on guard day and night.

Chuck told Bob Williamson, "We may even catch up with you before you reach Independence Rock!"

Scraper left them with enough provisions for several days, and extra jerky for Yellow Hawk when he headed back to his village.

After the train pulled out, Chuck, Lucinda, and Tom set up camp close to the creek.

Chuck knew Yellow Hawk would have to have some kind

of protection on his journey when he was able to travel.

He found a dead oak limb and fashioned it into a bow using strips of rawhide for the string. He then searched the woods for good straight sticks for arrows, wrapped the ends with sharp pieces of bone, and placed feathers in the opposite end of each arrow. He folded a piece of leather and made a quiver to hold the arrows.

Lucinda prepared their supper and she took food to Yellow Hawk.

"Why you do this for me? I treat you bad and hit you hard," he said to her.

Lucinda asked Chuck what Yellow Hawk had said to her. When Chuck interpreted, she said, "You tell him I forgive him for treating me the way he did, and I hope he will learn a lesson from this and be a kinder brave from now on."

Chuck explained what Lucinda had said, and then told him, "Yellow Hawk, when you get to your village tell Chief Winnemucca that Strong Eagle, a Shoshone brave, saved your life. Maybe this will help make peace between the Paiutes and Shoshones."

"I do this, Strong Eagle; I tell him how you a Shoshone and the white man helped Yellow Hawk -- even after Yellow Hawk stole Strong Eagle's woman, he still helped. I tell him that."

The evening was soon upon them and in the dusky darkness around the campfire, they talked softly of their plans when they reached Indian Territory.

Even though all seemed calm and peaceful, they still stayed alert to the night sounds. The night bird's call or the howl of the coyote or the scream of a fox could be the renegade Indians communicating with one another.

Chuck told everyone, "It's been a long, tiring day, so you all go ahead and bed down; I'll take first watch -- and Tom, I'll wake you at midnight, okay?"

"Sure, Chuck -- at midnight."

The next morning Lucinda woke early, sat up and stretched and yawned and looked around for Strong Eagle. He was nowhere in sight.

She rose to her feet and looked at the sorrel sky, with storm clouds gathering above the horizon. Dark ominous clouds with bursts of lightning were moving toward the northwest, toward their camp.

Tom and Chuck came up from the creek together, both carrying armloads of leafy tree branches.

Chuck said, "Lucinda, there's a storm coming—we're going to have to build some kind of shelter... a lean-to is the fastest.

"See if you can find small flexible vines to braid together to make strong ties while Tom and I gather more limbs.

"Tom, we'll build it between these two low evergreens and tie it to their trunks -- they're spread out far enough to make a shelter large enough for all of us."

"Chuck, wouldn't it be better if we built it under one of the large trees for extra protection?"

"No, Tom; we want to stay away from the large trees because lightning strikes the tallest objects in the forest. Tying to the low-growing evergreens will root us to the ground and give the lean-to the stability to stay the wind."

They worked fervently on the shelter with the dark threatening clouds moving in fast. The wind began to blow hard, and large raindrops came down upon them, but the lean-to was completed and they moved their supplies and themselves under the shelter and waited for the storm to pass.

Lucinda sat close to Strong Eagle, with his arm tight

around her. He prayed, *"Please, Lord, protect us; keep us safe from this storm."*

The rain came down hard and the wind blew against the shelter, but just as Chuck had imagined, tying to the evergreens held the lean-to in place and strong to the ground.

The storm passed and as they emerged from the shelter, the sun burst through the battalions of clouds and a rainbow arced through the sky until it touched the earth.

Lucinda and Chuck, standing with arms around each other, viewed the serenity of the sky and Lucinda said, "Oh, Strong Eagle, the breeze smells so fragrant and clean after the storm… and look, God has filled the heavens with His rainbow to tell us all is safe and well."

Chuck spent the rest of the day hunting game while Tom stayed at camp with Lucinda and Yellow Hawk. The three had become friends, and Tom and Lucinda had learned enough of Yellow Hawk's language and he of theirs to communicate to some degree.

Chuck told Tom before he left, "Don't fire your gun unless there is danger from the renegade Indians or wild animals. There may be cougars or bears in the vicinity, but if you keep the campfire blazing, they'll more than likely stay away.

"I'm only going to hunt with the bow and arrow; gunshots may let Black Moon and his braves know we're still in the area."

Later that evening, Chuck returned to camp with two prairie hens and a pheasant. Lucinda cleaned and dressed the birds and placed them on a spit over the open fire. The birds were a pleasant change from the beans, bacon, and flat bread that they had been consuming.

The next morning Lucinda checked Yellow Hawk's shoulder and could see that it was healed over nicely, with no sign of any redness from infection.

Yellow Hawk said to Chuck, "I'm well enough to go to my people. I feel strong now and can go."

"Are you sure, Yellow Hawk? Are you sure you're strong enough? We can wait another day."

"No -- Yellow Hawk will leave this day!"

Tom spoke up and said, " Let him go, Chuck; he should know if he's well enough, and this way the wagons will be only a little over two days ahead of us."

Lucinda packed the rest of the fowl left over from the night before in Yellow Hawk's bag along with other provisions, filled his canteen with fresh spring water, and gave it to him.

"Lucinda, you are like summer rain that fall and give drink and nourish all it touch," Yellow Hawk said.

Chuck told Lucinda what he had said to her, and she was exceedingly moved.

"This name I give to you as Indian name, Summer Rain -- no longer just Lucinda, but Summer Rain."

Chuck said, "Yes, Yellow Hawk, that's a perfect Indian name for my Lucinda -- she is like a summer rain that nurtures everywhere it falls."

Yellow Hawk and Strong Eagle clasped their hands on one another's arms in the Indians' friendship way of saying goodbye.

Lucinda stood on her tiptoes, kissed Yellow Hawk on the cheek, and said goodbye. "I will miss you, my friend."

They all waved as the young warrior rode his Appaloosa off on the distant prairie, toward his homeland.

Chapter 19

Chuck, Lucinda, and Tom saddled their horses and filled their canteens, packed their provisions, and headed out toward the open prairie. They galloped their horses in a rhythmic pace and the distance unrolled before them.

"At this rate, we should catch up with the train before they reach Independence Rock," Chuck called out to Lucinda and Tom.

Tom said, "Yes, but we don't want to push the horses too hard."

"That's right, Tom, and we'll give them plenty of resting time. We've been riding hard all morning and I think it's time to stop. Looks like a brook up ahead. We'll stop and water the horses and have something to eat, but I want to make it to Soda Springs by nightfall."

They did reach Soda Springs before night came; they rode their mounts close to the cool rushing water and set up camp for the night. Lucinda slid off Jack, loosed the cinch, and pulled the saddle off his back. She then hobbled him and set her mount to grazing on the wild grasses. Tom's sorrel and Chuck's Star soon joined Jack, and all were peaceful and contented.

The campfire was readied, and much- welcome coffee was made. Lucinda prepared their supper for the evening and they all settled back in the flickering firelight and enjoyed the tranquility of a cool evening breeze and the star-studded blue-black sky.

Tom removed a French harp from his pocket and began to play a beautiful mournful tune.

Lucinda said, "Tom, that was just wonderful-- I didn't realize that you were so talented. I didn't recognize the tune you were playing…what is it called?"

"It's a song I wrote called 'The Lonesome Trail,' and I'm glad you liked it. This is the first time I've played it for anyone," Tom said shyly, but with an expression of gratitude.

"Tom, play us another tune. Do you know 'My Sweet Rose of Sharon'?" Chuck asked.

"I sure do, Chuck; one of the old favorites."

Tom played the soft melody and Chuck and Lucinda sang the lyrics. The early evening passed and they all settled down for the night's rest.

Lucinda spread her blanket close to the campfire and placed the saddle for a headrest. Chuck lay down close to her and Tom took the first watch.

The night air had become quite chilly and Lucinda, turning over and drawing her knees up, began to shiver.

Chuck, watching her, noticed her trembling and going down on his knees, spread his blanket over her. She looked up at him with her hazel eyes and said, "Thank you, my Strong Eagle."

He bent down and ever so gently kissed her and said, "Now sleep well, sweetheart."

The next morning they got an early start, anticipating the possibility of catching up with the wagons before the day was finished.

They rode east along a dusty trail until they came to a steep, rocky incline. Chuck dismounted Star and led him down. Lucinda and Tom followed suit.

Chuck said, "The wagon train must have had a hard time getting the wagons down this steep hill, which must have slowed them down considerably. They may not be that far ahead; hopefully we will catch up before they arrive at Independence Rock."

After descending the incline, it put them into the river valley and not far from Sweetwater. They reached the river in a couple of hours and stopped to water the horses and take a short rest, letting the horses graze on the bountiful thick grasses.

Lucinda walked out onto a protruding rock and sat down, and pulled her boots off her tired feet. As she dipped them in the cool river water, Chuck came out and joined her.

"Sweetheart, I know you must be exhausted, but hopefully we'll be at Independence Rock before the train arrives and we can all have a day of rest before we head out to Fort Laramie."

"I'm all right, Strong Eagle; I'm really stronger than I look. My papa toughened me up all those years of working with him on the farm."

"How can anyone be as beautiful and womanly as you, Lucinda, and be as strong as you claim? I just want to take you in my arms and protect you always."

"And I continually feel protected when I'm with you, Strong Eagle; you're the strongest, dearest man I've ever known, and I love you with all my heart!"

Chuck looked at her intensely and gave her one of his big smiles and said, "Well, now you better get your boots on -- we need to push on."

They followed the river for some time. Chuck said, "When

we see Devil's Gate, we'll know we're close to the rock."

They rode for miles, following the river with very little communication -- just the subdued ripple of the river and the clippety-clop of the horses' hooves and the whispering breeze in their ears—and then in the distance, there it was: the tall band of rocky mountain with a narrow gorge that looked like a giant arrow from the heavens had split the rock in two and made a path for the river to flow through.

Tom said, "Look -- that must be Devil's Gate!"

"Yes, sir -- Tom, that's Devil's Gate, all right!"

Chuck took out his field glasses and looked toward the distant gate. He turned the glasses and saw the wagon train in the far-distant valley and said, "I see them only a few miles away!"

Chuck turned Star toward the wagon train, gave him a kick in the side, and said, "All right, boy, let's get goin'!"

Lucinda reined Jack around toward Tom and said, "Let's go, Tom, and catch Chuck and Star!"

They galloped the horses until they were breathing hard for air, and then they slowed to an easy pace and gave the horses time to catch their breath. It wasn't long until the horses were rested and raring to go with a steady gallop!

Lucinda thought to herself, *I wonder if we'll ever see Yellow Hawk again?* She prayed, "*Please, Lord, take care of him and help him to mature into a good, strong, and kind Indian brave, one that I know he has a good start in becoming. Help him to remember our kindness and friendship toward him.*"

Chuck yelled, "There they are -- there's the wagons just up ahead!"

Bob Williamson and Henry Shelton saw the three riders coming. Bob cupped his hand at the side of his mouth and yelled to the rest of the train, "Riders are coming -- three riders coming this way!"

Others echoed the message down the train, and to the soldiers up ahead.

Henry Shelton said, "Wait a minute -- is that who I think it is? Yes, it's Chuck McCord, Miss Lucinda, and Tom!"

The wagons all came to a halt and the women and men jumped down from the wagons and ran back to see the three approaching. Helen and Mary, Tommy and Maggie were all jumping and waving as the three riders came close and rode into camp.

Lucinda climbed off Jack, and Helen met her and gave her a big hug; little Maggie clasped her around her legs, and Tommy was there to shake her hand, but instead Lucinda grabbed him and gave him a big hug and said to his momma, "This is my little hero -- I may not have been saved from that menacing Black Moon if Tommy hadn't acted so quickly!"

Helen responded by saying, "Yes, I know, Lucinda, and we're all very proud of him."

Tommy's face turned scarlet with embarrassment and with his face to the ground he kicked his toe in the dirt and said shyly, "It twer'nt nothin' anyone else wouldn't have done."

Tom and Chuck stepped their weary bodies out of their saddles and the men gathered around them, with handshakes and pats on the back.

The train made it to the rock before nightfall. They all settled down around the campfire, and Chuck and Tom told them how they and Yellow Hawk had become good friends, and how he had been anxious to get back to his village and give his chief the message of how the white man and a Shoshone half-breed had saved his life.

The next day they took a day of rest before the long trip to Fort Laramie. Some carved their names and the day's date into the large looming granite rock, as so many migrants had done down through the years.

Helen, her two children, and Henry Shelton went to the rock together and carved their names and wrote under their names, "married soon."

That evening while all were gathered around the main campfire, Henry and Helen announced their engagement.

Lucinda and Mary hugged Helen and said how happy they were for her and the children.

"Henry is the kind of man I have been looking for. He's strong and dependable, and he loves me and the children."

"Helen, I have a wonderful idea -- why don't we have a double wedding when we reach Fort Laramie?" Lucinda suggested.

"Lucinda, you wouldn't mind?"

"Of course not, silly -- I wouldn't have suggested it if I hadn't thought it a wonderful idea. I have already asked Mary to be my maid of honor. I'm sure Elaine Elis would be glad to stand up with you, Helen."

"Then it's settled, a double wedding. I have to go and tell Henry!"

Helen was so excited that she ran up to the campfire where a lot of the men were gathered and announced the news. "Henry, we're going to have a double wedding when we get to Fort Laramie!"

Henry jumped up and put his arm around Helen and with a wink and a grin said, "That's wonderful, darlin', but when did we decide all this?"

Everyone laughed, and Helen was embarrassed. She said, "Oh, I'm sorry, Henry --is it all right with you?"

"Well, of course it is -- whatever you want is fine with me as long as we get married!"

The crowd laughed again and most rose to their feet and congratulated the two, and everyone was excited to get started to Fort Laramie and the activities that were to occur.

Chapter 20

The next morning as they headed east, Bob Williamson told them it would be an easy journey because there was only flat prairie from Sweetwater to Fort Laramie, and if they had no trouble they should be there in a couple of days.

When they arrived, Chuck's uncle, Captain JR McCord, was there to greet his nephew with a warm handshake.

"Your father sent a telegram to let me know you were coming this way. I'm to let him know when you arrive."

"I have even more news to tell him, Uncle JR. Come with me and let me introduce you to the woman I'm going to marry."

"Well now, when did this happen? Your father will be surprised!"

"Well, actually we met at Fort Boise. Father and I met her at the dinner dance given for those on the wagon train she was with. She is a very special lady, and we plan to be married here at Fort Laramie."

"You mean a wedding here and now! Charles, this is wonderful news, and I am really happy for you!"

They arrived at Lucinda and Helen's wagon. Chuck went to the back of the wagon and said,

"Lucinda, are you in there? I have someone with me that I want you to meet."

With Chuck's help, Lucinda stepped down from the wagon, and with his arm around her waist he introduced her to his uncle.

"I'm very glad to meet you, Miss Lucinda. Charles has told me good things about you, and I want to welcome you to the family.

"I hear the wedding is to be right away, here at the fort. I feel very privileged to be able to attend -- I so wish Chuck's father could be here, but at least I am here to fill in for him."

"Thank you, Mr. McCord; I'm glad to meet you too. Chuck has told me how highly he thinks of his Uncle JR, and one of the reasons we decided to get married before we reached Indian Territory was because he knew you would be here at Fort Laramie and would want to share in our joy."

"Well, he was right about that, little lady -- and you don't have to call me Mr. Please, Lucinda, call me Uncle JR."

It was a beautiful double wedding. Hanna, Captain McCord's wife, offered Lucinda her wedding gown.

She said, "Lucinda, I saved my wedding dress thinking that my daughter would someday wear it, but you see JR and I have two sons. Would you honor me by wearing my wedding gown?"

"Oh, yes, Hanna -- you are truly a blessing to me, and it is I who would be honored to wear the gown."

It was a beautiful old-fashioned gown with an underlay of white taffeta and overlaid with brocaded lace. The bodice was underlaid with taffeta from the waist to just above the bust. From the bust up to the neckline was the sheer brocade lace only, and the gown had long fitted sleeves that came to a peak over the hands.

The ladies at the fort helped Helen with her dress and the decorations and food for the festivities.

Bob Williamson walked Lucinda down the aisle, and Troy

Elis was obliged to escort Helen.

It was a beautiful double wedding. The brides each carried a bouquet of wildflowers, made up of golden aspens and white daisies.

Chuck told Lucinda, "As you walked down the aisle toward me, I thought you were the most beautiful bride I had ever seen, and the golden flowers you carried were reflected in your beautiful hazel eyes."

After the wedding and the reception, JR came to Chuck and said, "I received a return telegram from your father, and he said to give you his congratulations and tell you that he wished that he could have been here. He also said to tell you that he is contacting someone in Washington concerning a job for you when you get to Indian Territory.

"He wants to know if you would take a commission as an Indian agent for the Muskogee nation.

"He said they are desperate for men with good character who would be fair to the Indians. So many of the agents take advantage of their position and steal the provisions allotted for the Indians and sell them to line their own pockets.

"Many of the reservations are now self-supporting and are making a good living for their families, but some are still in need of help from the government."

"I have to know more of the details of the job before I give an answer," Chuck replied.

"Also, Chuck, your father said something I didn't understand, but he said you would. He said to tell you, 'Remember why your mother named you Strong Eagle.'

"Chuck, what did he mean by that? What does your Indian name have to do with whether you take this job or not?"

Chuck explained about his mother's vision before she died,

and the meaning of his name.

He said, "My mother with her dying breath made my father promise that my name would be Strong Eagle. When I was of age, my grandfather, the great Chief Pocatello, gave me this necklace shaped like an eagle that you see around my neck.

"Grandfather told me, 'Your mother, before she died, saw in a vision that your name would be linked with the eagle and you would have to be strong like a mighty eagle because of your divided heritage.'

"He said, 'Your mother's prayer was that you would use that divided heritage to help make peace between the two nations, the red man's nations and the white man's.'"

"Well, Chuck, it seems this may be your destiny -- your chance to fulfill what God had planned for you."

"Uncle JR, if I hadn't met Lucinda and fallen in love with her, I wouldn't be going to Indian Territory.

"I knew from the first time we met that we were meant to be together. I believe that she is the wife God wanted for me, and that our meeting would lead us onward to the destiny He wants for us. That destiny must be in Indian Territory. I will discuss it with Lucinda, and if she is of the same opinion I'll let Father know that I will take the appointment."

Lucinda agreed, and the telegram was sent.

The train stayed a couple more days at Fort Laramie, but then Bob Williamson said that was all the time they could spare; they had to move on to keep on schedule.

Some of the men who were occupying wagons talked it over and decided to bunk together and provide a wagon for the newlyweds, Chuck and Lucinda.

Henry and Helen could have their wagon all to themselves, of course, except for Tommy and Maggie, but even their nightly presence was taken care of -- they were invited to spend a couple of nights with Mr. and Mrs. Elis and their two children.

The five wagons of the overland teachers' expedition arrived in Indian Territory the 24th day of August, 1852.

The train's destination was Fort Gibson in the eastern central part of the territory. This was where they would get their instructions as to where they would be assigned their particular teaching position, according to their qualifications.

Lucinda explained her familiarity and friendship with a Wasco Indian tribe. With her knowledge of Indian ways, they assigned her to teach in an Indian school on the Creek Reservation in east central Indian Territory.

With this teaching established for Lucinda, Charles took the assignment as the Indian agent for the Creek (Muskogee) Nation.

The Creek Nation was considered one of the Five Civilized Tribes, which meant they were considered civilized by Anglo-European settlers, and had adopted many of their ways.

The Creeks had become skillful in farming in this rich topsoil with a good clay base, especially in growing corn and other vegetables that they used to feed their families, but also sold to white settlers for profit.

They also grew large fields of cotton and they used their black American slaves, three hundred in all, to help them work the fields, working side by side in those fields, the slaves and the Indians that owned them.

The land was rich with wildlife: white tail deer and fowl of all kinds, pheasant, quail, and wild turkeys.

The Creek Indians were a peaceful people and had generally good relations with their neighbors.

The government wanted Lucinda and Chuck to live among

the Creek Indians, to learn their language and to teach the children how to speak and write English, to teach them reading, writing, and arithmetic that they might be prepared to adapt and make a living in the white man's world.

The government allotted one hundred and sixty acres of Indian land to Chuck, in the center of the Creek reservation.

With the money Chuck had saved, they built a large log home and barn and began to gather and break the wild horses in the area, breeding and raising quarter horses and some mustangs.

Chuck's stallion that he brought with him from Idaho was a mustang, and he planned on using him for breeding.

He and Lucinda named their ranch "The Wild Horse Prairie Ranch."

The first year they were in Indian Territory, Chuck and Lucinda had their first child, and named him after Chuck's father and Lucinda's, Joseph Scott McCord. Two years later, their daughter Margret Ann was born.

The chief of the Creek Nation was now Chilly McIntosh -- an enormous role to fill of "walking in his father's footsteps."

His father, William McIntosh, had been Chief of the Creek Nation between the turn of the nineteenth century and the time of Creek removal to Indian Territory.

William McIntosh married a Creek woman and they had a son named Chilly who became Chief of the Creek Nation after the death of his father.

William McIntosh, whose Indian name was White Warrior, was half Scots and half Creek Indian. His father, being Scots-American Captain William McIntosh, was connected to a prominent Savannah, Georgia family. White Warrior's mother was a Creek Indian woman.

Charles Edward McCord became good friends with Chief

Chilly McIntosh; after all, they had the same heritage: Scots and Indian. With this in common, they worked well together.

Because of their Scots/European influence in Washington, they were able to help the Creek Nation in many ways, and the years were peaceful…that is until the Civil War broke out in 1861.

The war divided the Creek Nation. Some wanted to keep their slaves and fought with the Union, and others with the Confederate army.

Chuck McCord followed the lead of his father, Scott McCord, and fought with the North, which for a time, until the war was over, placed a schism between Chief Chilly and McCord.

After the war was over and slavery was no longer lawful, some of the blacks left the Creek Nation, but many remained. For the most part they had been treated well by their Indian masters, and now with the freedom to make up their own minds, and the promise of being given a proper wage for their labor, they stayed.

The land didn't produce the bounty that it had before for the Creek Indians, but they still scratched out a good living, and the black Americans also prospered and were able to make a good enough living to build modest homesteads on the Creek reservations.

McCord and Chilly resumed their mutual governing of the Creeks; at first somewhat strained, but soon old disagreements were forgotten and the friendship returned.

Scott McCord, Chuck's father, was killed at Gettysburg and Chuck mourned his father's death for many months.

The little family flourished on their hundred and sixty acre ranch on the Creek Nation in Indian Territory.

Chapter 21

Oregon Territory, January 1867

It was a cloudy cold January day when old man Williams' son Jacob came knocking at the front door of Rose Collins' home.

Rose opened the door and said, "Hi, Jacob. I haven't seen you in a long time. Won't you come in out of the cold? You look half frozen."

"Yes, thank you, Miss Rose. I rode over here on my horse instead of bring our buggy. The buggy's much warmer than that old sorrel of mine."

"Well, just come over here by the fire and warm yourself. Would you like a cup of coffee? I just put some on the stove."

"Oh, yes -- if you don't mind, that would be most appreciated, Miss Rose!"

Rose brought the coffee and a tray of cookies and placed them on the table in front of the fireplace.

"Please, Jacob, help yourself."

"Much obliged, Miss Rose; don't mind if I do," Jacob said as he picked up a cookie.

Jacob and Rose sat on chairs close to the fire and sipped the coffee and ate cookies—Jacob nervously balancing the dainty blue willow cup and saucer on his knee—and chatted for a few minutes, and then Rose said, "Jacob, is this just a social call, or do you have something else on your mind?"

"Well, Miss Rose, I heard that your land and homestead are for sale."

"That's right. I have several interested parties, but no contract has been signed. Are you interested in buying, Jacob?"

"Yes, I'm very interested. If the price is right, I'm ready to sign that contract."

Rose told him how much she was asking, and he said that was a reasonable price for such a fine place.

"Judy and I and our three children have been waiting for a place like this, Miss Rose. I know it's been hard for you, losing your papa and now having to sell the farm, but I hear that you and Alford Claybrook are getting married soon and moving to Indian Territory."

"That's right, Jacob, and if I have to sell the farm I would be very happy for a young family like yours to have it."

"Well, Miss Rose, I've already made an agreement with the bank, so if you will just meet me there tomorrow, I'll make the arrangements and we can sign the papers."

"Jacob, I probably don't even need to say this, but my family burial plot is on the land, and I have written in my contract that whoever buys the land is to take care of the cemetery. It can be used for the family that buys the land, but no one else can be buried there, and if I ever return to this land I want to be able to visit that cemetery plot."

"Of course, Miss Rose -- I will definitely agree to that. I would never keep you from that cemetery plot!"

As Jacob rose from his seat, Storm came scampering into the parlor, a good-sized puppy by now, and ran up to Rose and then over to Jacob. Jacob reached down to pet him and said, "You sure are a pretty boy! Miss Rose, he kind of looks like Papa's white husky."

"I know, Jacob, and I believe the husky is Storms papa. His momma was a gray wolf and I found him after his momma and other siblings had been shot by wolf hunters.

"I've tried to keep it a secret about Storm being half wolf but I don't think it really matters that much now, because we will be taking him with us when we leave for Indian Territory. But I still would appreciate it if you wouldn't spread it around that he is half wolf."

"I won't, Miss Rose, but I'm glad you told me that you think our husky is his papa. The way Sam runs with the wolves, there probably are more white ones out there."

Jacob was able to buy Rose's property, but it was entered into the contract that she wouldn't vacate until after she married, and the wedding was planned for the 25th of February, and then she would move into the back of the mercantile until they were ready to leave for Indian Territory.

Alford had a buyer for the mercantile store, with the same stipulation that they couldn't take possession of the property until they left in the first part of March.

Alford had been in touch with the railroad and had made an arrangement to rent one of the cars for the belongings that they would take with them: some of their special pieces of furniture, dishes, and other belongings.

They also planned on taking their horses, Snowflake and Jo, and had the railroad reserve a car for them. It would cost them extra to take so many of the belongings, and the horses and dog. Rose couldn't even think of leaving Snowflake and Storm behind, and Alford felt the same about his dappled gray.

Alford and Rose didn't want a large wedding -- only family and close friends.

Rose asked her best friend Susan to be her matron of honor, and her husband Eddy was Alford's best man.

Doc Davis was honored to walk Rose down the aisle. Rose was dressed in her mother's long lacy wedding gown, and carrying a bouquet of winter Lenten roses and pink Oregon grape flowers.

Jenny and Alice were her bridesmaids. Little Danny was the ring bearer, and Jessie Adams' little girl Janie was the flower girl.

It was truly a beautiful wedding and the after festivities were beautiful as well.

The Davises took Danny, Jenny, and Alice home with them for a few days.

As the newlyweds drove the carriage up to the mercantile store, Alford said to Rose, "I can't believe you are truly my wife -- it seems like a dream, and I'm going to wake up and it won't be so."

"It is true, my darling, and I'm yours forever -- but I do understand how you feel; it seems that way to me, too. We are so blessed to have found one another, and we can thank God every day for such a blessing."

"Yes we can, sweetheart -- but now let me take you to your new home."

Alford lifted Rose from the carriage and carried her to the front door. He managed to turn the doorknob without setting her down, and carried her over the threshold.

Alice said to her brother, "Alford, I don't want to move to Indian Territory. All my friends are here and I won't know anyone there."

"I'm sorry, Alice, but you are part of our family and you can't stay here by yourself, you know that; so just make the best of the situation. Think of this as an exciting new adventure, which we know it will be. You will make new friends!

"Won't it be good to see your sister Lucinda and meet little Joseph and Margret Ann? And what about Lucinda's husband Chuck, or even better known as Strong Eagle? He sounds like quite an interesting character, and I can't wait to meet him!"

"It's not that I don't want to see my sister and her children and her husband -- but it's so far away from all that I've ever known!"

"Just trust me, sis, you will adjust to your new surroundings and you can write and tell your friends all about your adventures. Now that the Continental rail, is active maybe your friends can even come visit. Rose is expecting Susan and Eddy to come see us."

"Really, Alford, that makes me feel a lot better, and the whole thing does sound exciting—a little scary, but exciting. I'm going to go tell Jenny what you said and make her feel better; she's feeling a little frightened too."

Alice wasn't like her sister Lucinda. She had been a momma's girl and a little spoiled. She had soft lily-white hands and a complexion to match. She was a pretty little thing, with big brown eyes, long brown hair down her back, a slight and dainty little figure—and she could cook, made the best apple pie in the county—won the blue ribbon at the county fair two years in a row.

Chapter 22

Rose and Alford woke at the sound of the old red rooster's crow.

"Come on, sleepyhead -- this is the day that our new adventure begins," Alford said with a stretch and a yawn.

Rose set up in bed and brushed her jumbled auburn hair back from her face, threw the covers back, and stepped into her house slippers. She pulled her long cotton gown up over her head and said, "It won't be long until I'm dressed, my darlin', and I'll make us a quick breakfast. When you get dressed, would you wake the children and tell them to hurry and get ready?"

"Yes I will, sweetheart; I'm so excited that this day has finally come."

Storm was sleeping at the foot of their bed. He jumped to the floor and followed Rose down to the kitchen. She opened the door to let him outside and said, "Now Storm, don't go very far -- you hurry back I'll give you your dinner."

Storm was learning a lot of words, and this was one of the first that he had understood, for he had a big appetite and knew what Rose meant when she said the word "dinner."

The train was to pull into the station at ten o'clock; they were to have all their belongings and horses at the station by that time.

The family had gathered their belongings that they would take to Indian Territory, and had them sorted and crated, along with the selected pieces of furniture that they decided on.

The two wagons had been loaded the day before and were just waiting to be pulled into position to be loaded into the rented boxcar.

Alford constructed a cage for Storm, where he would ride in the car with the horses. Rose had wanted to keep him with her on the train, but the Transcontinental Railroad wouldn't allow it.

Alford told Rose, "Eddy's here, and he and I are ready to drive the wagons to the train station. We have already taken the horses."

Even though it was the first of March, the sky was a misty gray, and the north wind gusting off the snow-capped mountains was chilling to the bones. The children were dressed in their warm coats and scarves and were ready to leave; Susan drove up in her carriage to give them all a ride to the train station.

It was an exciting day and a little frightening, for none of them had ridden a train before. They were used to the haunting sound of the train's engines and whistles as they pulled into town—many times Jenny had taken her little brother Danny to the station to watch the trains come in.

Those huge locomotives with the bellowing black smoke and the gigantic squealing wheels were especially exciting to Danny, and he had aspirations of someday becoming an engineer so he could pull that whistle and wear one of those blue and white striped hats.

Susan, Rose, Alice, and the children arrived at the station just as the train was blowing its whistle, coming close to its arrival. As they walked along the platform, the train was just pulling in, with billows of stream shooting out from under its squealing wheels.

Alice said, "Look -- it's the Jupiter that will carry us to Indian Territory! That's the famous locomotive that met at Promontory Summit during the Golden Spike ceremony, commemorating the completion of the first Transcontinental Railroad!"

"Alice, how do you know all that?" Rose asked.

"We studied all about it in school. Look how magnificent it is with the black engine and red cab and pilot plow, and its name is trimmed in gold. Just look at its headlights decorated with big brass ornaments -- isn't it just grand, Rose? I couldn't even imagine that we would be riding to Indian Territory in the Jupiter!"

The conductor and some other men jumped down from the train and ran back to where Alford and Eddy were waiting with the horses and two wagons to unload.

The conductor said, "You will have to load your animals onto the stock car. There are some cattle in there, but they are partitioned off from where your horses and dog will be. There is still plenty of room for your animals."

The two wagons were unloaded into the baggage car and the conductor said, "I have a schedule to meet, so you folks get aboard the train right away!"

Susan hugged Rose and said, "Rosie, you just don't know how much I'm going to miss you."

"Yes I do, Susie, because that's how much I will miss my very best friend -- but I will write and tell you everything!"

"I'm counting on that, you know -- and Eddy and I…we'll come visit; you just wait and see!"

"You know, Susie, I'm counting on that!"

The hugs and handshakes and tears were over, and the little family was mounting the steps to the train. They all found seats close together and settled down for the long journey.

The conductor was waving his arms and shouting, "All aboard!" He mounted the steps and clicked the guardrail shut. The Jupiter's wheels began their creaking and sputtering and wheezing with a chuff…chuff…chuff. The car jerked forward, the car behind slamming into it; finally the jerking and bumping smoothed out and they were all watching the trees whiz by.

Even in the coach, the pungent smell of the coal dust was ripe in their lungs. Alford and some of the other travelers opened a few windows and let in fresh air. Even though the air was cold, it was more appreciated than the black coal dust.

"Papa, I'm awful cold," Danny said with a shiver.

"Son, go sit by your Auntie Alice and snuggle up with her— she'll keep you warm."

Alice gave him a welcome smile and opened her red wool coat, and Danny jumped down from his seat and climbed onto his auntie's lap and cuddled close. Alice closed the coat around the little fellow and his shivering ceased.

There was a potbellied stove at the end of the coach, and Alford rose from his seat and walked down the narrow aisle and stoked up the fire, and added another bit of fuel to help compensate for the open windows.

The train consisted of a coal car behind the engine, the coach with seats for the passengers, a sleeping car lined with bunks concealed behind heavy drapes, a dining car, and two cars behind the dining car: one for luggage and the passengers' personal belongings, and the car for livestock and the red wooden caboose at the end.

The dining car served a scant breakfast of coffee and pow-dered milk, and a sweet roll or other cakes. Lunch was a variety of different cold cuts and cheeses made into sandwiches, and dinner was canned stew warmed up on the top of the potbel-lied stove and served with soda crackers.

Of course, the passengers were able to eat at the train stations, or when the train made its stops for water, or they could buy food to take with them. Usually at these stops Alford and Rose would see to the horses and Storm. If there was enough time, Rose would let Storm run and play with her and the children.

Little Danny loved to talk to everyone who would listen. The second day out, when they had stopped at a large tank to take on water, Danny was telling Mr. Hampton, who was busy positioning the hoses to fill the water tank on the train, "I sure would like to be able to do that, mister, and I'm gonna be an engineer when I grow up so I can blow that whistle and drive a big train like this one."

With a big grin the man said, "Oh, is that right? Do you think you could handle a big train like this one?"

"Well…not yet I can't, but when I grow up and get big like my papa I can, I betcha!" Danny said confidently, with his hands on his hips.

Alford walked up and said, "Danny, I've been looking for you -- you need to leave Mr. Hampton alone so he can get his job done."

Mr. Hampton, looking at Alford, said with a wink, "Oh that's all right, Mr. Claybrook, Danny and I were having a good conversation about what he wants to be when he grows up. He wants to be an engineer on a train like the Jupiter. Would it be all right with you if we let Danny climb up in the train engine before we leave this stop, and he can try out the engineer's seat and blow the whistle before we leave?"

"Well, it's all right with me, sir, if it's all right with Danny," Alford said to Mr. Hampton with a grin and a wink.

"I sure want'a do that! It's just fine with me, Papa! I'm gonna go tell Jenny and Auntie Alice and Momma Rose!"

With his little legs flying and his arms waving in the air, he ran to tell the whole family what he was going to get to do.

Mr. Hampton told Sam Jones the engineer his plan, and with the water loaded and everyone on the train except the Claybrook family, Mr. Hampton pushed Danny up the ladder and into the cab of the engine.

Sam Jones said, "Well, Mr. Danny, I hear you're looking to be an engineer someday."

"Sure am, mister! Gonna drive a big train like this one, too!"

"Well, you can try my seat out, then -- and here, you wear my official striped engineer's hat."

Danny said, "Wow -- I can wear the hat, too?"

Jones set the hat on little Danny's head, and he sat down in the engineer's seat.

"Now, Danny, it's time for this train to pull out -- one of the jobs of an engineer is to keep on schedule, you know."

"Oh yes, sir, I know that!"

"Well then, you better pull that whistle so we can get this train moving down the track."

"Yes, sir!"

Danny grabbed hold of the line and pulled as hard as he could. The whistle blew loud and clear, and the whole family clapped and cheered. Mr. Jones handed Danny down to his papa, the family joined the other passengers, and the train was again rolling down the tracks, bringing the Claybrook family closer to their final destination.

Chapter 23

March 2

C huck and Lucinda were getting everything ready for the arrival of the family.

"Chuck, tell me when you and Joseph will leave to meet Alford and the family in Wichita."

"Well, sweetheart, they left the first day of March, and the trip by rail should only take five to six days. I'm thinking we should leave tomorrow morning. It's a good three-day trip, and we certainly want to be there in plenty of time; we never know what can come about on the trail."

"Well, my darling, I think that is wise and Joseph has been ready to leave ever since you told him he was needed to drive one of the wagons -- he's so excited about the trip.

"Chuck, I'm just so anxious to see my brother and sister, and little Danny and Jenny -- it seems like a lifetime since I've seen them. I don't think Alford could have found a better wife than Rose Collins; I'm eager to see her, too."

Chuck walked close to Lucinda and gently placed his hands on each side of her face, tipped her head back, and kissed her. He looked into her hazel eyes and said, "My sweet little Summer Rain, it won't be long now and you will have your brother and his family close to you from this time forward.

"It will be good for Joseph and little Margret to have their cousins and their aunt so close. By the way, where is Joseph? He's supposed to be cleaning out the barn, but I was out there and he was nowhere to be found."

"He should be back here anytime. I sent him over to Heyburn's store to pick up some flour and sugar. I want to have plenty of cookies and pies made when the family arrives. We have plenty of meat in the smokehouse and a cellar full of canned vegetables and fruit. There will be plenty of food."

"Mommy, Mommy – Joseph's back!" Margret exclaimed as she ran out the front door.

Joseph was a handsome lad, tall for fifteen, tall and slender with thick dark auburn hair. His Indian blood was apparent from his dark intense eyes, his olive complexion, and high cheekbones.

Little Margret Ann took her looks more from the Scots, with her clear light complexion, rosy cheeks, and blonde hair.

Chuck stepped out the front door and said to Joseph, "Son, take those things in to your momma, and come help me feed the stock and get the wagons ready for the trip. We're leaving bright and early first thing in the morning."

Lucinda said as she told Chuck goodbye, "I shan't sleep a wink while you're away!"

"Oh, now sweetheart, you know you will have to close those big beautiful eyes and rest. Besides, you won't have time to worry, with all the preparations that you will be making for Alford and his family."

Chuck hugged his little daughter and said, "Now Margret, you help your momma while we're gone. There are going to be a lot of extra chores with Joseph and me both away."

"I will, Papa; Momma and I will take care of all the chores."

"All right, then; I'm counting on you."

"Yes, Papa -- I know."

"Lucinda, if you need any help while we're gone, ask Standing Bear or Little Beaver, or Jack Montgomery. They all know we're leaving and have said you could count on them if you needed help."

"I know, darling, and I have asked my good friend Moon Flower to come help me with the chores and to just be here when she can and keep us company."

Lucinda hugged Joseph and said, "You take care of your papa…you both take care of each other, you hear!"

"I hear, Momma -- you don't have to worry," Joseph replied as he stepped into the wagon and picked up the reins.

Chuck called, "Let's move out -- time's a- wastin'!"

With the sky overcast with thick dark clouds, it was apparent that they might very well be in for a rainstorm, which could slow them down immensely, but as the day progressed, the dark clouds diminished and they were able to make good time that first day, following the Ozark trail north to their destination in Wichita, Kansas.

They bedded down that night under a full moon and a sky full of stars.

"Papa, tell me about when you were a little boy growing up on a military fort. Was it hard being called a half-breed?"

"Yes it was, Joseph, but I've always been proud of my Indian heritage and also my Scots. I've learned that God has a purpose for each one of us in this life. He made us the way we are, and He's watching to see if we are going to appreciate the way we're made and the gifts He has given and use them in a good way, or in the way of greed and selfishness.

"He expects us to love our fellow-man, whether he loves us or not. Sometimes we have to fight to protect the helpless, or in self-defense -- but fight only if you have no other choice; that's what my papa taught me.

"I did have to fight a few times growing up but mostly because I was always ready to forgive and help others, I was pretty well-liked and respected in those years at Fort Boise."

Chuck placed a couple of more logs on the fire and said, "We had better get some sleep now; we have a long hard day tomorrow.

Joseph woke to the singing of the robin redbreasts and the blackbirds, which were perched high up in the large oak where they had camped.

His papa had risen earlier and stoked up the coals in their campfire, and had the coffee hot and the pancakes and bacon ready to eat.

"I was just going to wake you, son, but I see our feathered friends did it for me, huh?"

"I should say, Papa -- those are the noisiest birds I have ever heard!"

"Well, eat up so we can be on our way."

The trail was long and rocky, and the wind blew across the prairie and through the blackjack and wild oak native trees, while high in the sky they saw a whitetail hawk circling the fields to find his dinner of a field mouse or small critters of some sort -- anything small enough to carry off.

Chuck called to Joseph, "Pull over here and stop your team! I think I saw Indians up ahead coming this way. Quick, let's pull our wagons over here—back of this brush thicket!

The teams and wagons were well-concealed, and Joseph and his papa watched the Indians approach, coming closer and closer until they were only a few yards away. Were they peaceful Indians, or were they out to make trouble and rob and steal any time they had the opportunity? Chuck wasn't taking any chances, especially with Joseph along.

The trail of Indians was long, with women and children and their belongings on litters pulled behind horses.

Chuck could see they weren't renegade Indians -- there were too many of them. They looked like a whole tribe.

"Wait a minute -- I know that Indian!" Chuck expounded to Joseph. "That's Yellow Hawk! What is he doing so far from his native land?

"Look Joseph, if I'm not mistaken that's the chief of the Cheyennes, Black Kettle -- what is Yellow Hawk doing with the Cheyennes?"

"I don't know, Papa -- maybe we better find out."

"I think you're right, son; let's find out right now!"

Chuck stepped out from behind the brush, with Joseph behind him. They both walked out onto the trail and raised their hands in friendship. Chuck called, "Yellow Hawk, it's Strong Eagle!"

In surprise, Yellow Hawk pulled back on the reins of his horse and said, "Strong Eagle! Is that really you?"

He threw his leg over his Appaloosa and slid off the left side of the mount—at first walking slowly toward Strong Eagle and the boy, and then running until he arrived on the trail where they were waiting.

The rest of the tribe had stopped and was watching.

They grabbed one another's forearms in friendship, and then brought their bodies together in a manly embrace.

Chuck said, "Yellow Hawk, this is my son Joseph. You remember Lucinda, to whom you gave the name Summer Rain?

She's his momma. We were married soon after your departure."

Joseph said, "I'm glad to meet you, Yellow Hawk; Momma and Papa have told me all about you, and now you're here! I never thought I would ever get to meet you."

Yellow Hawk smiled and said, "I'll see if Black Kettle will stop here for a rest, and we talk. Come now, Strong Eagle and Joseph -- you can meet Black Kettle, Chief of the Cheyenne."

When Chuck met the chief, he informed him of his position as the Indian agent for the Muskogee Indian tribes. Black Kettle responded by saying, "Chuck McCord, we have much to talk about, but first let us set up camp, and you and your son Joseph will come sit with us around the council fire."

The sun was sinking low in the western sky, and Black Kettle told his people they would make camp here. Dogwood Creek was nearby—a good place to camp for the night.

Chapter 24

That evening, many of the elders of the tribe along with Chief Black Kettle, Yellow Hawk, Chuck McCord, and his son Joseph were gathered around the council fire. Black Kettle said, "Chuck McCord, Yellow Hawk of the Paiutes tells me your Indian name is Strong Eagle and your mother was Princess White Willow of the Shoshones."

"My father was a white army officer and he loved my mother, but she died giving birth to me—before she died, she had a vision that I was to be named after the eagle. She made my father promise to give me the name Strong Eagle.

"I have pledged my life, to the best of my ability, to the pursuit of making peace between the white man and the red man."

"That's a noble pledge, Strong Eagle, but a difficult one to carry out," the chief declared.

"I have made much progress with the Muskogee tribe. They are prospering on their reservation and they have little trouble with their neighbors, the white settlers. They sell their crops to them for a good profit.

"I have to be honest with you, Black Kettle; some of the main problems with the reservations have been finding honest men as agents. In the beginning, the tribes need help to sustain themselves until they can hunt and raise crops to feed their families. The government supplies their basic needs -- food, blankets, farming instruments, and seeds for planting -- but much of the time, before they can get to the Indians, the agent steals the supplies for profit."

"Strong Eagle, because white man lusts for gold found on Cheyenne and Arapaho and other tribal land, we forced sign Treaty at Fort Wise, giving up most our land.

"Black Kettle with other chiefs made trip to Fort Lyon to tell white man we want peace. Even told we fly their flag over our lodge. We told by soldiers' camp, near fort on eastern plains, that our people be regarded friendly village.

"We camp near Sand Creek and we feel safe to leave family and hunt buffalo, but white man lie and send soldiers kill our women, children, old men. My people raise white flag with other flag, but they still kill my people -- no mercy, only slaughter!"

"I know, Chief Black Kettle; I heard about the horrible slaughter of your people at Sand Creek. The instigator of the horror was a man named Chivington. Black Kettle, he is an evil man full of hate. I want you to know that there were other officers leading the soldiers who ordered their men not to fire upon your village, against Chivington's commanding orders.

"There are evil men in all races, and then there are good decent men who are against and shocked at the brutality that took place at Sand Creek. One such white man is a man named Kit Carson. He fought sometimes on the side of the Indian and sometimes on the side of the white man, according to the situation. He also was married to an Arapaho Indian. I read the statement that he made concerning the massacre at Sand Creek; I considered his statement significant, so I cut it from the paper and have kept it with me."

Chuck put his hand into the inside pocket of his jacket and

brought out a leather wallet; he opened the wallet and retrieved the folded clipping, opened it, and began to read:

Jis to think of that dog Chivington and his dirty hounds, up thar at Sand Creek. His men shot down squaws, and blew the brains out of little innocent children. You call sick soldiers Christians, do ye? And Indians savages? What der yer s'pose our Heavenly Father, who made both them and us, thinks of these things? I tell you what; I don't like a hostile red skin any more than you do. And when they are hostile, I've fought 'em hard as any man. But I never yet drew a bead on a squaw or papoose, and I despise the man who would.

"I feel same way, Strong Eagle. Some men evil, some men good. Some red men full of hate, attack innocent settlers and kill women—children. I try teach them not do this, but they don't listen.

"Strong Eagle, we were forced to sigh the Medicine Lodge Treaty. The Cheyenne and Arapaho have to leave our homeland in what the white man calls Kansas and Colorado. We have been forced to move south to Indian Territory to reservation west where the Washita River flows."

"I know that territory, Black Kettle. There is good rich land there, and an abundance of wildlife and fish in the streams and rivers.

"I will help you in any way I can. I'll use my influence to try and get you an honest agent, and if he's not fair with you, he will answer to me!"

"I've taught my people to make peace with the white man. There is no need to fight—too many soldiers—we have to make peace. But some young warriors don't listen to Black Kettle.

"Before we left Kansas, some Cheyenne, allied themselves

with Arapaho, Kiowa, and Comanche and attacked white settlements in Kansas and Colorado. Some of the raids were along the Solomon and Saline Rivers. These Indian rebels killed and raided white settlers against Black Kettle's warning.

"At Fort Lyon, while we in Kansas, Cheyenne and Arapaho Indian agent Wynkoop, talked one my chiefs Little Rock, and he tell what he learned about raids.

"Little Rock say, 'War party about two hundred from camp above forks of Walnut Creek went out camp tending to go against Pawnee. Instead raid white man's settlements along Saline Solomon Rivers.

" 'Some of warriors returned Black Kettle camp. Little Rock learned from them what took place. Little Rock named warriors most guilty for raids agreed to try to have them delivered white authorities.'

"Wynkoop thought best we move out Kansas make our way to Indian Territory. He said no delay before we be accused of harboring those rebels."

"Black Kettle, my son and I are headed for Wichita, Kansas to meet my wife's family, who are coming in by rail. After I return and have the opportunity, I'll come see the Cheyenne and Arapaho in the west of Indian Territory. I'll also pay a visit and check out the agent who has been assigned to your tribes."

"That good to know, Strong Eagle; we be glad you visit."

Later when Chuck and Joseph were alone with Yellow Hawk, Chuck again asked him why he had left his homeland and was traveling with the Cheyenne and Arapaho.

"I stayed with Paiutes many years. Because of message I took Chief Winnemucca, relations between Paiutes and Shoshones much better.

"I left village. I want search out other land; I want see other country. I hear you marry Summer Rain and come Indian Territory. I want see you again. I hear Cheyenne and Arapaho coming this way. I travel with them here -- I meet you and boy!"

"I'm glad you decided to come see us, Yellow Hawk, and I know Lucinda will be glad to see you! Is there any reason why you can't come with me and Joseph in the morning?"

"No reason, Strong Eagle; we leave together when morning come."

Yellow Hawk, grabbed Joseph by the upper arm and said in a half-joshing way, "That strong arm for young brave -- this boy a good hunter, Strong Eagle?"

"He brought down his first buck a few days ago," Chuck replied.

"Then he good hunter!" Yellow Hawk said, jovially shaking Joseph by the arm.

Morning came and Chuck, Joseph, and Yellow Hawk bid goodbye to Black Kettle and the Cheyennes and Arapahos, Chuck reassuring Black Kettle that he would visit them on their reservation in the near future.

Yellow Hawk tied his Appaloosa to the back of Chuck's wagon and slid into the seat beside him. They talked about the relations now with the Paiutes and Shoshones, and the progress that was being made for peace between the two tribes.

"Soldiers killed Black Moon and some of his braves; rest went back to Paiute village and has not caused trouble anymore," Yellow Hawk explained.

"Glad to hear that, Hawk. There's a saying among the white man, that 'one rotten apple can spoil the whole barrel.'"

"Yellow Hawk think that good saying. It be true -- Black Moon bad man, caused many young braves to be killed."

"Maybe you'll find what you're looking for in Indian

Territory, Hawk. Lucinda and I have a horse ranch. We've gathered a good herd of wild horses and we're raising quarter horses to sell. How are you at breaking and training horses?"

"I good at that job, Strong Eagle."

"Do you want to come and work for me, then?"

"I come work for you a little while, see how I like it."

"It's a deal, then -- we'll see how you like working on our Wild Horse Prairie ranch. That's the name we gave it."

"I think that good name, my friend; that real good name for horse ranch."

The lumbering wagons rolled down the rocky Ozark trail toward the Kansas border until evening was upon them and the sun was sinking low into the western horizon, sending amber shades of light onto the waving, rustling grasses.

Chuck said, "I think this is a good place to stop for the night, Hawk."

Chuck called to Joseph, who was up ahead, that it was time to stop and set up camp.

After they unhitched and hobbled the horses, Yellow Hawk said, "I go hunting, bring back meat."

"It's kinda late; you think you can snag something before time to eat?" Chuck asked.

"I good hunter, Strong Eagle; you see, I bring back grub. You and Joseph have fire ready."

After Yellow Hawk left, Joseph asked, "Papa, do you think he's really going to bring back something to eat that soon? He sure seemed confident, didn't he?"

"He sure did, son—we better get the fire going anyway, just in case."

Joseph and Chuck set up camp, with a well-built campfire surrounded by rocks, and they waited for Yellow Hawk to return.

Yellow Hawk slipped through the woods, his moccasin-covered feet treading quietly, with bow and arrow ready, looking for signs of deer or quail or pheasant. He thought to himself, *I better find grub soon. I act like big shot hunter; better take something back to eat.*

Just then a covey of quail flew up from the tall grasses, and Yellow Hawk quickly aimed and shot his arrow. More flew into the air, and he shot again and again! He downed enough meat for the evening meal and some to save for the next day! He was so proud.

He thought to himself, *I think Yellow Hawk is good hunter!*

Yellow Hawk returned to camp with his catch, and prepared them for roasting over the open fire.

As they ate the tender succulent meat, Joseph said to Yellow Hawk, "When we get back to our ranch, maybe we can go hunting together and you can show me how to hunt like an Indian. Like you, Yellow Hawk."

Yellow Hawk, with a mouth full of meat, looked at Joseph, wiped his mouth with the back of his hand, smiled a big smile, and nodded his approval.

After they had satisfied their hunger and the shadows of evening were upon them, it was time to settle down for a night's rest. Joseph took his harp out from his pocket and began to play a delightful little melody.

Chuck and Yellow Hawk lay back on their bed rolls while the music flowed through the air and into the darkness of the night. It was such a bewitching peaceful melody that the two men were soon fast asleep.

Joseph placed the harp back into his pocket, closed his eyes, rolled over, and dozed off into a deep and peaceful slumber.

Chapter 25

The next morning while they were eating their breakfast, Joseph asked his papa, "Do you think we'll reach the Kansas border today?"

"Yes, I think we will be there by noon if we don't run into any trouble -- in fact, we may reach Wichita before the day's end."

"Well then, Papa, if we do make it today we will be there at least two days early."

"That's all right, Joseph; it will give us time to look the town over and do some shopping. I'd like to take something back for your momma and Margret Ann.

"Son, I know you've wanted your own guitar, and your momma told me to see if we could find you one in Wichita."

"Really, Papa? My own guitar?!"

"Yes, son; then you can give back the one you borrowed from Mr. Smith. He told me and your momma that you have an inborn talent for music -- and he should know, with his experience."

"Mr. Smith has taught me all he knows about playing the guitar. He told me I learn fast and have a special gift. His encouragement made me want to work even harder."

"And you do, son -- not only in playing musical instruments, but also you have a good singing voice."

"Thank you, Papa!"

"Don't thank me, son; thank the Lord who gave you those talents. One way you can thank Him is to play the kind of music that would please Him."

"Yes, Papa; I plan on playing inspiring songs -- songs that tell a good story. I've been working on one, and I have it almost completed."

Chuck, Joseph, and Yellow Hawk pulled into the town of Wichita late evening. They found the livery stable, turned the teams over to the proprietor, and headed for the hotel to rent a room.

The desk clerk looked at Yellow Hawk and said, "We don't allow Injuns in this hotel, so you're gonna have to get him out of here!"

"I'm a government agent for the Muskogee Indian Nation in Indian Territory just south of here. This man, Yellow Hawk, is a friend of mine and I insist that he be allowed to stay with me and my son in our room; otherwise I will report this incident to Washington authorities."

"All right then, but I hold you responsible for him -- any trouble that's caused from the other patrons in the hotel or its restaurant, I'm not responsible for!"

Chuck signed the registry "Charles Edward McCord and party," but out of the corner of his eye he saw two young men looking their way, whispering and laughing to one another.

The desk clerk said, "You better watch out for those two; they just like to hang around the hotel and see what trouble they can cause.

"The sheriff lets 'em get away with it 'cause their daddy's got money and a lot of clout in this town."

As Chuck, Joseph, and Yellow Hawk walked up the stairs toward the room that had been assigned to them, Chuck whispered to Yellow Hawk, "We're gonna have to get you into some more appropriate clothes -- those Indian breechcloths and leggings have got to go!"

The Indian's eyes snapped, looking at Chuck with condescension! Give up his Indian garb? Wear white man's clothes? But when Chuck's look came back with the steel-eyed determination that Yellow Hawk had seen before, he relented.

"The dry goods store will be closed by now. You're closer to Josephs size; he'll loan you some of his clothes until tomorrow."

When they were in the room, Chuck and Joseph unpacked their satchels. Joseph had brought an extra pair of blue jeans and a chambray shirt.

"Here, Yellow Hawk, see if these fit," Joseph said.

Yellow Hawk reluctantly tried on the clothing and said, "What kind of hide these pants made out of, Strong Eagle?"

"No hide -- they're made from cotton and some kind of metal woven into them; makes them strong for hard work. They're called blue jeans—all the farmers and cowboys are wearing them now."

Yellow Hawk strutted around the room with his thumbs in the front pockets of the denims and said, "These pants feel pretty good on Yellow Hawk. I think I like wear blue jeans."

Yellow Hawk ran the rawhide belt that held his scabbard with the eleven-inch hunting knife through the loops in the pants.

He left the first few buttons of the chambray shirt undone to expose his bear-claw and turquoise beaded necklace.

He removed the band around his head that held the eagle feather, and Chuck gave him a comb to straighten his black shoulder-length hair. After he combed his hair he proceeded to wrap the band back around his head, but Chuck said, "Yellow Hawk, I think it would be better for now if you left that off your head."

"Okay, Strong Eagle -- I do what you say."

Yellow Hawk was strikingly good-looking with his intense, expressive eyes that sparkled when he laughed. He possessed full lips and a strong, masculine jaw, and a slight indention in his chin.

"I'm starving -- when are we going to go eat?" Joseph said to his papa.

"When you're ready," was Chuck's reply.

"Well, let's go then, 'cause I'm ready. How about you, Yellow Hawk? Are you ready to go eat?"

"Yes, Joseph, I ready go eat big steak. That's what I want -- big steak!"

"That sounds good to me!" Chuck expounded, "The biggest steaks in the house --that's what we want!"

The three found a table and sat down. A pretty girl came to the table and asked what they would have.

Chuck said, "We'll have three of your biggest steaks, with lots of potatoes and all the trimmings."

"Yes, sir; right away, sir," was her answer.

While enjoying their dinner, Chuck noticed the entrance of the two young men the desk clerk had called troublemakers. They both took seats at the bar, ordered whisky, and told the bartender to leave the bottle.

Chuck heard the bartender saying, "Now Newt, you and Slim, I don't want any trouble from either one of you today." Then the bar keeper brought out a wooden club and laid it on the bar.

The young men just snickered and poured another shot of whisky. They turned and looked toward Chuck's table, and whispered and laughed to one another.

After they had finished eating, Chuck said, "I'm going to check on the horses -- you two want to come with me?"

"I come with you, Strong Eagle, see if my horse Straight Arrow is all right."

"I think I'll just hang around here," Joseph said.

Joseph walked to the bar and ordered a sarsaparilla, and struck up a conversation with the man next to him.

Newt and Slim, having downed half of their bottle, with the bottle in hand staggered over to Joseph and Newt said, "Hey, you there plow boy -- you drinkin' that sarsaparilla stuff? Let us show you what a real drink tastes like."

Joseph held his glass up and said, "No thanks, fellows; this is strong enough for me."

"Ah, come on now. Have a drink with us."

Slim grabbed Joseph's arms and held them behind him, and Newt grabbed him by his hair and was going to pour the whisky down his throat, but the bartender came out from behind the bar with his club in hand raised over his head and said, "You two get out of here before I use this on you -- go home and sleep it off, and don't cause no more trouble -- you hear me?"

Newt pulled his gun and said, "Old man, someday you're gonna be the one in trouble."

"Put that gun back in the holster and get out of here!" the bartender retorted.

Slim said, "Ah, come on, Newt -- let's get goin'. We've got other things to do."

Joseph was pretty shook up and he decided to head for the livery stable to find his papa and Yellow Hawk.

He stepped out of the hotel onto the boardwalk, down the steps, and onto the packed dirt street.

It was a dark night, and the only light was from the hotel windows and the dim light cast from the oil lamp somewhere down the street.

Joseph headed toward the livery stable, but he felt like someone was following him. It was the two troublemakers, but when Joseph looked back, they would duck into a dark alley.

Newt and Slim went down the alley and around to the darkest corner where Joseph would have to turn on his way to the stable, and they lay in wait for him.

Chuck and Yellow Hawk were on their way back to the hotel a couple of blocks from where the two hoodlums were waiting for Joseph.

As Joseph turned the shadowy corner, the two jumped out in front of him and said in a slurred drunken voice, "Hey, it's that sarsaparilly kid. Looky here; we want to talk to you about that Injun that you were with. Are you an Injun lover?"

"That's Yellow Hawk. I wouldn't mess with him, if I were you -- and my papa's half Shoshone, and I would advise you to stay on his good side. Those who've got on his bad side were not happy afterward."

"What about you? We're gonna name you the Sasaparilly Kid. are you as tough as your papa and his Injun friend? Wait a minute -- if your papa's a half-breed, then that makes you a no-good Injun, too."

Newt came at Joseph, intending to hit him in the stomach with his fist, but as fast as lightning Joseph grabbed him by the wrist with his right hand, put his left hand under his elbow, and threw him to the ground!

Slim came at him from behind and Joseph whirled around

on one foot and hit him under the chin in a high kick with the other foot; by that time, Newt was up from the ground and grabbed Joseph's arms from behind, and Slim hit him in the stomach hard!

Before they could hit him again, Chuck and Yellow Hawk came out of the shadows. Hawk grabbed Newt, hit him on the jaw, turned him around, and secured him in a body grip. Chuck grabbed Slim by his hair and pulled him away from Joseph.

Before Chuck could stop Hawk, he had pulled his knife and had it at Newt's throat!

Chuck yelled, "Yellow Hawk, don't cut his throat!"

Yellow Hawk yelled back, "He need his throat cut, Strong Eagle!"

"Please let me go, Injun -- I promise I won't cause no more trouble!" Newt said, weak-kneed and trembling.

"Yellow Hawk, give him a swift kick in the seat of the pants and let him go!" Chuck yelled as he held Slim by the hair with one hand, and his arm twisted behind him with his other. "I'll do the same with this other hoodlum."

As they turned them loose, the two ran down the street and disappeared into the darkness.

Chuck turned toward Joseph and asked, "Are you all right, son?"

"Yeah, Papa -- I was doin' pretty good at first, and then you and Yellow Hawk showed up just in time!"

"Well, we've had enough excitement for one night. Let's head back to the hotel and get some rest. I don't think we'll have any more trouble from those two cowards."

The hotel room was equipped with two beds, and Chuck told Yellow Hawk he could have one, and he and Joseph would sleep in the other.

"Me not want sleep in white man's soft bed; me sleep on floor."

"Okay, then -- suit yourself," Chuck retorted, and tossed him a blanket.

The next morning Chuck rose early, walked to the train station, and inquired as to when they expected the Jupiter to arrive.

He was told the train wasn't expected until tomorrow morning, possibly by eight.

Chuck thought, *That will give us the whole day to look over the town and do our shopping.*

The first place they visited was a dry-goods store, to buy clothes for Yellow Hawk.

"Strong Eagle, I be sure and get blue jeans, okay?" Yellow Hawk asked.

"Of course, blue jeans -- what else?" Chuck answered, looking at Joseph with a wink and a grin.

They purchased two pairs of blue jeans, and chambray shirts and a buckskin coat and vest for Yellow Hawk.

While Chuck was busy looking for a possible gift for Lucinda, he turned and noticed Yellow Hawk admiring a wide-brimmed felt hat.

Chuck walked over to him and said, "You like that hat, huh?"

"It look like good hat to me -- and look, Strong Eagle, it got porcupine quills and beads on band."

"Well, why don't you try it on and see how it feels?" Chuck said.

Yellow Hawk asked Chuck, "You buy all this for me -- how I pay you back?"

"You can pay your debt by working for me when we get back to the ranch."

"Okay, Strong Eagle -- I work for you till at least I pay back debt."

"Well, friend, I hope you stay longer than that."

They purchased the hat, and when they returned to their room at the hotel, Yellow Hawk placed his eagle feather in the band of the hat and looked in the mirror, pleased with the reflection of himself and his new hat.

Before the day was over, the guitar for Joseph and the gifts for Margret Ann and Lucinda were purchased.

Chapter 26

That evening after supper, the three and some of the other townsfolk sat on the benches in front of the hotel. It was a lovely evening; the moon was full, and a gentle breeze drifted in from the south.

Joseph began to strum his guitar and sing some of the old ballads that most people knew, and those who were listening sang along.

He sang, "*There once was an Indian maid, a shy little prairie maid—she sang all day a love song gay for her lover far away.*

"*Oh, tonight the moon shines bright on pretty Red Wing, the breeze is sighing, the night bird's crying, far oh far beneath the stars her brave is sleeping, while Red Wing's weeping her heart away.*

"*She watched for him day and night, she kept all the campfires bright, and under the sky, each night she would lie, and dream about his coming by and by;*

"*But when the braves returned, the heart of Red Wing yearned, for far, far away, her warrior gay, fell bravely in the fray.*

"*Now, the moon shines tonight on pretty Red Wing the breeze is sighing, the night birds crying, for afar beneath his star her brave is sleeping, while Red Wing's weeping her heart away.*

"Joseph, that very sad song, I feel sorry for little Indian Red Wing. You think it true story?" Yellow Hawk asked.

"I don't know, Yellow Hawk. The song was written a long time ago, so no one really knows if it was a true story or not."

"Well, it sad story, but it make me think someday I want find me an Indian maid, maybe someone like Red Wing. That pretty name, don't you think, Joseph?"

"Yes, a very pretty name."

The next morning they rose early with excitement, for this was the day for the families' arrival.

Joseph had never met his Uncle Alford and Aunt Alice, or his cousins, Danny and Jenny.

With the horses hitched, the wagons waiting to be loaded, and Yellow Hawk's palomino tied to the hitching post, the three anxiously waited at the station for the train's arrival.

The Jupiter pulled into the station and the steam spewed out from under the heavy wheels—the gigantic iron horse, festooned with gold and red, came to a screeching halt.

The conductor opened the guardrail, stepped down onto the ground, and pulled the heavy steps out for the passengers.

Passengers hurriedly streamed from the train, first stepping onto the platform and looking for the ones waiting for their arrival.

An astute-looking man stepped onto the platform and Joseph said, "Papa, is that Uncle Alford?"

"No, no -- I don't think so," Chuck replied.

Lucinda had shown Chuck a picture of Alford when he was just a young man, but would he be able to identify him now?

Alford stepped out onto the platform, and Chuck immediately recognized him.

"That's him -- that's your Uncle Alford -- and that beautiful lady with him must be his new wife, Rose!"

Chuck and Joseph jumped down from the boardwalk, hurried over to the train, and arrived just as Alford helped Rose down the steep steps and onto the gravel, with Alice, Danny, and Jenny behind her.

"I believe you're Alford Claybrook, if I'm not mistaken?" Chuck said, holding out his hand in friendship.

"No, you're not mistaken -- and you must be Charles McCord, Lucinda's husband. I've waited a long time to meet you; Lucinda's told me so much about you in her letters," Alford said as he shook Chuck's hand.

"Chuck, this is my wife Rose, and this is my sister Alice," he said as he helped her down the steps. "Also I'd like you to meet my two children, Danny and Jenny."

"So glad to meet all of you -- and this is my son Joseph."

Yellow Hawk had stayed on the boardwalk, hesitant to come down until Chuck motioned for him. He jumped down and walked over to the gathering.

"I would like all of you to meet my friend Yellow Hawk. He surprised us a few days ago and now has decided to come work for me at the ranch."

"Yellow Hawk, Lucinda wrote about you in her letters -- seems she thinks a lot of you," Alford said as he held out his hand to him.

"Summer Rain fine lady; she very forgiving to become my friend after way I treated her in beginning."

Chuck said, "Well we better get these wagons loaded -- the train's going to want to pull out soon."

"Joseph, would you come help me unload my dog and our two horses?" Rose asked. "I could sure use your help."

"Yes, ma'am; I'd be glad to help!"

Yellow Hawk spoke up and said, "I be glad to help too -- I good with horses."

"Wonderful, Yellow Hawk. They're down this way in the stock car."

The horses and Storm were reclaimed and the wagons loaded, and they all headed down the trail for their long journey back to Indian Territory and the family ranch.

Storm was so glad to get out of that cage and to be close to Rose again that he wouldn't let her out of his sight; all the rest of that day he was either close to her heels or by her side when she was walking, or in her lap when she was seated.

Storm was now five months old and a little big for Rose's lap, but he didn't seem to realize that difficulty.

Alice thought she would help the situation by making friends with the little fellow and giving Rose a rest.

Alice said, "Storm, you little wolf -- come over here and pay attention to me for a change."

Storm ignored her as if she hadn't even spoken to him. Rose said, "Go ask your brother for a stick of jerky,' Storm loves that stuff."

When Alice returned with the jerky, she enticed the pup by holding it out to him. He took the bait and walked over to her, and as he ate the food out of her hand, she rubbed his head and scratched behind his ears.

They stopped early to make camp that first night on the trail. With the long train ride and the loading of the wagons and just the excitement of meeting one another, they were all tuckered out early that evening.

After a good hot supper when all were gathered around the campfire, the night being cool and breezy, Joseph began to strum his new guitar.

"I've written a ballad that I would like to sing to all of you. Even my papa hasn't heard the song. I was gonna wait until we returned to the ranch and include Momma and Margret Ann, but I am just so anxious for someone to hear it -- and I can still sing it for them when we get home."

"Oh yes, Joseph, we would love to hear your song!" Rose said, and everyone joined in, encouraging him to sing.

Joseph said, "The name of the ballad is 'Sundancer.' And he began to play and sing:

There was a young lad of twelve years, it is told and a gold-coated stallion that had never been rode.

He tamed the young stallion, taught him all that he knew, and loved the young stallion, and he loved him too.

They rode o'er the meadows and the hills they did roam, and he named the young stallion Sundancer was told.

(Chorus) Sundancer, Sundancer don't leave me alone, we'll roam the high pastures, bring the lost doggies home.

We'll round up the cattle, drive 'em into the pen, then ride in the meadows through to warm summer's wind.

The day's work was ended, and time for some play, and Johnny and Sundancer rode out that day.

They ran through the meadow, picking up a fast pace, when a dip in the ground brought the Sundancer down.

The poor boy he tumbled and rose to his feet, but his Sundancer lay there broken and weak.

His father came running as he saw the horse fall, and the crack of the gunshot and poor Johnny's' call.

(Chorus) Sundancer, Sundancer don't leave me alone, we'll roam the high pastures, bring the lost doggies home.

We'll round up the cattle, drive 'em into the pen, then ride in the meadows through the warm summer's wind.

The lad lay a-sleeping that night in his bed, and a vision of Sundancer danced in his head.

Johnny stood on a cliff at the edge of the sky. It thundered, and lightning lit up the black night -- and there on the cloud was his Sundancer friend; his eyes flashed like lightning, and his mane in the wind.

He turned his great body and rode through the wind, away from poor Johnny, who was calling to him.

(Chorus) Sundancer, Sundancer don't leave me alone, we'll roam the high pastures, bring the lost doggies home.

We'll round up the cattle, drive 'em into the pen, then ride in the meadows through the warm summer's wind.

Sundancer he turned, and he galloped the way back to his friend Johnny, who was calling his name.

They rode off together into the dark night, to visit the moon and the star-studded sky.

(Chorus) Sundancer, Sundancer don't leave me alone, we'll roam the high pastures, bring the lost doggies home.

We'll round up the cattle and drive 'em into the pen, then ride in the meadows through the warm summer's wind.

A call from his father woke Johnny from sleep; Come with me, come with me, I want you to see...

There stood in the shadows a gold- coated foal, born in this first nighttime; it was Sundancer's colt.

His momma has died and left him alone; he needs you, he needs you so he won't be alone...

(Chorus) Sundancer, Sundancer don't leave me alone, we'll roam the high pastures, bring the lost doggies home.

We'll round up the cattle, drive 'em into the pen, then ride in the meadows through the warm summer's wind.

Everyone clapped with enthusiasm as Joseph completed his song.

Rose and the girls wiped the tears from their eyes and Rose said, "Joseph, that was a truly beautiful, moving ballad -- it was sad, but very beautiful."

"Yes, Joseph sing sad songs -- some happy song, some sad; but I like that song Sundancer. It sad, but I like it," Yellow Hawk mused.

Back at the ranch Lucinda and Margret were having their supper and Margret said, "Momma, I wonder when they're going to be here?"

"I suspect it will be a couple more days, daughter. We'll just have to be patient and pray that they will have a safe trip with nothing to slow them down -- but I know how you're feeling, Margret; I'm as anxious as you are to see my brother and sister and all the rest."

"Yes, Momma, but these are family I've never met -- aunt and uncle and cousins -- oh, I am just so excited to meet them all…and a little nervous too, Momma. Do you think they'll like me?"

"Of course they'll like you. What's not to like?" Lucinda said as she smiled and gave Margret an encouraging pat on the shoulder.

"You just be yourself and they will love you!"

"Oh, Momma -- you know I can be kind of ornery sometimes."

"Ornery but sweet, daughter."

"Oh, Momma; you always say that."

"Tomorrow is our bread baking day and we will need to bake a lot of extra for our company—Moon Flower is coming to help us. We had better get to bed now; we will have a busy day tomorrow."

The next two days were full, eventful days for Lucinda, Margret Ann, and Moon Flower. They made extra pies and cakes and had the house clean as a whistle.

Some of the men from town and a couple of Indian friends had helped with the horses and other stock, cut wood, and stacked extra hay into the barn loft.

Chapter 27

"Uncle Alford, how much farther is it to your ranch?" Jenny inquired as she rode up close to her uncle's wagon.

She and Rose's horse had become well- acquainted; Rose let her ride Snowflake, and Joseph rode Alford's stallion Jo much of the trip, Jo being a little more temperamental and needing a stronger hand.

"We're almost there -- only about three miles to go," Alford answered.

Joseph asked his papa, "Can Jenny and I ride on up ahead and let Momma know the wagons are coming?"

"Yes, you can; that's a good idea! Tell her we'll be there soon!"

"Is it all right with you, Aunt Rose and Uncle Alford, if we ride your horses on ahead?"

"You've proven you're good riders; go ahead," Alford said, and Rose nodded in agreement.

"Yellow Hawk ride with them, surprise Summer Rain," Yellow Hawk said enthusiastically.

"Oh, she'll be surprised all right -- good that you're riding with them," Chuck exclaimed as they rode away.

Margret Ann was coming from the barn with a pail full of

milk and she saw the three riders coming. She ran to the house sloshing milk onto the ground, calling, "Momma, Momma -- someone is coming!"

Lucinda burst through the front door and into the yard, her hand over her forehead to shade the sun from her eyes. She turned back toward the house and called, "Moon, where are you? Come and see -- three riders approaching!?"

Moon came out the front door, wiping her hands on her apron.

"Look, it's Joseph riding a dappled gray, and a girl on a white horse…there's another man with them; looks like an Indian," Lucinda said.

As they drew closer, Lucinda exclaimed with excitement, "It's Yellow Hawk! I can't believe it, that's really Yellow Hawk!"

As Joseph rode up he said, "Momma, this is Jenny, Uncle Alford's daughter."

Lucinda walked over to Jenny and Snowflake and helped Jenny to dismount. She held Jenny by both hands and said, "Well, little Jenny, it's so good to finally met you." And she pulled her to her breast and gave her a big hug.

Yellow Hawk was still mounted on his appaloosa waiting for Lucinda. She walked over to him and said, "What are you waiting for? Get down off that horse and tell me what you're doing here!"

"I come see my good friends Summer Rain and Strong Eagle."

Lucinda held out her hand and shook Yellow Hawk's with enthusiasm, and said, "My friend, I never thought I would ever see you again -- but I'm so glad you're here! Welcome to our ranch!"

Joseph said, "Papa wanted us to tell you that he and Uncle

Alford are only a few miles back; they should be here soon."

Moon Flower was standing back waiting to be introduced when Lucinda said, "Jenny and Yellow Hawk, I would like you to meet my good friend Moon Flower, of the Muskogee tribe."

Jenny walked over and said, "Very glad to meet you, Moon Flower."

Yellow Hawk was tending to his horse when he turned and saw Moon Flower. He thought to himself, *This lovely young Indian maiden --more beautiful than I ever saw.*

Moon Flower's raven-black braided hair hung almost to her waist. Her dark eyes sparkled as she looked at Yellow Hawk and held out her small hand in friendship.

"I very glad to meet you, Moon Flower -- you are very beautiful," Yellow Hawk said as he took her hand in his.

Moon felt the blood rush to her cheeks and she lowered her head in embarrassment at Yellow Hawk's boldness, but she thought to herself, *He is very handsome, and I'm glad he is so bold.*

"Well, all of you come into the house and have something cold to drink. I have some fresh lemonade," Lucinda said.

It was a short time before the two wagons pulled up into the barn yard. The families came together in joyful camaraderie. It was a night for celebrating, with a bountiful feast around the rustic large oak table, and after dinner there was music and dancing, Joseph playing his guitar and Alford the fiddle; they played and sang well into the night.

Yellow Hawk and Moon Flower strolled together in the misty moonlight, and he told her all about himself -- how he had gotten mixed up with Black Moon and helped kidnap Lucinda, and how even though he did this, she and Strong Eagle nursed him back to health from the bullet he had taken in his shoulder.

"We became good friends and I help Strong Eagle and Shoshones by going back to Paiute camp and telling chief and tribal elders what Shoshone and white man do to help Yellow Hawk. This help make peace between Paiute and Shoshone tribes."

"Are you going to stay here in Indian Territory, Yellow Hawk, or are you just here for a short visit?" Moon asked.

He looked intently into Moon's dark eyes. "I tell Strong Eagle I work for him for a little while and then I go…but now I may be here longer," Yellow Hawk whispered as he leaned down and kissed Moon's warm full lips.

The next few weeks were chock-full with activity. Alford and his family stayed with the McCords until they could find suitable dwellings.

Running a general mercantile was all that Alford knew, and he considered building one in the area until he was informed that the proprietor of the Heyburn trading post had died. The family had placed the establishment up for sale.

The trading post was a rustic natural rock building with living space in two back rooms and a log storage house out back.

Alford told Rose, "It can't compare with the mercantile I had in Oregon Territory, but the price is right and it can be a beginning -- a start for us in this new land. We can live in the back rooms until we can have a house built close to the store, and then we can always add to the mercantile later."

"Yes, Alford, and it's close to the school where Lucinda is teaching, and the children can go there."

Yellow Hawk was telling the truth when he said he was good with horses. He had a true gift of communication with the animals; he understood their language, and could win their trust.

Chuck also was a good horse trainer and the two refined the horses with patience and sensitivity.

By the time the wild horses they had captured were trained and ready to be sold, the two were proficient in their training techniques, and neighbors were bring their horses to Wild Horse Prairie Ranch to be gentled and trained: young ones that hadn't been broken to the saddle, and older horses to be "tuned-up" to be better-trained mounts.

Their new breed of mustangs and quarter horses were coming of age and would be ready to sell in a couple of years.

Business was booming on the ranch and Yellow Hawk, with orders from Chuck, had set in to teach Joseph the skills of horse training.

Joseph woke early; he was excited at the prospect of learning to train the horses. He had learned to sit a horse well, but he wanted to acquire the skills of understanding and communicating with the magnificent four-footed creatures.

Yellow Hawk told Joseph, "First thing you learn is make friends with horse, show him he not fear but can trust that you not harm him. Come with me now, Joseph -- I show you how."

They both walked over to the corral. Yellow Hawk had turned a beauty of a black and white pinto into the fencing.

"Joseph this wild horse only captured few days ago. Now you watch; I make friends."

Yellow Hawk ever so quietly opened the gate and stepped inside.

He stood his ground with his head bowed, not looking at the mount. The horse saw him out of the corner of her eye and trotted around the enclosure with her head in the air and her tail high.

Yellow Hawk stood in his position until the horse settled

down, as she was before. Then with his head still bowed, he bent his body over from his waist, bent his knees, and walked slowly toward the mare, making sure not to make eye contact with the animal. As he approached, the mare turned her head toward him and nickered. He stood at her side as another horse would stand, and she seemed to accept him as a natural companion, as she would have one of her own kind. He then lowered his head and slowly walked back and through the gate.

"Yellow Hawk, that was amazing -- how did you get her to accept you so soon?"

"Joseph, I approach horse in nonthreatening stance with head down and body bent. Not look horse in eyes. When look horse in eyes, it thinks you make challenge. When I walk up to her, she accept me, and I stand by her like other horse would do. Now you make friend of mare. Don't fear her, Joseph; she good mare. She know if you afraid."

Joseph followed exactly as Yellow Hawk had told him, and the mare accepted his friendship just as she had Yellow Hawk's.

The Indian turned the pinto out with the other horses, and brought in an Appaloosa that he had been working with for some time.

"This horse is friend, but not been trained to saddle blanket or saddle. Only halter. Now I show you how we get him used to something on his back."

Yellow Hawk placed a long rope on the halter. He held on to the halter with one hand and began to throw the rope in the air over the animal, and it would fall down onto the horse's back. Over and over he threw the rope; all the time he was doing this procedure, he was stroking the gelding's jaw with the back of his hand as he held on to the halter.

"In few days horse will except blanket on his back, and then saddle. Now I show you how I calm nervous horse.

"When horse's head up high, neck muscles tense, he not relaxed. Have to make him lower head -- this how we do it.

"Take hold of rope with one hand and put finger in side of horse's mouth. Rub back and forth on tongue and make horse open his mouth and lick with tongue -- when he do this, pull down on rope; he bring head down a little. Rub tongue more and pull on rope, he lower head more. When head down low, horse relaxed -- not nervous anymore.

"I show you now, how break horse after he used to saddle. We take horse and go to pond."

"I don't understand -- what has the pond to do with break-ing horses?" Joseph asked.

"You see, Joseph, when we get there."

As Yellow Hawk and Joseph were walking the path to the pond, Joseph asked, "Yellow Hawk, have you decided to stay here on Wild Horse Prairie Ranch?"

"I stay here Indian Territory, Joseph. I keep working for your papa as long as he have me to."

"Momma and Papa want you to make this your home, and Papa depends more and more on your help with the horses and the work around here."

"I know that, Joseph, but I also have other reason for staying."

"I bet I know what that other reason is, Yellow Hawk. It couldn't be that pretty little Moon Flower that you've been seeing, could it?" Joseph said as he playfully bumped Yellow Hawk's shoulder with his.

"You smart boy, all right -- figure that out right away," Yellow Hawk said as he grinned and gave Joseph a push with his open hand.

Yellow Hawk led the horse to the water and let him drink.

He then began rubbing his muscles and down over his neck and under his belly. The horse let out a big sigh and relaxed. Yellow Hawk then began to back into the pond, leading the horse into the water. The horse resisted at first, but slowly he followed Yellow Hawk into the water, up to his flanks.

"That deep enough; now I back him out of water. You see, Joseph, we get horse used to water, and when we ready to ride him first time we take him in pond even deeper, then get on his back and it hard for him to buck. He give up and we ride him out of water broke to ride --easier on horse and rider."

Joseph learned quickly, and in the matter of a few months was filling in for his papa while he was away attending to his responsibilities as Indian agent for the Muskogee tribe.

He was also helping Black Kettle and his people as much as time would allow. The agent that had been assigned to the Cheyenne and Arapaho was a relatively honest man, but didn't do all that he could to see that the Indians had enough food and the farming techniques and equipment to become independent, as the Creek Indians had become.

Chapter 28

The Cheyenne and Arapaho had been nomadic people for generations, as far back as their ancestry would carry them. They were used to following the buffalo from one place to another, and it was a hard adjustment to have to stay on the reservation and learn to be farmers and hunt game only in their assigned area.

The government had sent food provisions, blankets, and some farming equipment, along with seeds for planting, but hadn't given instruction on how to use the tools or how to plant.

Their second year in Indian Territory, Chuck told the Cheyenne, "You aren't the first Indians to raise crops. The Aztec Indians grew corn for generations before they even came in contact with the white man. Corn's a good foodstuff, and the climate is good here for raising corn. The kernels can be fed to livestock, and it can be ground into meal to make bread to feed your people."

"That sounds good, Strong Eagle. You teach us how to raise corn," the chiefs and council determined.

"It's too late in the season to plant, but next spring we will learn how to plant corn. Now we just have to see you have enough provisions to make it through the winter," Chuck explained.

Chuck had influential friends in Washington DC -- friends who had also been friends of his father's: men who had the same values as he and his father, and used their influence in every way they were able to help the Indians and see that they were treated fairly.

They had informed Chuck of an ostentatious young man who had made a name for himself in the civil war by his exhibitionistic exploits: executioner of Confederate prisoners at Front Royal, Virginia; destroyer of homes and barns in the Shenandoah Valley; and now in his vainglorious insolence, he was striving to further his career by slaughtering the red man. His name was George Armstrong Custer.

One gentleman informed Chuck of Custer's assignment over the Seventh Cavalry.

"Chuck, another dark ominous cloud is gathering; those who want to destroy the red man have given this narcissist an unbridled power force in the Seventh Cavalry."

Chuck informed Richard Simons, the assigned agent for the Cayenne-Arapaho, concerning this new information. He and Chuck, with the new possible danger evolving, asked for a meeting around the council fire to inform the Cayenne and Arapaho of the danger.

Black Kettle said, "Strong Eagle, Simons, Black Kettle, Little Robe of Cheyenne, and Big Mouth and Spotted Wolf of Arapaho made trip to Fort Cobb talk to William Hazen and said to him, 'The Cheyennes, when south of Arkansas River, not wish return to north side because we fear trouble there, but we continually told we better go there, to be rewarded with goods.

" 'We told when we leave Kansas reservation be south of river now you want us go north.

" 'Cheyenne not fight at all on south of river, but on north of Arkansas they almost always at war. When lately north of Arkansas, some young Cheyennes fired upon and then fight began. I always done my best keep young men quiet, but some will not listen; since fighting began I not been able keep them all at home. But we all want peace. I would be glad to move all my people to Fort Cobb; I could keep all quiet near camp if close to fort.

" 'My camp now on the Washita, forty miles east Antelope Hills, I have there one hundred eighty lodges. I speak only for my own people; I cannot speak nor control Cheyennes north Arkansas.' "

Big Mouth of Arapahoe's said, "I tell Hazen, I never would have gone north of Arkansas again, but Indian agent sent for me time after time, saying it was place for my people; finally I went. No sooner we get there than trouble start. I not want war, my people not want war, but we come back south Arkansas, soldiers follow us and keep fighting -- we want you send out and stop these soldiers from coming against us.

"Simons and Strong Eagle, Hazel tell us, 'I am sent here as a peace chief, all here south of river is to be peace, but north of the Arkansas is General Sherman, the great war chief, and I do not control him, and he has all the soldiers who are fighting the Arapahoes and Cheyennes. Therefore, you must go back to your country, and if the soldiers come to fight, you remember they are not from me, but from the great Chief Sherman, and with him you must make peace.'

"As we begun trip back to Washita weather turn bad and snow start fall; snow deep before we come here. After we return Indian scout, Black Dog, come tell us he hear General Sherman tell Hazel move all peaceful Indians to Fort Cobb.

Indians not at Fort Cobb considered hostile.

"Strong Eagle, we peaceful, not want war; but Hazel not allow us to move people Fort Cobb. Black Dog hear that General Sherman already declare all Cheyennes and Arapahos not at Fort Cobb be hostile and subject to attack by US Army."

The council's meeting with the principal men of the village, with Chuck McCord and Richard Simons, lasted well into the night. The council decided that after the foot-deep snow cleared they would send out runners to talk with the soldiers and clear up misunderstandings, and make it clear that Black Kettle's people wanted peace. Meanwhile, they decided to move the camp next day downriver, to be closer to the other Indian camps.

Chuck and Simons were given a lodge for the night and were planning on leaving the next morning.

They reassured the chiefs that they would also do all that they could to convey the chiefs' feeling to the soldiers, as soon as weather permitted travel.

Unbeknownst to Black Kettle and the other chiefs, that very evening 150 warriors, which included young men of the camps of Black Kettle, Medicine Arrow, Little Robe, and Old Whirlwind, had returned to the Washita encampments. They had raided white settlements in the Smoky Hill River country with the Dog Soldiers.

When Black Kettle returned to his lodge, his wife, Medicine Woman, was waiting for him. She was very troubled and spoke to him of a vision that she had this night while sleeping.

She said, "As I stood and looked out into the night, I saw dark shifting shadows in the snow, and there beneath the willow tree a wounded mother wolf mourning its little ones who had been scattered and killed by a mighty enemy.

"This vision was a warning, my husband --you need to move our people this night, down river closer to the other tribes!"

Black Kettle said, "We move when morning come. Now come and sleep, Woman."

But Medicine Woman would not sleep; she walked out into the dark frigid night and stood for a while outside the lodge, angry and in deep thought.

She hesitated to go against her husband, but she understood from her vision that it was imperative that she shield her children from the shifting shadows.

She moved quietly to the lodge of her good friends, Sly Fox and Sunny Woman. She whispered to them to awake, and stepped into their lodge.

She explained her vision and told them her concerns and Black Kettle's decision.

"I want you to go wake my children -- take them to Black Kettle's nephew Whirlwind's camp, five miles downriver. Must be in secret; Black Kettle must not know I go against him," Medicine Woman explained.

Sly Fox with his wife Sunny Woman quietly woke their children and the four children of Medicine Woman and Black Kettle, dressed them warmly, and headed through the snow to Whirlwind's camp, arriving a few hours before dawn.

Chapter 29

November 27, 1868

The evening before, 150 young warriors, who had come from raids with the Dog Soldiers, quietly rode in and joined their tribes.

On November 26th, Custer's Osage scouts located the trail of the Indian war party. Custer's troops followed this trail all day without a break until nightfall, when they rested briefly until there was sufficient moonlight to continue. When they reached Black Kettle's village, Custer divided his forces into four parts, each moving into position so that at first daylight they could simultaneously converge on the village.

Just before dawn on that icy November night, Strong Eagle suddenly woke from a troubled sleep -- he dreamed of violent black horses descending upon the village. It was as though he could hear their hoofbeats pounding in the packed snow, coming toward them.

"Simons, wake up -- there's trouble coming."

Simons sat up, rubbed his eyes, and said, "What's going on? I don't hear anything."

"Just get your pants and boots on. I know there's trouble on the way," Chuck expounded.

"All right, all right -- but how do you know there's trouble coming?" Simons asked as he yawned and fumbled with his breeches.

"I had a warning dream."

"You had what? A dream? Oh come on now, Chuck -- I'm going back to sleep!" Simons said with disgust in his voice.

"You get up from there and get your pants on before I have to dress you myself!" Chuck said, as his temper flared.

They were both soon suited in their warm boots and coats. They stepped out of the lodge and looked around.

"Chuck, everything's quiet, isn't it? It was just a dream you had because you've been worried about that Custer fellow."

"Maybe you're right, Simons, but I'm going to have a look around just the same."

With rifles in hand, the two walked among the lodges -- all was still except for the cry of a papoose in a distant lodge and the yaps of dogs fighting over a half-devoured squirrel. Then Chuck stopped in his tracks. "Did you hear that?"

"Yes, Chuck -- a rustling in the woods…" Before anything else could be said, soldiers came vaulting on horseback toward the village from all directions.

Chuck instinctively fired his rifle in the air and he and Simon cried, "Soldiers, soldiers!"

A flaxen-haired man on a gray mount appeared, bounding over a fallen tree, his eyes wild with brutal excitement, with a blazing Colt in his right hand!

Black Kettle emerged from his tepee, the old leader shouting to arouse his people. Thoughts of Sand Creek massacre raced through his mind as his trembling fingers struggled to untie his pony, which was tethered close at hand. He climbed on the pony with his squaw up behind.

As Black Kettle rode to the banks of the Washita, a barrage of shots rang out from the woods across the water. Black Kettle fell from his pony into the icy stream. More shots, and Medicine Woman slipped into the bloody torrent next to her chief.

The Cheyenne warriors, women, and children hurriedly left their lodges to take cover behind trees and in deep ravines.

A squaw was carrying her papoose and hurrying, her little boy in front of her—a trooper headed straight for them with sword high, ready to cut them down!

Chuck ran fast, jumped on the back of the horse, and threw the soldier to the ground. The trooper fell on his sword and didn't move. Chuck jumped off the horse, picked up the boy, and hurried them to the bushes.

Within minutes the village was taken, with only two soldiers killed and three wounded, but many braves lay still, either dead or dying.

The yellow-hair motioned to the women and children to come out of their hiding—some responded and others ran through the icy water to try to escape, but all that weren't lying dead were rounded up and brought to the center of the village, along with the old men and young warriors that didn't escape.

Two troopers captured Chuck and Simons and forced them at gunpoint before Custer.

"What are you two men doing here?" Custer demanded.

"We are agents representing the Cheyenne, Arapaho, and Muskogee tribes. We were guests at the Cheyenne council, where it was determined that as soon as the weather cleared for travel, they would send out runners to go to the soldiers and clear up any misunderstandings—to let them know that the Cheyenne of Black Kettle only wanted peace. Simons and I also were to go to the authorities and tell them the same."

"Black Kettle may have wanted peace, but we followed a Cheyenne war party to this camp! This village was harboring warriors who had pillaged and raided settlements in the Smoky Hill River country. We followed their tracks here," Custer said angrily.

"That was no excuse to kill the innocent," Chuck said, his eyes ablaze with indignation.

"So be it -- if a village harbors lawbreakers, the innocent suffer!" Custer retaliated.

"Black Kettle wasn't aware of the young warriors' arrival into his camp," Chuck argued.

Custer came back with, "Oh, don't be fooled, Black Kettle; may have wanted peace, but from what we hear he has harbored these young renegades before -- now enough talk!"

Custer ordered many of the lodges to be burned, and he ordered the slaughter of many of their ponies.

He said with sadistic cold-heartedness, "This should teach them a lesson to stay on their reservation and to not harbor those who raid and take captive and kill white women and children."

Tall Bear, the Seventh Cavalry's Osage scout, came to Chuck and Simons in secret and said to them, "Custer not care what happen to Indian women and children. He's planning to take many with him as captives and use them as shields when he fights other Cheyenne and Arapaho. You must stop him doing this!"

"Yes, we must, Tall Bear -- he must be stopped!"

Simons said, "You sound awful sure he can be stopped. How are you going to do that?"

Chuck only gave him a sobering look and walked behind

the tepee and knelt down, bowed his head down to the ground, and beseeched God for help to save these innocent women and children from this terrible fate.

When Chuck came back from his prayer, Custer was rounding up the women and children that he would take with him. The children were crying and the women were fighting, but the soldiers were dragging them and putting them on ponies that they hadn't slaughtered.

All of a sudden, a trooper came running up to Custer, breathing hard till he could hardly speak, but he took a breath and blurted out, "Look over there, on the hill!"

There was a large gathering of Indians from upriver; when they began to move toward Custer and his troops, it seemed to their eyes that there were hundreds coming toward them.

Custer yelled, "Troopers mount up! Mount up and retreat, retreat! Leave the hostages! Retreat!"

When the Indians arrived, there were only twenty-five men and their horses.

Chuck, Simons and some of the other Indians helped bury the dead and salvage what they could from the burned lodges.

"There was a disgraceful travesty performed here today, with Black Kettle and his wife slaughtered, along with many others -- but you must still strive for peace, as your great leader Black Kettle had striven.

"Those young warriors who had returned to camp from raids with the Dog Soldiers gave Custer and his troopers an excuse to attack Black Kettle's village. If those warriors hadn't returned to Washita, Black Kettle would still be alive!

"Simons and I will return and bring supplies to help you through the winter, and when spring comes we will help you learn how to raise food for your families as the Muskogee tribes have learned to do."

The two agents said goodbye to the Cheyenne villagers, but in their farewell they reassured them that all the destruction caused here at the Washita by Custer and the Seventh Cavalry would be reported to those in authority in Washington, as they were eyewitnesses to the travesty.

Chapter 30

Chuck and Simons were two days on the trail before reaching home. They said goodbye at the crossroads—Chuck was anxious to see Lucinda and his children; it seemed such a long time since he had been in the warmth of his family, but in reality it had been only a few days.

As Chuck rode up to the house, no one was in sight. He wearily slid off his horse, tied him to the hitching post, and walked into the house. He called for Lucinda, but no answer.

The children must still be in school, he thought. *No, this is Saturday -- then where is everybody?*

He ventured into the barn and saw Lucinda with her back to him. She was busy brushing down her horse, Jack, and humming a tune that she often hummed when she was working. He slowly walked up behind her and grabbed her around the waist. Lucinda screamed and he whirled her around, and when she saw it was her Strong Eagle she kissed him passionately and then hit him playfully with the brush that was still in her hand.

"You scared me half to death!" she exclaimed, and then she kissed him again and he kissed her back with warmth and passion.

As they walked back to the house with arms around one another's waists, Chuck said, "Where is everybody?"

"Alice came and picked up the children to take them to Rose and Alford's for the day, and Yellow Hawk is out looking for our milk cow Daisy. She broke through the fence again. He shouldn't be long; she won't be hard to follow in the muddy ground from the melted snow."

"Sweetheart, I have much to tell you," Chuck said with a heavy sigh. "Not good news, I'm afraid."

"Well then, come on in the kitchen and I'll get you coffee and something to eat, and you can tell me all about it -- but I also have good new to tell you, my darling."

"I can sure use some good news; you tell me your news first," Chuck said as he sat down at the table and Lucinda poured him a cup of coffee.

"Moon Flower and Yellow Hawk are getting married; he finally got up the nerve to ask her."

"Oh, he did, did he?" Chuck said with a chuckle. "That rascal -- it's about time he settled down and stopped his wandering. That's good news -- real good news!"

"Chuck, my darling, there is more I have to tell you," Lucinda said as she stared down at her coffee cup. She brought it up to her lips and took a sip, and looked at Chuck with big eyes and a little smile.

"I hope you are as happy about it as I am."

"Well, what is it, sweetheart? Just spit it out, whatever it is...."

"We're going to have another baby."

"Another baby! That's wonderful, Lucinda -- but you're not as young as you used to be. That's my only concern!"

"I know, Chuck, but the doc says I'm in good health and he doesn't see any problems."

"Just the same, I don't want you overdoing it. From now

until the birth, I don't want you lifting anything heavy."

"Oh -- now darling, I've always worked hard and I'm strong; you know that."

"Just the same, you abide by what I say!" Chuck said with sternness in his voice, but then gently took her in his arms and said emotionally, "Lucinda, if anything happened to you, I don't know what I would do. I would be lost without you -- don't you know that?"

Lucinda looked up at Chuck and saw his furrowed brow and his dark eyes full of uneasiness, and she said, "I will abide by what you say. I will take every precaution. The doc said I'm three months along, so we should have our new addition to the family in the spring, sometime in the month of May."

"Have you told the children yet?"

"No, I was waiting for your return when we could tell them together."

"We'll tell them tonight after supper," Chuck decided.

"Now, darlin', what were you wanting to tell me about your trip to Washita?"

"You know, sweetheart, I think I'll wait on that news until later, maybe after supper when the children have gone to bed and I can tell you and Yellow Hawk together."

The children were excited. Just the thought of a baby in the house was exciting.

Margret Ann said, "I hope it's a girl so she can play with my dolls, and I'll teach her to sew and make biscuits like Momma taught me, and…."

"Margret, slow down now -- it'll be a while before you can teach your little sister or brother any of those things," Lucinda said.

"Yeah, Margret -- besides, I think it'll be a boy, and I can teach him a thing or two!" Joseph spoke up and said.

"Oh, now, you two, we just hope and pray that the baby will be healthy, whether boy or girl, all right?" their momma said with finality in her voice.

"Yes, you're right, Momma, just so it's a healthy baby, we'll love it no matter whether it's a little boy or girl," Joseph said, and Margret Ann agreed with a nod of her head.

The children were retired for the night and Chuck, Lucinda, and Yellow Hawk settled down in comfort in front of the large natural rock fireplace.

Chuck added another log and said, "I really am tired tonight -- it's been a long day, but I want to tell you both what happened at the Washita."

Chuck described the whole atrocity in detail, and Lucinda and Yellow Hawk were very saddened to hear it, especially of the murder of Black Kettle and Medicine Woman.

"He was great leader of Cheyenne, a good man," Yellow Hawk said.

"My hands were tied, I couldn't stop the killing!" Chuck lamented with his head bowed and in his hands.

Lucinda said, "But Chuck, if you hadn't been there, things would have turned out even worse. God answered your prayer and saved the women and children from captivity. That was a great miracle, Strong Eagle!"

"Yes, I mustn't forget that God listened to me and saved those women and children."

Yellow Hawk stood up and said, "I leave now -- you need to rest, Strong Eagle. Things look better in morning after good night's rest."

"Maybe so, Yellow Hawk, but tomorrow I want to hear about you and little Moon Flower."

"I tell you all about it tomorrow -- now you go to bed!"

"Yes, sir, my friend; that's exactly where I'm headed."

The snow had melted and the roads were now passable. Chuck and Simons made their way together to the nearest telegraph office and reported their witnessing the massacre at the Washita River.

By early December the attack had provoked debate and criticism in the press. On December 9th, in the *Leavenworth Evening Bulletin*, an article read: "Generals Sanford and Tappan, and Col. Taylor of the Indian Peace Commission, unite in the opinion that the late battle at the Washita with the Cheyenne-Arapaho Indians was simply an attack upon peaceful bands."

The December 14th *New York Tribune* reported, "Col. Wynkoop, agent for the Cheyenne and Arapaho Indians, has published his letter of resignation. He regards Gen. Custer's late fight as simply a massacre."

The *New York Times* published a letter describing Custer as taking "sadistic pleasure in slaughtering the Indian ponies." It alluded to his forces' having killed innocent women and children.

Because of the outrage in the press, there were orders from Washington that the Cheyenne and Arapaho would be allowed to consider their reservation south of the Arkansas, and were allowed to stay in the vicinity of the Washita where they had been assigned to begin with. Also, all the supplies that were needed to see them through the winter were soon available for distribution.

Chapter 31

Moon Flower was the daughter of Chief Broken Arrow. The chief would have rather his daughter married into the Muskogee tribe. Yellow Hawk was a Paiute, and Broken Arrow didn't know much about Paiutes, but he would not stand in the way of Moon Flower and Yellow Hawk's happiness so he did give his blessings to them, with the stipulation that Yellow Hawk give ten horses for his daughter.

"Ten horses, Strong Eagle? That lot of horses! Moon Flower worth it, but where I get that much horse flesh?" Yellow Hawk questioned.

"I'll give you five of the horses you have broken for the ranch as a wedding gift, but the other five you will have to go after in the wild and gentle them to be ridden."

"That take time, Strong Eagle, and I ready to marry Moon."

"I know, but good things are worth waiting for, Yellow Hawk -- and it won't take that long for you to bring in five horses, will it?"

"Maybe not; I get started right away."

"I tell you what -- I'll send Bob and Jo with you and bring in all the horses that you can round up for the ranch, and then you can cut out the five you want. Hawk, if you want, I will help you build a cabin for you and Moon to live in after you're married."

"That be good, Strong Eagle, but not know where we live yet."

"Why don't you live here on this land that has been allotted to me and my family? The north forty acres is good land, with a creek for water close by."

"That sound good -- I like be close to you and Summer Rain. Why you so good to me, Strong Eagle?"

"Don't you know by now that you are like family to me and Lucinda?"

"That good to hear -- I feel same way 'bout you and Summer Rain and children. That Joseph like my brother."

Yellow Hawk and the men rounded up the wild horses, and he cut out the ones he wanted to gentle.

Chuck told Yellow Hawk that if he were to help him build the cabin, it would have to be during the winter months before spring came; they would all be too busy with planting after that.

So they set out to build a log cabin, and produced the roof with heavy wood shingles made by hand from wood on the land. It would be only a one-room cabin for now, but could be added onto later. The floor was made by using straight logs and splitting them to the desired thickness.

On the north wall they made a large natural rock fireplace with a swinging cast-iron pot, where Moon would prepare their food.

Yellow Hawk and Moon Flower were married on the first of February, and they settled into their new home on the forty acres adjacent to the McCord's.

Lucinda was now heavy with child, and Moon Flower spent much of her time helping Lucinda in the kitchen and with other chores. They shared the bread and other baked goods from Lucinda's kitchen, and the milk that was retrieved from the McCords' milk cows.

It was good for Moon to be there close to Yellow Hawk and her best friend Lucinda. Hawk and Chuck worked well together, training the horses and taking care of their small herd of cattle.

Chuck had hired Jo and Bob a few months before and they were good workers for the most part, but Jo needed some watching, as he like to malinger when he had the chance.

Spring was almost upon them. The field needed plowing, where they raised a good-sized garden. The seed potatoes would need to be in the ground by the last of February.

Chuck and Simons had been in contact with the governing authorities who were in charge of placing the teachers in their assigned positions in Indian Territory.

Chuck remembered that Henry Shelton had told him that he was from a long line of farmers -- his father and grandfather had been farmers, and as far back as he could remember, the family had been farmers.

His father had expected him to take over the family farm after he was gone, but Henry had an exceptional bright analytical mind and had been inspired by Miss Godfrey, his high school teacher, to make something more of his life.

He decided that he wanted to be in a position to inspire other young people in the same way he had been inspired. This was why he chose a teaching career instead of farming.

He had told Chuck, "Although I want to teach the three R's, I also have a yearning to teach what I know about farming. My papa was brilliant in some of his farming techniques, and he passed them on to me. I suppose farming is in my blood -- whether I wanted to acknowledge it or not, the love is there."

Simons and Chuck McCord asked those in authority if it would be possible to assign Henry and his wife Helen to teach the Cheyennes and Arapahos on their reservation in the southwestern part of Indian Territory.

They had already started teaching north of the Arkansas, but if they agreed to the change, they could be transferred.

Chuck sent a telegram to Henry explaining the situation. Henry sent back and said he would be willing to make the trip and talk to Chuck and Simons before he made his final decision.

It took Henry a good week to make the trip. After Chuck explained the whole state of affairs, they all decided to make the trip to the reservation and look over the terrain, and introduce Henry to the Cheyenne council.

It was exciting for Henry Shelton to discover the rich land that had formed from the years of flooding of the Washita River. All those years, the land had never been cultivated. The soil was black and loamy from the silt, just waiting to grow whatever seeds were embedded in its richness.

Henry explained, through Chuck's interpreting, "You have been blessed with this rick land as your reservation. I can teach you how to grow enough food to feed your families and enough to sell for profit to the trading posts, who in turn will be sell to other Indians and white settlers. With this profit you can purchase livestock, cattle, chickens, sheep, horses, or whatever you desire.

"My wife and I will also start a school in this area for your children and any of the white settlers' children to attend. Your children need to be educated in speaking and writing English if they are to deal in the white man's world.

"The Muskogee nation has done well in farming and building substantial living quarters. They've prospered in raising cotton, wheat, oats, and peanuts on their reservation, and they live in peace with the white man in this Indian Territory. With our help, you can learn to do the same."

The council agreed that they would learn to farm the land and send their children to the white man's school, and they would do their best to live at peace with their white neighbors.

"Those Cheyennes and Arapahos that cause trouble by robbing and killing white settlers will not be tolerated; Cheyenne law will punish and turn them over to government authorities. But let it be known if soldiers fire upon my people first, there will be blood shed!" Chief Whirlwind declared.

Henry and Helen Shelton and their two children, Tommy and Maggie, moved to southwest Indian Territory and began a large one-room school house, roughly constructed of logs.

The contents were a large potbellied stove and long benches for the children's seats, an oak desk for the teacher, a slate blackboard, and several dozen McGuffey's readers and slates for the children. All the supplies were brought in by wagon.

In a couple of weeks after the agreement, plows and farming implements and seed were delivered, along with four large work horses to pull the plows. There were two milk cows and five head of cattle, one large bull, and a crate of chickens.

The Indians had already rounded up some wild cows for milking and had found the nests of wild chickens and pheasants, for eggs, but not enough to feed the many people of their nation.

The planting began, and with Henry's instructions the Cheyennes and Arapahos plowed the dark rich soil, planted seed, and watched the corn grow tall. They planted potatoes, onions, squash, and cabbage among other vegetables and grains.

It was now into the first week of the month of June. The McCord family, along with Yellow Hawk and Moon Flower and the Claybrooks, were anticipating the arrival of the new member of the family -- the baby that would soon be born.

"Lucinda, should you be out and about with your time so close?" Rose asked as she stood behind the counter of the Heyburn trading post, now owned by her and her husband Alford.

"Now Rosie, you're just like everyone else, trying to get me to stay in bed or off my feet. I'm a strong woman -- and besides, I had to come in and see Doc Martin," Lucinda said as she rubbed the soft furry back of the Claybrooks' old yellow tomcat, who was on the counter, his favorite place in the store.

"Yes, but I bet the doc would have made the trip to come see you at your home. What did he have to say about you making such a trip into town?"

"Well…he wasn't well pleased…but he did say that everything checks out and I should deliver on time…maybe a couple of weeks. Anyway, that's why I need to finish the baby's quilt before it gets here -- I just need some fabric for the border, and it will be completed.

"Rosie, give me a yard of that pretty lavender calico. Joseph is waiting for me, and we need to get back," Lucinda said as she noticed the time on the large round clock on the north wall.

"All right, Lucinda, but you tell Joseph and Chuck that I want to know when your time comes. I want to be there to help the doc in any way I'm needed."

"I will, Rosie; I'll tell them both," Lucinda said as she placed the package with the fabric in it under her arm, held on to the bottom of her tummy with that hand, and opened the screen door with the other.

When Lucinda and Joseph returned to the ranch, Lucinda spent the remainder of the afternoon in her comfortable chair with her feet up, quietly sewing the lavender fabric onto the baby quilt.

Moon had put a large beef stew on the stove and was busy making a blackberry cobbler for tonight's supper.

Margret Ann was helping make the cobbler dough when Lucinda rose from her chair, walked into the kitchen, and said, "Moon, you are just too good to me, and I know that you're working too hard—I can help."

"Nonsense, you need to rest -- the doc says only a couple of weeks, and then the delivery; and you're going to need to be rested and strong for your baby. Besides, Margret Ann and I are doing just fine fixing this supper -- aren't we, little miss Margret?" Moon said as she winked at Lucinda.

"We are, Momma -- you don't have to worry,'cause we have everything under control," Margret Ann said as she raised her flour- covered hand up and scratched her cheek, leaving her jaw and the tip of her nose covered with flour.

After supper, when Yellow Hawk and Moon had left to return to their cabin and Joseph and Margret Ann had gone to bed, Lucinda lay on the lounge and Chuck sat on the buffalo rug next to her.

"Tell me, sweetheart, how are you really feeling -- and what did Doc Martin have to say about your condition?" Chuck asked as he gently stroked her arm with his callused hands.

"Strong Eagle, you mustn't worry so much. I'm a little tired, but the doc said that was normal. He also said that I'm doing good to be in my last few days before I'm due.

"This baby is going to be an energetic little one—if he is as active after he is born as he is now. There he goes again; Chuck, put your hand here and feel him kick!"

"Wow, that's a strong kick -- does it hurt when he does that?"

"No, silly, it doesn't hurt!" Lucinda said with a teasing laugh and a push on Chuck's shoulder.

Chuck rose up on his knees and put his arms around Lucinda's distended tummy and said, "Hey, little one -- what are we going to name you? Are you to be Scott after your Grandpa McCord, or Rachel after your Grandma Claybrook?"

Chapter 32

The days passed and Lucinda had to spend more time resting and off her feet. When Doctor Martin came to make his house call, he told her that she might have the baby earlier than they had calculated. He said, "Lucinda, have you been drinking your raspberry tea?"

"Yes I have, Doc, ever since you told me to start drinking it."

"That's good, Lucinda; it will make your delivery much easier. Some in the medical field think natural medicine does no good, but I believe in using the herbs God created and placed on this earth for therapeutic purposes. The tea will make your uterus relaxed and supple."

Also he said, "Lucinda, there's a full moon next week -- and not that I understand it, but there are more babies born on a full moon than any other time of the month."

"Really, Doc? I never heard that one before."

"Just the same, I'm going to be on the alert at that time, and it would be best if you would be, too. Make sure you're not alone when the moon turns full. I know that will come about a week or so before your due date, but just the same, I expect you to have someone with you, you hear?"

"Yes, Doc, I hear -- and I will be sure I have someone with me when there's a full moon, all right?"

"Well, be sure you do, young lady." The doc turned and said as he walked out the front door carrying his black bag and heading for his carriage, pulled by his old gray horse, Samuel.

The whole family was informed as to what the doc had cautioned.

"Well, I'm going to make sure I stay close when that moon turns full!" Chuck decided.

Moon Flower spoke up and said, "Yes, I've seen that happen. More Indian babies are born on a full moon."

The men had been working long hours, training the new horses recently brought in, helping Moon and Margret Ann with the large garden area, building fence and all the other demands of running a horse and cattle ranch.

Joseph was well-trained now in taming the horses, and his papa relied on him more and more. He loved working with the horses, but what he loved most was his music. He spent every evening playing his guitar and singing his songs.

Lucinda especially loved to hear her son's music -- it was so soothing to her, and she said, "Joseph, when you play and sing, the music seems to soothe this little one, too. It settles down, and I think it must go to sleep."

The busy work-packed days went by fast and everyone forgot even to notice the moon until one balmy summer evening just after supper, Chuck and Yellow Hawk walked out of the house and down to the barn to check on one of the mares who was about to foal. They noticed the restlessness of the ponies in the corral; their whinnies and snorts as they uneasily trotted around the enclosure.

The mare in the barn also seemed fidgety and Chuck said, "Hawk I think she's gonna have that colt tonight."

"Why are the horses so excited? You don't think there are

wolves close, do you?" Chuck said, scratching his head, but just then he looked out of the barn window toward the east and noticed the large full moon peeking up over the trees on the far horizon.

"There it is, Hawk -- that's why the stock's so restless; this is the first night of the full moon!

"Strong Eagle, you think there's anything to this full moon business make babies come?"

"I don't know, but I'm going to be close at home just in case."

The mare had her foal that night, just as Chuck predicted, but there was no change in Lucinda's condition; she slept soundly through the night.

The next morning, the silvery full moon could be seen high in the eastern sky.

Lucinda rose from her bed and stretched and yawned. Chuck had gotten up early, made the coffee, and had headed out to check on the new foal and the mare.

Lucinda slipped her house shoes on and picked up her housecoat from the foot of the bed, slipped it on, and walked into the kitchen, poured herself a cup of coffee, and proceeded to prepare griddle cakes for their breakfast.

Her lower back felt tired and achy, but otherwise she felt she was doing fine for being over eight months pregnant.

Chuck came in from the barn and kissed Lucinda good morning and said, "How are you feeling this morning, sweetheart? That old full moon's still up there," Chuck said with a little tease in his voice.

"Oh, it's still there, is it? Don't worry, I'm fine," Lucinda said, looking up at Chuck with a little chuckle.

"Oh, griddle cakes -- I'm ready for a breakfast of your

griddle cakes, sweetheart! Looks like we may get some rain -- there's a cloud bank in the west," Chuck said as he sat down at the table and forked a good portion of cakes into his plate.

Lucinda, pouring his coffee said, "I hope we get a good rain; the crops could use a good drenching."

Chuck finished his breakfast and left to see to his work. A short time later, Moon walked in the front door and Yellow Hawk headed for the horse corral.

Moon called, "Lucinda, where are you?"

Lucinda called from the parlor, "I'm in here, Moon."

Lucinda was sitting back in her easy chair and looking a little uneasy.

"What's wrong, Luc? Are you feeling all right?"

"My back just feels a little tired and achy; that's all."

"Are you sure that's all it is? You know there's a full moon now?"

"Oh, Moon -- not you too! I'm fine; just a little back ache."

"Well, all right then; I'm going out back to start the wash. If you need me, call."

Moon kindled a fire under the iron kettle, drew water from the well, and filled it. When the water was good and hot, she poured enough in the wooden tub along with cool water from the well, and began to scrub the clothes on the washboard.

As she rubbed the square bar of lye soap on the shirt she was washing, she looked up into the western sky and thought, *It looks like a storm is coming. I may not be able to finish this wash.*

The storm was moving in fast; the dark threatening clouds cast their shadows across the silver moon, and the bright rays of the sun disappeared.

Since Indian Territory had very little law enforcement, it was a welcome refuge for rustlers and outlaws.

After attempting to rob a bank in Wichita, Kansas, the Jenkins gang barely made their escape to their horses. With bullets flying from the sheriff and his deputy Billy, the youngest brother took a bullet in the shoulder just before the three disappeared into the thick forest.

The Jenkins brothers were a notorious outlaw gang. Their papa was a harsh tyrannical man with very little sympathy for his boys. He taught them how to steal and rob and kill. Sometime after his death, the boys set out to follow the road their papa had paved for them.

Even though Drake and Homer were hardened to the core, the youngest brother, only seventeen, had never killed anyone and still remembered his mother and her kind heart toward him—before she died from the harsh treatment of his papa, she had said to him, "Son, try to get away from your papa and your brothers. Make a life away from them in any honest way you can!"

He had no use for his papa, but he had a deep affection for his momma; he wanted to obey her last words to him, but he knew no other way of life. He had no other family to turn to and now, here he was, riding into unknown territory with a searing pain in his shoulder, hardly able to stay in the saddle.

The three rode south, heading for Indian Territory. When they were sure no one was following them, they stopped by a flowing stream and Homer saw to Billy's wound.

"The bullet's still in there, Drake -- we've gotta get him to a doctor."

"And just where do you think we're gonna find a doctor out here, you numskull? You're gonna have to dig that bullet out yourself."

"No. I've got the bleeding stopped; I say we ride on and see if we can find a doctor."

"All right, then -- but if we don't run into some civilization before long, you're gonna have to dig that bullet out yourself. Besides, there's a storm comin' and we need to find some kind of shelter."

The three rode on, but the wind began to kick up and the rain began to fall, and the light began to diminish from the dark storm clouds all around.

Chuck and Yellow Hawk secured the stock into the barn before the fast-approaching storm was upon them.

Joseph ran to the house and began to close the shutters over the windows when Moon came to the door and excitedly told Joseph, "Hurry, get your papa -- your momma needs him!"

Joseph ran to the barn and delivered the message.

"What's the matter, Joseph? Did she say?"

"No, Papa -- she just said come quickly!"

They hurriedly ran to the house and Chuck rushed through the door and said to Moon who was standing there waiting, "What's going on? Where's Lucinda?"

"She's in the bedroom; she's gone into labor, Strong Eagle. Someone needs to go for Doctor Martin!"

By this time, the storm was over them. The thunder was booming, there were great streaks of lightning crashing down, and the wind was raging!

"Lucinda wants you here with her; she doesn't want you to leave," Moon said.

"Strong Eagle, is that you?" Lucinda called from their bedroom.

Before Chuck hurried to her side he turned to Yellow Hawk and said, "Bring the doctor as soon as you can -- you know I'm counting on you."

Yellow Hawk ran to the barn, through a torrent of rain and the wind pressing against him. He quickly saddled his Appaloosas and headed toward the settlement.

Pounding on the doctor's door, Yellow Hawk yelled, "Doctor, Doctor -- open up!"

Doctor Martin opened the door and Yellow Hawk said, "She's having the baby, Doc -- you need come quick!"

"Hang on to your pants, Hawk! Go around to my barn and hitch up my buggy while I tell the missus and get my bag!"

Chapter 33

The wind blew hard against the carriage and the rain came down until it was hard to see the road, but old Samuel's steady trot was unaltered, and soon they pulled up in front of the McCord homestead.

Yellow Hawk rode his horse into the barn, unsaddled him and gave him hay, and then made his way to the house.

Moon met the doc at the front door and told him, "Her pains are now four minutes apart. Doctor, what can I do to help?"

"Right now just make a strong pot of coffee; the men are going to need it. Now take me to her -- where is she, Moon?"

Moon escorted the doc to Lucinda's bedroom, where Chuck was sitting in a chair close to her.

"Chuck, you want to step out while I check Lucinda?"

Chuck hesitated to leave but Lucinda said, "It's all right, Strong Eagle; I'll be in good hands."

After Chuck had left Lucinda told the doctor, "Doc, my water broke some time ago, and the pains are getting stronger."

"Just try to relax, Lucinda -- and before long, you'll have a fine little one."

"Up ahead, I see some houses up yonder, looks like a store!" Homer exclaimed.

The three rode up to the Heyburn trading post. Drake said, "You two stay here and I'll go see if there's a doctor around."

He opened the door and walked up to the counter just as Alford was coming out of the back storage room.

"Can I help you? Bad storm out there."

"Is there a doctor around here? My brother's sick and needs a doctor."

"About a half mile down the road you'll see his home and office; you can't miss it."

Drake turned and headed out the door with no thanks, just a hard look and a grunt.

Alford thought, *That was sure a rough- lookin' hombre; maybe I should ride down to doc's and make sure everything's all right.*

Drake pounded his fist on the doctor's door and Mrs. Martin opened it.

Drake pushed his way in without waiting to be invited.

"Where's the doctor, missy?"

"He's not here right now; he's out on a house call."

"He's out in this kind of weather? Tell me where he went so I can take my brother there --he's real sick."

"What's wrong with him, mister? Maybe you can bring him in out of the weather and wait for the doctor until he returns."

"Can't do that, missy. You tell me where he went!" Drake said harshly, raising his voice.

"He went to deliver a baby at the McCord ranch," Mrs. Martin said, trembling and giving directions.

"You don't tell nobody where we went or I'll come back and…ya just don't tell nobody, ya hear!" Drake said with an intimidating growl in his voice.

"No, sir; I won't tell a soul," Mrs. Martin said as she shrank back.

As they were leaving, the doctor's wife peeked out between the shades and saw the young man with blood on the shoulder of his coat, and favoring that shoulder -- she perceived from a gunshot wound.

The doc's wife thought, *Should I go to Alford's store and tell him what happened? It'll be hard to get there by foot in this storm -- oh, what should I do?*

Just then Alford stepped in the door and said, "Mattie, is everything all right? I sent that fellow down here, but he was sure rough- lookin.' Has he already left? Where's the doc?"

"Oh, Alford -- I didn't know what to do. I sent that fellow and the other two with him to Chuck's house because a short time ago Yellow Hawk came after the doctor...Lucinda had gone into labor.

"That man threatened me -- he said if I told anyone where they went, that he would come back here after me! After he left I saw out the window, and his brother's not just sick -- he has been shot. Alford, those are bad men. What are we going to do?"

"Mattie, you're not going to do anything! I'm going to take you to Rose and you stay with her until the doc and I get back."

"All right, Alford, whatever you say -- but you better go over there armed."

"You don't worry about that now."

Alford escorted Mattie to their home and told Rose to take care of her, and then he saddled Jo and checked his rifle to make sure it was loaded and headed out through the storm to the ranch.

The three desperadoes rode up in front of the homestead, tied their horses to the hitching post, and walked up to the front door, Homer half carrying Billy.

Drake pounded his fist on the door and Moon started toward the door, but Hawk intercepted and said, "You stay back; I answer door."

When he opened the door Drake said, "We're here to see the doctor. Our brother Billy's been shot."

"Well, come on in then." As they brought Billy in Chuck said, "Take him over here and lay him on this couch. I'll go get the doctor. Moon, you and Margret Ann come with me."

When Chuck got in the bedroom he told the doctor about the three men. "I don't like the looks of them, Doc, and those two are both wearing guns."

About that time, Lucinda screamed out in pain. "I can't leave her now, Chuck -- the baby's coming!"

Chuck took his revolver from the dresser and stuck it in the band of his pants under his shirt and he said to Margret Ann, "Under no circumstances do you leave this room!" And then he went back into the parlor and said, "The doc's delivering a baby and can't come just now -- but this little lady--" he gestured to Moon, "will look after your brother until the doc can get loose."

Drake drew his gun from the holster on his side, and Homer did the same.

"You let this little missy take care of the women, and you tell the doctor to get in here or she gets it first! You, Indian -- get over here where I can see you!"

Hawk moved over close to Chuck, Joseph, and Moon.

"You, missy -- go tell the doctor to get out here, or we'll start shootin'!"

Hawk said, "It's all right, Moon, do what he says."

"Moon, the baby's coming -- I can see the head. When it comes, just cut the cord!"

Lucinda screamed in pain!

Doctor Martin came out and said, "You can put away those guns. I'll tend to your brother."

Drake said, "Just shut up and take care of him -- and if he dies, you die, too!"

The doctor removed Billy's coat and shirt and could see the wound had become infected. He poured disinfectant over it and had Chuck and Yellow Hawk clear the kitchen table and lay him on it.

"I'm going to have to have one of these men to help me."

"All right, you, get over there!" Drake said gruffly to Joseph.

"Joseph, hold this cloth over his face until he's asleep," the doc said.

"What's that you're doin'? What is that stuff?" Homer said.

"It's chloroform; your brother will sleep and not feel the pain."

"He better wake up, or you're dead!"

Lucinda screamed from the bedroom, and Chuck started toward her. Drake pulled the hammer back on his pistol and Chuck stopped in his tracks and said, "Let me see about my wife!"

"You try that again and you're dead!" Drake thundered.

Just then, Alford rode up slowly to the barn. He could see the three strangers' horses tied in front of the house.

He circled around behind the house and quietly stepped up onto the porch from the south. He peered in the window and saw the two men with their backs to him, but they were turned enough that he could see they held everyone at gunpoint.

Hawk and Chuck faced the window; Alford held his rifle up to the window and waved it. Chuck saw him, winked at Hawk, and rolled his eyes toward Alford.

Chuck put his hand on his shirt where his pistol was hidden

in hopes that Alford would understand he was armed. Then Chuck nodded, and Alford fired his rifle and shot Homer! Drake cocked his gun just as Chuck fell to the floor, rolled over, and came up to a sitting position with his gun firing! Drake fell to the floor and breathed his last.

Homer was wounded and lying on the floor. He raised his gun toward Chuck; Hawk pulled his knife from his boot and threw it into Homer's heart!

Alford came through the door and could see their captors were dead.

"I never shot a man before -- and I hope I never have to again."

"I know, Alford, but it couldn't be helped. If you hadn't come, I don't know what would have happened," Chuck said, patting Alford on the back.

Chuck hurried into the bedroom to see about Lucinda. When he arrived, Lucinda was holding their tiny little girl. "Come over here Chuck, and meet our little Rachel Sue."

Chuck, Alford, and Hawk carried the two men out in a secluded spot and buried them.

When Billy became conscious, Chuck told him his brothers were dead.

He said, "I know I maybe shouldn't feel this way, but I'm glad to be free from them. They were my brothers and I think in their own way they cared about me, but they were mostly cruel and heartless.

I never wanted to be like them, and our momma had told me before she died that I should get free from my papa and my brothers and try and make something good of my life -- maybe I can now. Mr. Chuck, you ain't gonna turn me over to the law, are you?"

"You just rest now, Billy; we'll talk again later."

Billy closed his eyes, and with a big sigh, passed into a deep sleep.

"Doc, before you head back -- and Alford, you too; I know you're both anxious to get back to your wives, I'm sure they're both worried -- but we need to talk about this young man Billy," Chuck said with a very serious countenance.

"We all need to be in agreement on this --including you, Hawk, and your wife Moon, and of course Lucinda -- I will talk to her a little while later after she has had some time to recover.

"As we all know, there's no law enforcement in this territory. We know little about the background of these brothers, only the little that Billy told me a few minutes ago.

"His brothers are dead and buried and he seems glad to be free from their grip and wants to make a new start. He said that's what his momma wanted him to do before she died -- to get free from them and their papa. I assume from the way he talked that both his parents are dead.

"This young man is about the same age as my Joseph, and maybe that's why I feel so inclined to help him.

"What do you say? Should we just keep this incident to ourselves? Those here, and Mattie and Rose, are the only ones that know about it.

"Billy's brothers are dead and buried and can do no more harm to anyone. If we all agree, I'll take full responsibility for him. What do you say?"

"I say Chuck, you're taking on a lot. That boy could just be fooling you," Alford responded.

"He may be, although I don't think he is -- but if he isn't sincere, I'll face that if it happens," Chuck replied.

"None of us want to see such a young man turned over to the law and possibly sent to prison, to those hell holes! If young men aren't corrupted when they enter those places, they will be before they get out!

"I'm with you, Chuck -- let's give the young man a chance in life to make something of himself," Doctor Martin exclaimed!

Hawk, Moon, and Alford all agreed, and they all were in a unified agreement to keep what had happened this day a secret. Doctor Martin and Alford said they would tell their wives the decision that had been made.

Chapter 34

Lucinda and Chuck agreed to keep Billy in the house until he was well enough to move onto a cot in the back room of the barn.

Billy healed fast; the doc came several times to check on his progress and to change his bandages, but on his last visit he said, "This boy's well enough to do some work -- not anything too strenuous, but some work will help him get his strength back."

Chuck asked, "Billy, you like horses?"

"I sure do, Mr. Chuck!"

"Well, you'll be taking care of them soon enough. You know, Billy -- you don't have to call me Mister. Just Chuck will do."

"Well then…Chuck, Miss Lucinda told me your Indian name, that it was Strong Eagle. She also told me about your momma and papa and why you were given that name.

"I think that makes you a great man, and I'd be proud to work for you…Strong Eagle. Is it all right if I call you by your Indian name?"

Lucinda was standing close by holding little Rachel Sue; she smiled at Chuck and Chuck winked at her and he turned to Billy and said, "Billy, you call me whatever you want -- by either name, which ever you choose. Billy, I think you're well enough now to move into the back room of the barn, and Joseph can have his bed back. I also expect you to keep the room in the barn neat and tidy. Tomorrow you can start work, cleaning out the stalls and brushing down the horses. Have you ever milked before?"

"Yes, I have, but not in a long time."

"Well, it'll come back to you. As soon as your shoulder is well enough, you can start helping Margret Ann with the milking. Right now, your only pay is room and board and a couple of dollars a week. If I see you're going to make a good hand, I'll up that pay."

"Two dollars a week -- that sounds good to me!"

"Also, Billy, until I decide you can be totally trusted, I don't want you carrying a firearm. Can you understand that?"

"Well, yes -- I guess I can, but you'll see, Chuck...you can trust me."

"Well, time will tell, Billy -- time will tell," Chuck said as he headed to the front door.

Lucinda had taken a liking to the boy, and so had the rest of the family. He did lack manners, though; the first time he was able to sit at the dinner table with the rest of the family, he dived into the food before Chuck could ask the blessing.

As Billy eagerly reached for the platter of meat, Lucinda gently placed her hand on his and said, "Now, Billy; you have to wait until after the blessing before we begin."

Billy, embarrassed, pulled his hand back, looked down at his plate, and said, "Sorry, I didn't know."

"Of course you didn't, son; it'll just take a little time for you to learn all of our ways," Chuck told him.

Rose, Alice, Danny, and Jenny came to visit, along with their dog, Storm. Storm was full- grown now, and a smart, playful fellow, but also a zealous protector of the family. He was gentle for the most part, but a hint of his still- untamable wildness could be seen in those slanted amber eyes and the full-teeth snarl if Storm thought there was danger from a predator.

Margret Ann and Lucinda came out of the house when they saw the company pull up in the carriage.

Lucinda said, "Oh, Rosie -- I'm so glad to see you! come on in the house and I'll make us some tea.

"You girls come in too if you want, but I figured you'd rather see the new baby kittens in the barn. Rachel's down for her nap and you can see her when she wakes up."

"Oh, yes -- we want to see the kittens. Come on, Margret Ann, and show us!" Alice said.

Alice, Jenny, and Danny headed for the barn following Margret Ann, with Storm following close behind.

There was a basket sitting back in the corner of the barn, and Margret Ann's calico cat was in it with her four little kittens, just a couple of days old, with their eyes still unopened. Two of them were black, one was brown, and the other one calico like the momma.

They all gathered around the basket, sitting on the hay-strewn wooden floor, Storm lying close by.

They had all picked up kittens and were rubbing their tiny little heads and talking, giggling, and cooing over how cute they were, when unbeknownst to them Billy walked into the barn and saw them.

He began walking toward the group when he heard a low snarling growl. Billy stopped in his tracks and Storm came out from behind a stack of hay with his head down, the fur up on his back, and his fierce teeth shining and dripping with saliva.

"Hey, whose dog is this? Call him off, call him off!" Billy yelled.

Jenny jumped up and yelled, "Storm, it's all right -- he's a friend!"

Just as quickly as he had become vicious, Storm raised his head and wagged his tail, and walked over to Billy.

"Wow, boy -- I thought you had me there for a minute, but look at you now...you've decided to be friendly?" Billy said as he gave Storm a pat on the head.

Jenny walked over to where the dog and Billy were standing and said, "Hi, I'm Jenny, and this is my dog Storm -- he's half wolf."

"Really? Half wolf, you say? What's the other half...cougar?" Billy said with a grin.

"No, silly; his daddy was a white husky. Who are you, anyway?" Jenny inquired.

Margret Ann said, "This is Billy Jenkins; he's staying with us and working for my papa."

"Well, then -- glad to meet you, Billy Jenkins," Jenny said as she looked at him with a flirtatious smile.

"How old are you, Jenny?" Billy asked.

"I'll be fifteen next birthday."

"Fourteen, then, and still wet behind the ears... but you are kinda cute," Billy teased.

"You better be careful, Billy Jenkins, or I can still tell Storm to get you."

"Well, I don't know -- I think he likes me now anyway... Jenny, almost fifteen.

Billy walked over to where Alice was still sitting with two of the kittens in her lap and said, "And who is this pretty lady -- and how old are you?"

"Don't you know it's not polite to ask a woman's age?" Alice said curtly.

"Well, excuse me; I didn't know I was talking to a woman -- maybe a girl not yet a woman?" Billy teased.

"I'll have you know I'll be eighteen next month!"

Margret Ann interrupted and said, "Billy, meet my Aunt Alice."

"Your aunt? Well, Alice, I guess then you are a woman?" Billy said with such a big grin that Alice had to grin back at him.

"I don't have time to talk any longer, girls and guys; I've got to get back to work, but it was good to meet you…and you too, Storm!" Billy said as he passed by the dog and gave him another pat on the head.

After Billy left, Jenny said, "Alice, he is real cute, don't you think?"

"Yeah, I guess so, Jenny -- but he's too old for you."

"How old is he, Margret Ann?"

"I think Papa said he was seventeen, or something like that -- he said about Joseph's age, and my brother turns seventeen next month," Margret Ann said as she scratched her head and rolled her eyes in thought.

"Come on, Jenny -- come and push me in the wheelbarrow -- they got a big wheelbarrow!" Danny said with a whine in his voice.

"Oh, all right, Danny; just once around the house, and that's all. Then I want to go in the house and see baby Rachel."

"Aw Jenny, more than just once!" Danny said, standing with his hands on his hips and looking sour.

Storm followed them twice around the house, wagging his tail and barking.

Chuck and Hawk came to the house for lunch and when Chuck saw Storm, he said, "Come here, boy -- I haven't seen you in a while."

Storm put his front feet up on Chuck. Chuck rubbed his ears and head and said, "Storm, you have really filled out and made a big boy. I think Rose is feeding you plenty."

Billy was coming from the barn and saw Chuck petting Storm. He said, "Hey, Chuck; that's some wolf dog they've got."

"How'd you know he was part wolf?"

"I surprised him in the barn and he showed his teeth, and I sure thought he was gonna attack me, but Jenny called him off. She told me he was half wolf."

"Oh, you met Jenny?"

"Yeah, and I met her little brother, too."

"Yeah, he's a handful," Chuck said with a smile.

By that time, Billy had walked up to where they were standing. He reached down and rubbed Storm's head and said, "We're good friends now, boy, aren't we?" Storm turned his head and licked Billy's hand.

"Well, come on in the house and we'll all have lunch and talk some more," Chuck said, putting his hand on Billy's back.

A couple of months passed, and Billy became like a member of the family.

He worked hard and did what he was told, even though it was sometimes dirty work.

Billy wanted to help Joseph and Hawk train the horses. He wanted to learn the gentling techniques they were using.

Chuck had upped his pay, enough that he could begin to save some of his earnings. He also gave him permission to carry a firearm.

"Billy, I think you have earned the right to carry a gun, if that's what you want to do, but remember it's only for protection, and a rifle for hunting.

"Billy, the way we train the horses takes a lot of patience -- you can't lose your temper with them. The training in the round corral is something that takes time to learn, and a lot of patience with the pony you're working with," Chuck explained.

"Chuck, I really want to learn and I will keep my temper, I promise. You'll see if you give me a chance."

"All right, Billy; I'll have Hawk begin your training when he has some free time, but this training has to be done when your other work is completed."

Chapter 35

The next Sunday, Jenny asked her momma if she could ride Snowflake over to Uncle Chuck's and see if Joseph would go riding with her.

"Please, Momma, can I take Storm along?"

"Well, of course you can; I wouldn't want it any other way, and he'll protect you and Snowflake and whoever is with you. Why don't you take lunch along and have a picnic?"

"Oh, that's a great idea; I'll go fix it right now."

"Jenny, there was meatloaf left over from supper last night -- you can make sandwiches with it if you want, and there are plenty of cookies."

Jenny tied the picnic blanket on the back of her saddle and headed toward the McCord ranch. She said, "Come on, Storm -- you get to go too."

She rode up in front of the house and slid off Snowflake's back, tossed her long black hair over her shoulder, and let her wide-brimmed Western hat fall to her back, the cord catching under her chin.

Jenny Claybrook's figure was beginning to show. She was no longer a little girl, but was blossoming into a lovely young lady.

She walked up to the front door, knocked, and walked on in. Lucinda saw her enter and said, "Hi, Jenny, come on in; I'm here in the kitchen."

"Hi, Aunt Lucinda. Where's Joseph and Margret Ann? I thought if they weren't busy maybe we could go horseback riding and have a picnic."

"Joseph's out at the barn and Margret Ann's outside somewhere -- I bet you can find them," Lucinda said as she wiped her hands on the dishtowel.

Joseph and Billy were in the corral and Hawk was giving Billy some pointers in his horse training when Jenny walked up and said, "Hey, you're not supposed to be working today...don't you all ever take a day off?"

"Hi, Jenny -- what are you doing here?" Joseph asked.

"Well, cousin, that's not much of a greeting. Aren't you glad to see me?" Jenny retorted.

"Well, of course I am -- I see you rode your momma's Snowflake."

"Yes, and I've got a picnic lunch waiting on her if anyone's interested and wants to go riding with me."

"Hey, that sounds pretty good -- how about it, Hawk? Enough training today?"

"Sure, Joseph, enough today -- you kids go and have a good time, maybe more training next day."

"Hey, Billy, you come too -- saddle up that paint over there, and I'll ride Sam," Joseph said.

"Sounds good to me. Jenny, you have enough vittles for me too?"

"I brought plenty, hoping you would come."

"Oh, hoping he would come, huh?" Joseph teased.

Jenny lowered her head, but her dark-brown eyes were on Billy, and as he looked her way, she smiled.

"Joseph, where's Margret Ann? Do you think she would

want to go too?" Jenny said when her attention returned to Joseph.

"You bet she will. I don't know where she's off to, but I'll saddle the small pony she rides, and you go see if you can find her."

"Come on, Storm, and help me find Margret Ann."

Storm ran past the house and into the woods headed for the creek, Jenny close behind. They found Margret Ann down on her knees with a fishing net, trying to catch tadpoles. Storm went up to her and licked her face.

"Storm, what are you doing her, boy!?" Margret Ann said with surprise as she put her arms around his thick white hairy body and gave him a hug.

"He's with me, Margret," Jenny called, "and we've been looking for you. Do you want to go on a picnic with us or not?"

"What picnic? I didn't know anything about a picnic?" Margret said as she rose to her feet.

"Well, come on, and I'll tell you on the way back to the house."

While they were getting everything ready to go, Lucinda made lemonade, chipped some ice from the block in the icebox, then chopped it up even smaller and put it in two canteens and poured them full of lemonade.

"Here, Joseph, take these two canteens -- you carry one and give the other to Billy to carry, and don't you kids be gone too long—no more than four hours at the most, you hear!"

"Yes, Momma -- no more than four hours, all right?"

"You hear me now; if it's any longer, I'll have your papa come lookin' for you!"

"All right, Momma; don't worry."

"Joseph, I want you to take your papa's rifle. I don't want to scare you, but George Smith told your papa that he saw a black bear on our property a few days ago," Lucinda said as she handed her son his papa's rifle.

"Sure, Momma, a good idea to take the rifle…a black bear, huh?! We'll be on the lookout, that's for sure."

"You take care of your sister now!"

"Yes, Momma, I will."

Joseph pushed the rifle in the scabbard on the saddle, hung the two canteens over the saddle horn, rode up to Billy and handed him the other canteen, and said, "Is everybody ready? Then let's go!"

"Aren't you taking your guitar, Joseph? I thought you took it everywhere," Jenny mused.

"Well, I would like to take it with me, but I didn't know whether my playing would be a nuisance or not."

"Yeah, it can get on a body's nerves and be a nuisance," Margret Ann said, rolling her eyes and giving a deep sigh.

"I know what you think, little sister -- you tell me often enough."

"Well, Joseph I love your music, and don't get to hear enough of it. I thought you could serenade us while we were having our picnic," Jenny said, giving Margret Ann a disapproving look.

"Hey, I like your music too, Joseph," Billy spoke up, giving his opinion.

"I'll just be a minute," Joseph said as he dismounted and ran into the house. He came back with his guitar in hand, and hung it from its shoulder strap on the back of his saddle.

It was a balmy summer day, with a beautiful cobalt blue sky and a scattering of ashen-white cumulus clouds.

The four rode down the country road until they came to the northwest meadow, which was strewn with golden color from the abundance of Black-eyed Susans growing there. They galloped their horses across the meadow until they came to the creek that separated them from the field that was their destination.

They stopped at the water's edge and let the horses drink, and then rode them through the slow-moving steam and over the slippery rocks, and up and over the bank to the other meadow.

As they started through the field, Jenny said, "Come on, I'll race ya -- bet Snowflake can beat you all!

"You're on, let's go!" Billy said with enthusiasm.

There wasn't anything Snowflake liked better than a good race, and she stretched her long white body out in a full run! For a few yards, Joseph and Billy's horses ran side by side with Jenny's, Margret Ann's small pony falling behind, but then Snowflake pulled out ahead and rode like a windstorm across the meadow, reaching the other side long before the others.

"Wow, what a horse!" Billy said as he rode up close to Jenny.

"Yeah, I should have known we didn't have a chance -- I've seen her run before. But it was fun anyway, wasn't it?" Joseph said with a chuckle.

"Hey, I thought so!" Billy said. "But now we better rest these ponies, don't you think?"

"I think this is as good a place as any to have out picnic. Look over there, under that large oak -- we can spread our blanket there," Jenny suggested.

"I think if we just drop the reins on these horses they will just graze and not run away, especially as tired as they are," Joseph said.

That's what the four of them did, and they spread the blanket in a cool shady spot under the large oak tree.

Billy made sure he sat next to Jenny. He did it as nonchalantly as he could manage; he wanted to be close to this spirited little lady with the long dark silky hair that shimmered auburn in the sun.

They ate their lunch of meatloaf sandwiches and tomatoes, onions, and radishes from the Claybrooks' garden, and sweet lemonade to wash it all down with. Storm had one of the sandwiches too, which he wolfed down in a very short time.

After they had finished eating Joseph took his guitar, lay back against a large sand rock, and began to sing and play. He played songs that they all knew and that they could sing along with him, then he sang his special song, "Sundancer," which Billy had never heard.

"Wow, I like that song, Joseph -- it's real special," Billy said as he lay back on the blanket with his arms folded under his head.

"Here's a song a little more lively," Joseph said as he began to play:

Skip, skip, skip to my Lou
Skip, skip, skip to my Lou
Skip, skip, skip to my Lou
Skip to my Lou my darling!

I got another girl prettier than you
I got another girl prettier than you
I got another girl prettier than you
Skip to my Lou my darling!

Fly's in the buttermilk shoo fly shoo
Fly's in the buttermilk shoo fly shoo
Fly's in the buttermilk shoo fly shoo
Skip to my Lou my darling!

They all jumped up and began to dance to the bouncy music! Billy grabbed Jenny and held her in the dancing posture, and they skipped around in a circle, keeping time with the music, and then he took Margret Ann by the hand and twirled her round and round. They danced until they were exhausted, and they all fell down on the pallet laughing and out of breath!

They drank some more lemonade, and Jenny brought out some cookies from her saddle bag that she had been saving for a surprise, and they ate and talked for a long while until finally Joseph said, "Don't you think we should be headed for home? Momma wouldn't want us gone much longer, you know."

"It's still early, Joseph. I brought some lines, sinkers, hooks, and bobbers -- how about let's fish some in the creek, and see if we can surprise Aunt Lucinda with some fish for supper?" Jenny said.

"Yeah, why not? I know where there's a deep pool in the creek where I've fished before. All we have to do is cut some poles."

The boys cut poles and fastened them with string and hook; the girls dug in the dirt and found worms for bait, but they really didn't want to bait their hooks with those crawly worms, so Billy baited Jenny's and Joseph's his little sister's, and they all settled down on the creek bank and waited for the fish to bite.

Only a short time passed before Jenny's cork began to bob up and down.

"Look, Jenny -- you're gettin' a bite! Don't jerk it yet," Billy hollered.

The cork disappeared into the murky water!

"Now, Jenny, now -- jerk the pole!" Billy said with excitement.

Jenny jerked the pole so hard that the fish and line flew through the air and landed on the bank.

"Look here, it's a big mouth bass!" Billy said as he picked it up from the ground and held it high.

"I bet it'll weigh at least four pounds," Joseph said.

They fished a little longer and didn't catch anything and Joseph said, "We better head for home now; I don't want to worry Momma."

They pulled their lines in and began to gather up their belongings to head back to where the horses were tied.

"Here, Jenny; let me carry your fish for you," Billy said, his intent being to walk her back to the horses.

Jenny gave him the fish to carry and secretly was glad he wanted to walk so close to her, although she didn't want to show she was so pleased -- she didn't want to appear that audacious.

As they turned and started up the bank, Storm began to snarl and growl toward the thicket.

"What's out there, boy?" Jenny said as she turned back to look at Storm.

Joseph said, "Oh, no -- what's he snarling at? Wait, I hear something in there too!"

"Come on, Storm -- let's get out of here!" Jenny yelled.

Storm wouldn't leave; he just kept barking, snarling, and running toward the thicket!

"Come here!" Jenny yelled. "Come on, Storm -- come this way!"

A large black bear came through the brush, headed toward them, but Storm came at the bear from the side, viciously, causing the beast to rise up on his hind legs, roar, and snarl violently at Storm.

This was Storms chance to divert the bear until the group could get away! The dog ran behind the bear circling him and staying just out of the reach of his menacing giant paws!

Billy said, "Run! Now's the time to get away!"

"Oh, if I only had the rifle -- I left it with the horses!" Joseph shouted.

"There's no need to worry about that now --just run!" Billy screamed.

"What about Storm? That bear's going to kill him!" Jenny said, as she turned to run.

"There's nothing we can do for Storm now. I think he gave us this chance to get away from that beast, so let's not disappoint him -- run!" Joseph exclaimed.

"Oh, poor Storm," Margret Ann said as Joseph pulled her up and over the steep creek bank.

As Billy was climbing up to the top of the bank, he noticed he was still lugging the looped rope with the fish. He thought, *Maybe, just maybe this would work!*

He turned and started scooting back down the bank! Joseph screamed, "Billy, come back here -- you can't help Storm now!"

"Yes, I can!" Billy said, breathing heavily.

Billy ran toward the bear and tossed the fish through the air and it landed directly in front of the beast. He called, "Come on, Storm -- let's get out of here!"

Storm immediately ran toward Billy while the bear picked up the fish and disappeared back into the woods.

Storm was bloody, with one ear torn and a gash on his shoulder. With Billy's help, Storm made it back to the horses and Jenny spread the blanket for Storm to lie on. Storm lay there breathing heavily and whining in pain.

"I don't think Storm can make it back to the ranch. Billy, you stay here with Storm, and Jenny and Margret Ann and I will ride back to the ranch and tell Momma, and we'll bring the buckboard for Storm."

As Joseph was starting to mount his horse, he called Billy over to him away from the girls and said, "Billy, you take this rifle -- that bear is still out there and could still attack, or come after more fish. I'll be back as soon as possible."

Chapter 36

J oseph and Margret Ann rode their horses at a run, and when they arrived, Joseph told Margret as he dismounted, "Go in the house and tell Momma what's happened while I hitch the horses to the buckboard."

"Momma, Momma -- where are you!" Margret called as she went into the house.

Lucinda heard her call and could tell something was wrong. She came hurrying from the bedroom.

"What's the matter, daughter? Where's Joseph? Is he all right?"

"Yes, Momma, Joseph's fine. It's…it's Storm…he's hurt bad!" Margret said, almost in tears.

"What in the world happened to Storm?"

"A big black bear got him, Momma, but I'll tell you all about it on the way. Joseph's hitching up the horses to the buckboard; we've got to go get Storm!"

Storm was still bleeding from the gash in his shoulder. Billy said, "Jenny, don't you have some cloths that you used to wrap the food in?"

"Yes, there in my saddle bags."

"Well, would you get them, please?"

As Jenny retrieved the cloths, Billy told her, "We've got to stop the bleeding; he's losing too much blood. Take one of the cloths and fold it several times, put it over the wound, and keep pressure on it until the bleeding stops."

"I don't think he's going to like me doing that!"

"Talk softly to him, Jenny; let him know you're doing it to help him. You don't have to press too hard to stop the bleeding -- just do it gently but firmly. I've got to keep my eye out for that bear -- he may be back for more fish."

"Oh, Billy, I hadn't thought of that! Maybe he'll stay away because he doesn't want to tangle with Storm again," Jenny said, looking up at Billy with fear in her eyes, but then she said, "But Billy, you do have the rifle."

Billy thought, *Oh, those big brown eyes! She's depending on me for protection and I won't disappoint this pretty, sweet girl.*

"Yes, and if that bear shows up, I want you to know I won't hesitate to use this rifle!"

Storm lay still while Jenny laid the folded cloth on his shoulder. He seemed to know that she was trying to help him, and even though the pressure on his wound hurt terribly and he flinched when she first pressed, then he lay motionless and the pain lessened.

It wasn't long before Lucinda and Joseph were there with the buckboard. They left Margret Ann at home so she could inform her papa when he returned.

On the way there, Joseph had told his momma all that had happened with the bear, how Storm had diverted the bear's attention for them until they could get away, and how Billy had saved Storm by backtracking and giving the fish to the bear.

Lucinda checked Storm's wound and said, "Jenny, I think you can let up on the pressure now. It has stopped bleeding, but I don't think this is his only wound. He may have internal injuries -- so carry him carefully, boys."

They carried Storm and laid him in the buckboard on the blanket that Jenny had brought. Jenny crawled up next to him.

"Joseph, you better tie Jenny's horse to the buckboard -- and when we get to the doctor's house, Jenny, you need to ride on and tell your momma and papa what happened and where we are."

"Poor Storm. I'm so sorry you got hurt by that old bear -- and Storm, I know you wouldn't come when I called you because you were protecting us. I know that, Storm; you are truly our hero, and we love you, boy. You're going to be all right -- you'll see; the doc will fix you up and make you feel better," Jenny said in Storm's ear as she lay on her stomach by his side in the buckboard, consoling him.

Storm whimpered, moved his head toward Jenny, looked at her with his wild but placid amber eyes, and licked her hand.

When Jenny arrived home, her papa was just driving up in front of the store.

"Papa, we need to hurry to Doc Martin's house. Storm's been hurt, attacked by a bear!"

"Run in and get your momma and tell Alice I said for her to watch the store -- and tell Momma to hurry," Alford said franticly.

Danny was playing on the porch and Alford called to him to come and get in the buggy.

By the time Alford and Rose arrived at

Doc Martin's, the doc had examined Storm, but wouldn't do more until his owners arrived.

Rose, Alford, and the children hurried into the doc's office, and Storm lay on the examining table.

Rose went to him and oh, he was so glad to see his friend

Rose. He raised his head whimpering, and reached out with his paw for her hand.

Lucinda took him by the paw, rubbed his head, and said, "It's all right, Storm -- I'm here now, old fellow; just lie still and let the doc help you."

"Doctor, we appreciate you taking our dog into your examination room. We know this isn't exactly what you've been trained for," Alford said apologetically.

"No, it isn't. But I couldn't turn down helping this canine hero -- and he is just that, according to what Joseph has told me.

"I don't believe he has any internal injuries, other than some bruised ribs. I think that's his worst pain. Of course, he has this gash on his shoulder; that's a deep cut. Jenny and Billy did well when they stopped the bleeding by compression. He'll be sore for a few days and should be kept as quiet as you can keep him, but other than that, I think he'll be just fine.

"I'll have to take a few stitches in his ear and sew up his shoulder. Rose, do you think you can keep him still while I do that? I can give him laudanum, which will help, but I don't want to give him enough to put him to sleep. I really don't know what kind of effect laudanum will have on a canine."

"Yes, Doc, I'll help you -- and if I'm here talking to him, I don't think he will give us any trouble...will you, boy?" Rose said as she rubbed Storm's back, and bowed down and put her cheek on the side of his snout.

"Alford, it would be a good thing if you would stay, too. I may also need your help."

Everyone else waited in the doc's office. The doctor, Rose, and Alford came out after the procedure was completed, and the doctor told everyone the good news that Storm would be all right and should have a complete recovery.

Rose walked over to Billy and hugged him. It caught him by surprise and he said, "Miss Rose, what was that for?"

"That was for saving Storm, Billy. Storm's not the only hero here. You risked your life to save him, and I'll always be grateful to you for that. If there is anything I can do for you, just name it!"

Alford came over and shook Billy's hand and said, "We just don't know how to thank you enough for saving our Storm."

Billy just lowered his head, a little embarrassed by all the attention and praise, and said, "Anyone in the same position would have done the same."

Alford said, "We want to thank all you kids for taking care of Storm and getting him here in such a short time."

Rose said, "Yes, thank you all -- and I think this calls for a celebration. I'm inviting all of you to come to our home this evening and have supper and homemade ice cream. Joseph, be sure and bring your guitar -- and also, Lucinda, you tell Moon and Hawk they're invited to come, too."

"Yes -- thank you Rose, I'll tell them."

Storm was able to walk to the carriage. Alford picked him up and laid him across Rose's lap, and he seemed pleased to be there.

Chapter 37

The Claybrooks were still living in the back quarters of the store, not yet having their new home completed. Space was limited for a lot of company, so they strung up colorful oil lanterns to be lit after dark, and set up long tables and benches in their yard, with chairs here and there.

They spread the long tables with blue and white checkered tablecloths, and Jenny and Danny gathered wildflowers from the field for decorations on the tables. Alice and Jenny helped in the kitchen, preparing food and drink. The chicken was fried and the potato salad made, along with other dishes. Jenny made a large cake, while Rose baked a cobbler, and Alice made her award-winning apple pie.

"This should be plenty of food, topped off by the ice cream that your papa is going to make for us."

"Momma, I can't wait for ice cream -- it's been a long time since Papa made ice cream!" Danny said with a big smile.

"Oh, Momma -- this is going to be so much fun! I can't wait for everyone to arrive!" Jenny said.

"Everyone, daughter? Or is it especially Billy Jenkins that you're anxious to see again?" Rose teased.

"Well, Momma, he is kind of cute -- don't you think?"

"What I think is you're a little too young to be that interested in a boy that old."

"Momma, he's just a couple of years older."

"More like three years, daughter -- and you won't be fifteen for two more months. It's not so much that he's older… it's that you're still so young."

Chuck arrived home from his visit with the Creek chiefs, and Lucinda told him all that had happened that day, how Storm had saved them from the bear, and how Billy had saved Storm.

"Rose and Alford want to celebrate, and have invited us all to their home this evening. Rose also said to invite Moon and Hawk. I already told Moon about it, so I'm sure they'll be there."

"Well, that is just great, sweetheart, I'll go get cleaned up, and you tell Joseph and Margret Ann to get ready. Tell Joseph to go tell Billy he can ride with us."

When the McCords and Billy Jenkins arrived at the Claybrooks' party, there were other folks already there. Alford had also invited some of their closest neighbors, Janet and Samuel Williams, and their daughter Amy, who was about the same age as Jenny, and a good friend.

Jenny introduced Billy to Amy, and Amy asked Billy if he would be going to school this fall.

"No, I don't need any more schoolin'. My momma taught me all I need to know."

"You mean you didn't go to school?" Amy asked.

"My papa wouldn't let me go to school, but Momma taught me to read and write and do my numbers. She said I had a gift for numbers. I don't know exactly what she meant by that, but I can do figures pretty well in my head."

"Jenny, go get some writing paper and a pencil, and we'll

see if Billy can figure as good as his momma thought," Amy ordered.

"I don't know what you're tryin' to prove, but I'll go along. It's all right, Jenny. Go ahead and get the paper," Billy said.

Jenny came back with a tablet and Amy said, "Now Jenny, write down a column of numbers and then you add them up and put down the answer. I'll check your answer to make sure we have it added correctly."

This was completed and then Amy read each set of numbers going down the column, and without hesitation Billy gave the correct answer.

"Wow, Billy -- you did that fast! Let's try a longer column with larger numbers," Jenny said excitedly.

It was the same -- Billy gave the correct answer.

"That's fantastic! Your momma was right; you do have a gift with numbers." Jenny said.

"I just figured anybody could figure like that; I never knew they couldn't," Billy said, scratching his head.

"Can you write numbers too, Billy? Do you know how to write a problem down?"

"Well, yes; Momma taught me how to do that, too -- but you girls don't go spreadin' it around to everybody and embarrassin' me, all right?"

"All right -- then let's go get something to eat and listen to the music. Joseph's playing his guitar and Papa's playing his fiddle," Jenny said.

"Who's takin' care of the ice cream freezer if your papa's playin' music?" Billy commented.

"Well, I said Papa made the ice cream, but he's got someone else to turn the crank. Let's go see who's turning it and how much longer it's going to take before we can all have a bowl."

"Looks like Hawk and Chuck are crankin' right now -- come on, Jenny, and let's dance. I like that music!"

Billy motioned to one of the other boys to come and dance with Amy. Robert came over and said to Amy, bowing at the waist, "May I have this dance, my lady?"

Amy, playing along, took the corner of her dress, held it out, curtsied and said, "Yes you can, my good man!" They both laughed, and Robert grabbed her and swung her to the music.

"Who's that boy Alice is dancing with?" Billy asked Jenny as he whirled her around under the colored lights.

"Oh, that's Marvin Tucker. He and his family just moved into the area recently, and he seems to be interested in getting to know our Alice better. He's in his twenties, and ready to find a wife, Momma said."

It was a beautiful summer evening and as the sun sank in the western sky Alford lit more of the lanterns, and everyone sat back and visited after the fine food, and listened to Joseph play soft and easy music.

Jenny went to her momma and papa and said, "Can we talk for a minute, in maybe a private place?"

"Certainly, daughter -- come in the kitchen and tell us what's on your mind," Rose said with Alford's nod of agreement.

"Billy didn't want Amy and me to spread it around and em-barrass him -- but he is really talented with numbers."

Jenny told her parents how Billy had never attended a for-mal school, but had been taught by his momma. She told of how she and Amy had tested him and he hadn't known until that time that he was gifted, but his momma had known and tried to tell him so.

"Papa, I know you're needing help in the store so you can spend more time building on our house, and Danny and I will be starting back to school before long and won't be here to help. I thought…well…since Billy is so good with numbers…."

Alford interrupted, "I think that's a wonderful idea!"

Rose said, "We owe him that much after his saving Storm."

"Jenny, don't say anything about this to Billy or anyone else until I have time to talk to Chuck. He's working for the McCords and living out there, and I have to ask Chuck before I ask Billy -- do you understand?"

"Yes, Papa. I won't say a thing."

After Jenny had went back to the party, Alford said, "You know, Rose, I think this is as good a time as any to ask Chuck and Lucinda."

"I'll go ask them to come to the kitchen," Rose said.

After explaining the situation to the McCords, Alford asked if they would object if they offered the job to Billy.

"Billy has become like one of our family, and if he decides to work for you, it won't interfere in the way we feel about him -- we'll still be his family. The decision is his to make. You want to ask him tonight?" Chuck said.

"We might as well. Where is he now?" Alford asked.

"I'll go find him and bring him here," Chuck offered.

Billy was overwhelmed by their offer. "You want me to work in your store? Working at the counter, selling your merchandise? You would trust me that much, knowing my background?"

"Billy you've proven your trustworthiness over and over again with the McCords, and you've shown your bravery to us by risking your life to save Storm. This is a good opportunity for you to use the gift that God gave you in working with numbers, and you may discover other things that you can excel in by working in the store."

"Chuck, what do you and Lucinda think I should do?

Can I still live in the back room in the barn if I work for the Claybrooks? Oh, and can I still learn to train the horses? There is just so much I want to do!"

"Slow down there, son -- you can live on the ranch as long as you want. Don't you know by now that you are a part of our family? When you're not working for Alford and Rose, you can learn to train the horses in your spare time. We won't tell you what to do, but we will say that it sounds like a good opportunity for you to use and develop your God-given talents."

"All right, then -- I would be happy to work for you, Mr. Alford. When do you want me to start?"

"Be here bright an early in the morning, and we'll get you started. And you can drop the Mister -- we're all family here!"

"Yes, sir -- I'll be here bright and early, first thing in the morning!" Billy said as he turned to run and tell Jenny and Joseph his good news.

Billy worked out well in the store. He learned fast, and Rose and Alford were amazed by his ability with mathematics -- not only his gift with numbers, but he had a brilliant mind for re-membering prices of the items for sale.

There were more and more settlers moving into the area, taking up some of the reservation given to the Indians. With Billy's ingenuity and smart business practices, the little store flourished more than it had in the past.

Storm, while recovering from his injuries, spent, a lot of time in the store with Rose and Billy but when he was feeling well enough, he tagged along with Alford while he worked on the house, running through the woods and chasing rabbits.

Chapter 38

When Danny came home from school after homework, he and Storm would wander through the woods together and sometimes go over to see Danny's good friend Jerry Smith, who lived just a couple of miles as the crow flies...and that's usually the way they would go, through the woods and across Clear Creek, up over Rodgers Hill and down in the valley to Jerry's.

On their last trip through the deep woods, Danny heard the yapping and howling of what sounded like wolves or coyotes far off in the distance. Storm became restless, as if he wanted to go toward the sound.

"No, Storm -- you could get in trouble with those wolves."

Storm looked up at him with more wildness in his eyes than Danny had ever seen. He had a deep growl down in his throat that Danny had never heard. Then he looked up at the boy, whined, and turned toward the sound, hesitating for just an instant, and then running toward the wolves without looking back!

Danny ran after him, but Storm was too fast, and finally Danny, tired and scared, headed for home.

"Momma, Storm left me in the woods and went to join a wolf pack. I tried to stop him, but he wouldn't listen!" Danny cried, "What made him do that, Momma? It wasn't like Storm at all!"

"I know, Danny -- but he probably heard the call of a female wolf, and that's why he left you. When such things happen, dogs act different."

"Why, Momma? I don't understand!"

"Well, you ask your papa when he comes home and he'll explain it to you."

Two days passed before Storm came dragging his tired and ragged body up to the front of the store. He raised his bloody paw and scratched on the door. Lucinda thought, *Oh, I hope that's my Storm!*

She ran to the door and opened it, and there stood Storm with his head hung low, beaten up, with dried blood caked on his dirty white coat.

"Oh, you poor fellow -- come in here, boy, and I'll get you something to eat." Storm limped through the door and went straight to his water bowl, and drank as though he hadn't had water for some time.

Rose gave him food, and he ate sparingly, and then lay down on his bed and fell sound asleep.

Billy came in from the back and said, "There's old Storm -- I was afraid we'd never see that dog again. But wow, he sure is a bloody mess, isn't he?"

"Yes -- and he needs doctoring and a bath, but that can wait until he has rested, poor guy. As soon as he had food and water, he fell over and went to sleep."

"I wonder now if Storm thinks it was worth it going after that female wolf?"

"I don't know, Billy -- I hope he's learned his lesson, but we have to remember half of him is wolf, and he has that wild side about him."

Rose had an uneasiness in her heart that this wouldn't be the last time that Storm answered the call of his wild heart, and he would again wander into a wolf pack for female company.

Lucinda and Chuck's little girl was old enough to drink from a cup by the time school began. Moon offered her services in taking care of little Rachel Sue while her momma was teaching.

"Oh, Moon, would you? I wouldn't trust just anyone to take care of our little darling, but I won't worry or give it a thought when she's with you, my good friend."

"Well, Luc, I may need your assistance in a few months, helping me."

"What...what do you mean...oh Moon, are you...?"

"Yes, Lucinda, I am!"

"How far along are you?"

"Doc Martin said about three months, but don't say anything to anybody yet—not until I've told Hawk. I'm planning on telling him this evening -- after that, I don't care who you tell."

"Well, I guess I can keep quiet that long," Lucinda said with a smile, and then she walked over and hugged her good friend and said, "I'm so happy for you, Moon."

There was a bright full harvest moon shining in the dark indigo night sky and the great expanse was studded with thousands of glimmering stars when Moon and Hawk made their way to their cabin.

Hawk stretched his tired body out on the soft buffalo robe on the floor of their cabin, and Moon brought him something hot to drink. He propped himself up with two feather pillows covered with beaver pelts.

"Hawk, I've got something to tell you."

"Well, sweet, come sit by me and tell what's on your mind."

Moon lowered herself onto the buffalo pelt and crossed her legs, Indian style, her little brown hands reaching out over his, and said, "Hawk, we're going to have a baby."

Hawk looked into her eyes and said, "A baby of our own? Oh, Moon -- you make Hawk very happy! What it be, boy or girl, I don't care...but little brave would be nice, huh?" Hawk said with a chuckle.

Moon smiled and said, "A little brave, or maybe a little maiden would be nice also."

"God blessed Hawk with sweetest little maiden in world, that I not good enough to have such sweet wife, and now He will bless us with little papoose! I tell Strong Eagle tomorrow, Moon and Hawk will have little papoose."

"I love you, Hawk!" Moon said.

"Hawk also love Moon Flower...more than all stars in sky...more than all world, Hawk love Moon!"

Harvest time was upon the land now, and this had been a good year for the Cheyenne and Arapaho. They had learned much in the last few years about raising crops. The rains had been plentiful, and the warm sunny days had made the crops ripen in abundance.

Some of the corn was dried and taken to the mill and ground for baking, while they ate some roasted on the cob and made some into hominy.

They raised squash and beans, pumpkins, sunflowers, wild rice, and potatoes, and they dried a good portion to save to see them through the winter months.

Of course, along with vegetables they were also able to gather wild meats, deer, fish, turkeys, ducks, chickens and their eggs.

They took advantage of all the food stocks available in the wild -- mushrooms, berries, acorns, persimmons, pecans, and others.

The crops were abundant for all in Indian Territory that year, and there was coming a day of celebration, a day of thanksgiving, and plans were being made.

In the little country schoolhouse where Lucinda was teaching, many of her students were Indian, or a mixture of Indian and of white.

There had been some controversy at the beginning of the term, but Lucinda soon put a stop to that.

Tommy Jackson, a tall, yellow-haired boy, somewhat big for his age, had just moved into Indian Territory with his parents.

Tommy, because of his size, had a tendency to bully, and the first day he was in school he began to pick on some of the smaller Indian children.

Little Corn Flower came in from the playground with her dress torn and dirt in her hair.

Lucinda said, "Corn Flower, come over here."

The little Indian girl shyly walked over to Miss Lucinda.

"What happened to your dress, Corn Flower? And how come your hair is full of dirt?"

"It was that new boy, Tommy; he pushed me around and then held me and poured dirt in my hair. He said 'cause I'm an Indian I better stay out of his way -- but Miss Lucinda, I wasn't in his way."

Little Deer also had a bout with Tommy's bullying. He told Miss Lucinda that Tommy had said his papa had told him, "The only good Indian is a dead Indian."

"And then, Miss Lucinda, he hit me."

"Well, Little Deer, I'll make sure he doesn't hit you again."

"Well, he better not, 'cause I'm gonna bring my tomahawk to school, and he better leave me alone!" Little Deer said with his lips pooched out and his little brow furrowed, and his hand held up as though he already had that tomahawk in it.

"Oh now, Little Deer, you're not going to do any such thing. If you bring a weapon to school you are in trouble, you hear me!?"

"Yes, Miss Lucinda, but he better leave me alone!"

"He will; you don't have to worry."

That evening, Lucinda explained the situation to Chuck.

"Well now, Lucinda, you know we can't have this -- we have to nip it in the bud before trouble starts."

"That's what I thought you would say, Strong Eagle. It's a visit to the Jacksons' home?"

"Yes, and we better go this evening."

Chuck saddled their horses, and they rode together to Tommy's parents' home and knocked on the door. A large red-headed man with a heavy beard came to the door and said, "Can I help you?"

"I'm Lucinda McCord, and this is my husband Chuck. We would like to come in and talk to you about your son Tommy."

"Why, what's that boy done now?" Mr. Jackson hesitated and then said, "Well, you better come on in. Martha, we've got company," Mr. Jackson yelled.

A small chubby woman came in from the back room and said, "Howdy do -- can I get you something to drink? Coffee, maybe?"

"No thank you, ma'am," Chuck said.

"This here's Tommy's teacher and her husband; they've come here to talk about Tommy."

"Well, don't just stand there -- you two come over here and

have a sit-down, but I want you to know that my Tommy's a good boy," Martha said.

"I'm sure he is, Mrs. Jackson, but he's got some wrong ideas about some of the children in our school."

"What do you mean when you say, 'some of the children'?"

"Well, it seems that he's been taught, according to what he's telling the other children, that he's supposed to hate Indians. You see, Mr. and Mrs. Jackson, this school is on the Muskogee Indian reservation. There are more Native American children attending here than there are White American children.

"The Muskogee Indian Nation is a peaceful people, and they pretty much get along with the white settlers that live here. Why did you move here, Mr. Jackson, if you hate Indians?"

"It was them savages that burnt down our farm in Kansas and killed our little daughter Mary Ann!"

"We are truly sorry about your daughter, but there have been killings on both sides -- whole villages of Indians, women, and children and old men, who have been massacred by the white soldiers.

"There are evil men on both sides, but here at the Muskogee reservation, we have learned to live in peace. One of the reasons is that we don't allow troublemakers on either side, the white man or the Indian.

"In this regard, we can't have Tommy attending this school with his attitude and beating up on the small Indian children."

The Jacksons said they would make sure Tommy behaved.

"Mr. and Mrs. Jackson, we would like to invite you and your son to our Thanksgiving celebration that we have every year. I think if you'll attend, you will better understand our values here, and what we have accomplished."

Chapter 39

Tommy did behave himself after that visit, and the class could then get on with their plans for the Thanksgiving celebration that would come about in just a few weeks.

The weeks passed and the costumes were completed for the Thanksgiving play that the children would perform.

The costumes for the white children were patterned after the Pilgrims' garb on that first Thanksgiving Day in history. For the boys, there were black knee pants and socks, black jackets with white collars, tall black hats, and black leather shoes with gold buckles. The children made the buckles out of heavy paper, painted them gold, and pasted them onto their shoes and the hats.

The girls would wear long black dresses and bonnets, white collars and aprons.

The Indian boys would dress in their native garb: breechcloths and leggings, moccasins. and headbands decorated with feathers. The girls would be in fringed doeskin dresses and moccasins, and also wearing headbands and feathers.

The celebration was to be held at the McCords' ranch this year. Long tables were set up by village people and Indians. Decorations were gathered for the tables -- cornucopia baskets filled with fruit, and fall flowers strewn on the tables.

There were rows of chairs set up in view of the elevated stage where the children would perform their play.

The day arrived and Lucinda, Moon, Rose, and Alice all worked feverishly with the food. They had prepared turkey and dressing, and pumpkin pies, as well as bread and cranberries.

Others were showing up with food for the celebration -- many of the Creek Indian women came with their children, and white families from the village and neighboring farms.

The tables were overflowing with food and drink, and everyone found their seats. Alford, Rose, and Danny with Jenny sat together as a family.

Jenny made sure she sat last in the row, hoping to save a seat for Billy. Sure enough, Billy saw the empty seat next to Jenny and he walked over, smiled, and asked, "Jenny, is it all right if I sit here?"

She smiled back at him and said, "Of course! Who do you think I was saving it for?"

He set down beside her and moved his hand toward hers under the table. When he found it, he cupped his large hand over her small soft one. She turned hers over and ran her little fingers through his, and they sat that way with their hands clasped until they were ready to eat.

Chuck saw Mr. and Mrs. Jackson and their son Tommy driving up in their buckboard. He waited until they began to walk toward the crowd, and he rose from his seat and walked toward them and said, "Welcome -- I'm so glad you came. Tommy, some of the children are eating at that table over there, if you would like to join them. Mr. and Mrs. Jackson, come and sit by my wife and me. I was just about ready to ask the blessing so that we could begin to enjoy all this bounty!"

"Please call me Odis -- and my wife's name is Martha,"

Mr. Jackson said.

"We would be honored, Odis and Martha, to have you sit next to us," Chuck said.

Martha added the food she had brought to the table, and then she and her husband joined the McCords at the table.

Chuck stood up and said, "This is the spirit we found here on the Muskogee reservation when we first came to this part of Indian Territory -- and my wife and I, along with all who live here, have helped to nurture this spirit of peace and friendship between the two peoples. Let us celebrate this Thanksgiving Day, giving thanks for the blessings and freedoms that we all enjoy, and give thanks for this bounty that is set before us.

"Will you all join hands while we pray?" Chuck then bowed his head and said, "We give thanks to you, Father in heaven, for the bountiful crops that you have so graciously bestowed upon us this year, and for the blessed peace that we all enjoy here in this land of the red man and the white man living together in harmony. Please, Father, bless all who are gathered here this day, and thank you for this bounty set before us. May you cast your blessing upon it. In Jesus' holy name we pray, amen."

After the dinner was over and the food was cleared, the children gathered in the house to dress in their costumes.

Jenny and Alice helped Margret Ann with her costume, and they also helped some of the other children, and then Jenny slipped into hers. She and Joseph were the oldest ones in the play, but there were a few other teens who participated.

The children were all decked out in their costumes and waiting backstage.

Lucinda walked up the stairs and in front of the closed curtain and said, "The children have worked very hard on this re-enactment of the first recorded Thanksgiving Day in this nation, when first the red man and the Pilgrims came together in friendship. The Pilgrims landed on Plymouth Rock in the year 1620, in the month of December.

"They came to this continent for religious freedom from a land that forced them to worship the way they were told -- and if not, they were severely persecuted.

"They came to begin a new way of governance, which was later established by a constitution of freedoms.

"The third president of this union, Thomas Jefferson, the author of the Declaration of Independence, wrote: *We hold these truths to be self-evident, that all men are created equal. That they are endowed by their Creator with certain inalienable rights that among them are life, liberty and the pursuit of happiness.*"

Lucinda as the narrator spoke to the audience and said, "When the Pilgrims landed on Plymouth Rock and looked out on the bountiful land, they were excited and full of great expectation."

The curtain opened for the first act.

There was a large papier-mâché rock the children had made with wire, paste, and paper. Next to the rock was a large poster of a ship with the name "Mayflower" written across its bow. At the back of the stage and all the way across were pine tree cut outs, painted green, with white snow painted on the tops.

Joseph and Jenny walked from behind the rock. Joseph stood with his hand on his forehead, looking out across the land, walking forward; the other Pilgrims came from behind the rock, and all greeted the new land that was filled with abundance.

The curtain closed and the narrator said:

"The Pilgrims that landed on Plymouth Rock in the month of December were not prepared for the long cold winter months. With their food stock depleted and little food left, many were sick from the cold and lack of food, and many were dying."

The curtain opened for the second act.

The stage was strewn with white sheets to represent snow, and a number of the Pilgrims were huddled together shivering, and some were lying on the ground as though they were sick or dying, with others on their knees beside them in anguish, with the backs of their hands on their foreheads. Others were holding pots and showing that they were empty of any food.

The curtain closed, and the narrator said:

"The Native Indians saw the anguish of these strangers in their land and they said, 'We must help these peoples with buckles on their shoes and on their hats!'

"So the Indians gathered as much food as they could spare, and they went to the Pilgrims to offer the sustenance."

The curtain opened for the third act.

The children were still as they had been in the second act, except at the left of the stage a group of Indians were gathered, observing the colonists' anguish, with baskets of food in their hands.

As the Indians walked toward the Pilgrims with the baskets overflowing, the Pilgrims all rose up and walked toward the Indians and took the baskets of food and thanked the Indians, and showed their gratitude to their new friends, the Native American Indians.

The curtain closed and the narrator said:

"Because of the generosity of the Indians coming to the Pilgrims' rescue, they were able to survive their first winter.

"The harvest of 1621 was a bountiful one for the colonists. They decided to show their gratitude for the help the Native Indians had given them by inviting them to a Thanksgiving dinner with all the trimmings."

The curtain opened for the fourth and final act.

The Indians and the Pilgrims all sat around a long table, eating and celebrating. The table was decorated with the harvest baskets filled with fruit and flowers, and a scattering of food left from the dinner before.

They all rose from the table and joined hands -- Indian, Pilgrim, Indian, Pilgrim -- across the stage, and they all sang together" "*Oh beautiful for spacious skies for amber waves of grain; for purple mountains' majesty, above the fruited plain! America, America, God shed His grace on thee, and crown thy good with brotherhood from sea to shining sea.*"

Joseph and Jenny stepped forward and said to the audience, "Sing with us!" And they all sang with great enthusiasm, and when the song ended, they all rose from their seats with applause!

White Willow's vision for her son, Strong Eagle, had come to pass. He had helped in reconciling many of the Indians with the white settlers, and he had stopped or at least decelerated Custer and his Seventh Cavalry from their infinite slaughter of the red man.

His life was full with his beautiful wife Lucinda and their three lovely children. He had the ranch he was destined to possess, where he could also help his people -- both the red man and white man. He and Lucinda had their extended family near: Rose and Alford, Alice, Danny and Jenny; with others they had adopted as family: Billy Jenkins, Moon Flower, and Yellow Hawk, and their soon to be born little papoose.

CPSIA information can be obtained at www.ICGtesting.com
Printed in the USA
LVOW071118031112

305658LV00001B/2/P